A
Certain
Hunger

a novel

Chelsea G. Summers

The Unnamed Press
Los Angeles, CA

AN UNNAMED PRESS BOOK

www.unnamedpress.com

Unnamed Press, and the colophon, are registered trademarks of Unnamed Media LLC.

Paperback ISBN: 978-1-951213-43-5
Hardcover ISBN: 978-1-951213-14-5
eISBN: 978-1-951213-15-2

Library of Congress Cataloging-in-Publication Data
Names: Summers, Chelsea G.
Title: A certain hunger : a novel / Chelsea G. Summers.
Description: First edition. | Los Angeles, CA : The Unnamed Press, [2020] |
Identifiers: LCCN 2020033063 | ISBN 9781951213145 (hardcover) | ISBN 9781951213152 (ebook)
Subjects: LCSH: Food writers--Fiction.
Classification: LCC PS3619.U45943 C47 2020 | DDC 813/.6--dc23
LC record available at https://lccn.loc.gov/2020033063

Cover Art by Bernardino Mei
Designed and Typeset by Jaya Nicely
Manufactured in the United States of America by McNaughton & Gunn.
Distributed by Publishers Group West

First Paperback Edition: October 2021
26 25 24 23   9 8

To all the bad girls, but especially to Molly and Katelan.

A
Certain
Hunger

1

Corpse Reviver #2

*T*hey all look the same, hotel bars, even when they don't. The oak and the glass, the palms and the bottles, the lighting that casts that singular glow, wrapping you in its warmth and pin-spotting your loneliness. Hotel bars smell like class privilege, desperation, and hope.

I sat at the hotel bar, drinking a Corpse Reviver #2. Corpse Revivers, as connoisseurs of cocktail culture know, were created as hangover cures, those hairs of the dog encouraged by Aristophanes, who, so long ago in ancient Greece, looked to quell the storms that come from swilling an excess of wine. Like many of the best things, the origin of the Corpse Reviver family of cocktails is shrouded in mystery. The obscure siblings of the Corpse Reviver first appeared in the 1871 publication of *The Gentleman's Table Guide: Being practical recipes for wine cups, American drinks, punches, cordials, summer & winter beverages; Recherché bills of fare with service of wines & c., & c.* It is a heady title, and a heavy book, one that runs as dizzy a gamut as its title suggests. Every proper young man should peruse a copy; every improper one should own it.

Most contemporary cocktails date from Prohibition, a profoundly stupid time in American history, and while already soundly middle-aged in 1920, the Corpse Reviver found its stride during these years of dumb deprivation. Harry Craddock, the legendary American bartender at London's legendary Savoy Hotel, ushered the Corpse Reviver into the modern age in the Roaring Twenties, cementing the drink's status in 1930 with the publishing of his *The Savoy Cocktail Book.* Craddock's own prim, starched lines are not to my taste. I enjoy a man who's kissed with a yeasty beastliness. Craddock's staid and studied ersatz Englishness aside, I detect a rumpled rebel's raging heart beating in his white-coated breast, if only when I drink his creations. Craddock's Corpse Reviver #2 is an exquisite drink that sits on the lintel of anarchy: what makes it also breaks it. The splash of absinthe propels the Corpse Reviver #2 into the territory of the faintly hallucinogenic—the absinthe also dates and places the drink. Absinthe was, of course, unfairly banned in these puritanical United States for about a century, returning in 2007. Those were happy days when absinthe returned to North American shores, even with its severely decreased worm-wood percentage.

The hotel bar where I sat sipping my Corpse Reviver #2 was not the bar of The Savoy Hotel. There are not sufficient superlatives that one can lay at the feet of The Savoy Hotel, or at least there weren't; times change, likewise places. This historic hotel—home to Oscar Wilde's love that dare not speak its name; habitat of Sarah Bernhardt; domicile of Noël Coward; and abode to countless other filthy gorgeous stars—has fallen from grace, or at least from the grace of those who live graciously. Still, I love The Savoy, if primarily for its history, its unswerving devotion to the laws of luxury, and its inordinate British taste. Others may enjoy their sex acts tick-a-tack in tawdry motels, pilled acrylic under their backs, shag rug as pestilent as the fur of a feral dog beneath their feet, and the illuminating, flickering, cold blow of a television screen. To say I'm immune to the charms of no-tell hotels would be disingenuous. But there's nothing as heav-enly as sundry perversions perpetrated in rooms with views, high thread counts, Turkish towels, and price tags to match. Cheap is fine; expensive is almost always excellent. The Savoy is, above all things, expensive, even if more recent days you'd be likely to find me in the Hotel Café Royal or The May Fair. (The decoration is better, and, after all, only the superficial lasts.)

I was not in The Savoy, and the bar was not in London. It was the fall of 2013 in New York City, my hometown, and the bar belonged to the NoMad Hotel. I like to visit hotel bars, even when I'm in my own city. You sit at a bar and you're gifted with that feeling of utopia peculiar to places frequented by wanderers. Hotels are like train travel, like early-morning pillow talk with a stranger. They allow you to occupy a space that's caught in indefiniteness.

I sat at the hotel bar, alone, the Corpse Reviver #2 beading in the glass before me, a wicked shade of stepmother white. Five other humans, two pairs and a single, ranged down the bar, a wide slab of wood as smooth as fine Belgian chocolate and almost as dark. One pair: businessmen in business suits, doing business; the eyes of one stole over his raised glass to meet mine from time to time. The other pair: a couple, husband and wife, most likely, who stared past each other's dead eyes as they spoke. And the single: a young man, tall and thin, with long aristocratic fingers and skin the color of Brillat-Savarin. Though clearly here on business, he wasn't wearing a suit; his shirt gleamed lustrous, lavender as an old bruise. Unlike the man who flicked his glances toward me like a cigarette in the general direction of an ashtray, this young man met my gaze in the mirror and held it steady. Nothing spilled in that cocksure gaze.

I drank my Corpse Reviver #2, I took notes on my most recent meal (Vitals & Orts, a new gastropub helmed by Rupert Bonnard, the *enfant terrible du jour*, who gleefully dished up offal to foodies desperate for some new sensation, their mouths gaping as baby birds', as Egypt's Blue Hole, as porn-stars' assholes. The food was excellent, especially its duck liver toast—unctuous as a Vegas emcee, salty as a vaudeville comedian—and its steak-and-kidney pie—tender as a love song, rich as Warren G. Harding). I bided my time.

In the wide mirror, I could see the slender single man fluffing himself in preparation to approach me. First, he leaned into the bartender and gestured in my specific direction; a fresh drink was placed before me, an abject offering. Next, he caught my eye and nodded at me, a slight dip of his sharp chin. Then, he slid off his chair, smooth as a pat of butter oozing from a pile of hot flapjacks. I felt him slide beside me.

"You know," he said, "you pose an interesting challenge."

His voice was deep and kissed with an indeterminate accent. It dripped with excellent upbringing, winters skiing in the Dolomites, summers spent in a ten-room "cottage" on the Baltic, private school with British teachers. His skin smelled like expensive paper and sap.

"Do I."

He glided onto the stool next to me, sliding his long legs under the bar, every moment as calculated as the luster on his shirt. No man wears a sateen shirt without wanting to be petted. "You have what I call 'resting bitch face.' It's interesting," he said.

I looked at him and arched a brow. "Well, wait until you see it in full fucking action, little man."

Later, though not much later, I'd explore the inside of this young man's mouth with my tongue and my fingers; it would taste of bourbon and ennui. His mouth would explore the lemon and salt of my pussy; it would taste of multiple orgasms and poor judgment.

The young man in question was long and creamy. A delight; a cream puff stuffed to bursting with pointed sweetness and cum. He was remarkably well raised, brought up by his single mother, a British émigré from the USSR, a woman in possession of an undisputable fortune and inexplicable good taste. This young man seemed to have been reared by Gigi, had Gigi lived in Soviet Russia and served as the mistress of an unnamable party chief. This young man was tangentially involved in hedge-fund trading by day, but he wrote poetry by night, his long fingers tip-tap-tapping on the keyboard, wishing that quills were not so difficult and so pretentious.

One learns so much about a person when one merely wants to fuck him.

In retrospect, it's easy to see how I should have known better. At the very least, I should have known something. All the others were different, you see. I'd built years of intimacy with them, great sprawling manor houses of shared histories with vaulted ceilings and crepuscular cellars, secret rooms and libraries shelved with books we'd read, breathless, in the dark, together. In my time with Giovanni, Andrew, Gil, and Marco, we had built memory palaces that telescoped with extra wings, added rooms, flying dormers, baroque spaces that expanded with time and shared experiences. With Giovanni, with Andrew, with Gil, and especially with Marco, I had spent fat swaths of my life, and even if we'd not spent much of that time together, the points had intersected often enough to create the illusion of a straight line.

From a distance an ellipses looks solid.

This man, this Casimir, which is the name of the young man in question—and it should have told me something, a dirty translation of it means "destroyer of peace"—was a nothing to me, a single blip in the Morse code of my life, something too brief to read. He was a phoneme, a dangling modifier, a printer's orphan. He was an incomplete thought. Some cautionary voice peeped a quiet squeak as that long, white Russian took my hand and led me to his room, but I did not listen. I have always found it hard to listen when a man pulls my head back by my hair. I should have listened. I should have known. I did neither.

Preverbal, love is the smell of a known body, the touch of a recognized hand, the blurred face in a haze of light. Words come, and love sharpens. Love becomes describable, narratable, relatable. Over time, one love comes to lay atop another, a mother's love, a father's love, a lover's love, a friend's love, an enemy's love. This promiscuous mixing of feelings and touches, of smiles and cries in the dark, of half-hushed pleasures and heart-cracking pain, of shared unutterable intimacies and guttural expressions, layer in embellished bricolage. One love coats another, like the clear pages of an anatomy textbook, drawing pictures of things we can only ever see in fractions. With the coming of words, love writes and is then overwritten; love is marginalia illegibly scrawled in your own illegible hand. In time, love becomes a dense manuscript, a palimpsest of inscrutable, epic proportions, one love overlaying another, thick and hot and stinking of beds. It's an unreadable mess.

I didn't love Casimir. That relationship didn't even live in the same zip code as love. When Casimir approached me, wrapped in sateen and creamy skin and erupting in clumsy pickup lines, I should have listened. I look back at the loves in my life and I think I should've known, I should've seen, I should've listened. I didn't.

Instead, I fucked Casimir in his hotel room, the bed snuggled into an alcove like a broad white tongue into a groove. In addition to a fine hand with the hair pulling, this young Russian had, I remember, the straightest, narrowest cock I'd ever seen. It was slender as a ruler and nearly as direct. That night, we had sex for an hour or so, then ordered room service. I was hungry. My ill luck to have told the waiter to wheel the cart into the room—later, much later, he'd remember my face, wrapped as I was in nothing but the top sheet, and testify in court.

Inconsequential things would later return to haunt me. The room service waiter. The video cameras in the hotel lobby, elevators, and hallway. The bartender at the chocolate-silky bar who'd so adeptly made my Corpse Reviver #2. These trivialities would conspire against me, bear witness, place me in exact time and space, and will my actions into repeatable being. Later, much later, I'd see grainy black-and-white footage of Casimir and me groping in hotel hallways, kissing in hotel elevators, engaging in erotic acts altogether unseemly for public behavior. I looked, I thought, surprisingly good for a fifty-one-year-old. My cheekbones are formidable.

Not that I was stupid enough to have killed Casimir in his hotel room. I may have been shortsighted with lust, but I wasn't crazy. Nor, for that matter, was I prepared. It's not easy for a woman to kill a man.

Why, I wonder now, did I kill him. Oh, Casimir, you were so little to me, a screen for the projection of my desires, twelve feet high and luminous, silvered and flickering. That first night, I left you in a muddled heap in your hotel bed, dusted with room service crumbs and slumbering. As I stepped out into the gimlet dawn, sunlight was beginning to slip like white lies between the skyscrapers. The doorman held the door for me. I walked into the opalescent half-light, flagged a cab, and was gone.

I could've left well enough alone. It would've been easy. The real mistake wasn't fucking Casimir. The real mistake was fucking him *again*. And, I suppose, the next few times. I should have made it a one-off, a lone death-defying act in a high hotel room. Maybe I was bored; maybe I was lost. Maybe he was simply that toothsome.

Maybe he was my middle-aged madness, my little red Corvette, my last great gasp before I sloughed off into menopause and the attendant hormonal horrors that anti-puberty has to offer. Whatever Casimir was to me, he wasn't just once, and now, of course, he is with me forever. I am marked by Casimir. We are joined unto death, which is a little ironic, if you think about it, and I do.

Thus I passed weeks with Casimir, multiple nights in his hotel room, fucking. There was a hand job under a table, too, Casimir's fingers parting my labia as I slid forward on a banquette, sly paroxysms of bad posture and muffled orgasm. There was also, if memory serves, a luxe bathroom stall, the click-click-click of expensive heels on the vintage tiles, and the red-lipped "O" of a surprised woman who had too much to drink (and not enough dick). For weeks, Casimir saw me, neither of us knowing that his life was ending. It wasn't as if I planned it.

Just as I was not so crazy as to kill Casimir in his hotel room, I was not so stupid as to kill him in my apartment—Casimir never saw the inside of my apartment! Indeed, I can think of only three lovers who have seen where I live; my home is mine, and I don't like to share. If you followed the trial, and I assume if you're reading this that you paid attention to my trial, then you already know how and where I killed Casimir—or you think you know. You saw Nancy Grace call me bloodthirsty; you read how *Vulture* hung on my trial, rated my outfits, made GIFs of my face, and thrilled at the testimony of Emma Absinthe; you saw my episode of *Snapped*; you read the tweets and you liked them, stabbing that tiny red heart with your forefinger in a hot dopamine rush. What the tabloids named me: the "MILF Killer," the "Butcher Food Critic," the "Bloody Nympho." None got it right. You know only enough about me to be sufficiently interested to shell out money to hear me tell my story, or, if you're cheap, to snag a copy from your public library. You may think you know, but believe me, you don't.

I had keys to my friends' house on Fire Island. It was October. Apple and wood smoke bit the air, but the ferries were still running skeleton schedules. I invited Casimir to spend the weekend with me at a house in Robbins Rest, a tiny townlet tucked between Atlantique and Ocean Beach and the only central township that lacks a road. To get there, you had to hump your luggage hard over the soft sand—there was no packed path on which to roll your wooden wagon, no easy ingress or egress. If you drove to Robbins Rest, you drove on the beach, dipping into the townlet's small enclave of buildings like a toe into the wind-whipped Atlantic, but mostly you walked through sand. Easiness is not the virtue of Robbins Rest. Remoteness is.

Fire Island was barren, and it was beautiful. The air felt like a giant's clean hand brushing your hair back from your face. Around me, all was silent but for the rare car whooshing in the distance, the odd dog barking, and the ceaseless waves, beating like the heart of a great somnolent beast.

I met Casimir at the Dunewood ferry—not exactly at the ferry, but close to it. I ran late, as it happens. I had duck confit in the oven; it takes time. The only thing better than heating a cold house with the warm smell of duck fat is heating the house with the scent of baking bread. I had that, too, a large crusty loaf of saltless Tuscan bread. It's a lovely accompaniment to duck confit, and an ideal conveyance for duck fat. (There's so much you can do with rendered duck fat. Like God's own lard, duck fat is great emperor of fat, the most generous of lipids. Sauté anything in duck fat, and it tastes infinitely better. You can live without many things, but to live without duck fat is the very essence of privation, something with which I am now achingly, hallucinatorily, hungrily familiar.)

I found Casimir wandering dazed as a startled possum near the ferry landing. He kissed me continental style, and then I led him along the quiet paths. We walked, he and I, the sun dropping like a final consonant; soon the night would be navy as '50s velvet flocked with gilt stars. He tried to hold my hand. It's charming, really, that affectation of affection. A stand of three deer warily watched us as we passed, our feet clunking in heavy boots on the wooden walkway.

They watched, but did not scatter. The deer in Fire Island are so cheeky, insouciant in the way of *West Side Story* Jets, standing their ground, cigarettes rolled in their shirtsleeves, whistling a tune, singing an expletive-free song of defiance. Someone could so easily shoot them. Venison steak is best cooked rare and served with cherries, figs, or forest berries. Some meats do enjoy sweet things.

Casimir and I wended our slow way to the house at Robbins Rest, and he delighted at the secret, tree-lined walks. Fire Island feels like the place where the elves of Lothlórien go for vacation. In the October cool, it was empty, row upon row of homes quiet as the grave, dark as repressed desires. Here or there a house blazed alight, like a life raft in the wake of the *Titanic*.

The house, when we entered it, smelled good. Warm and inviting, reaching out with its savory tendrils, pulling us close to its breast. I had a hard time finding the salad spinner, but then it wasn't my house. I gave Casimir the job of chipping the ice for our cocktails with an old-fashioned ice pick. There were cubes, of course, but cubes are frustratingly angular and unforgivably pedestrian.

I lit the fire (the trick is to soak wine corks in denatured alcohol in a mason jar). We sipped Old Fashioneds and ate Marconi almonds as the duck sizzled in the oven. Later, we ate the duck with our fingers, skin like oiled paper crackling in our mouths, grease happily coating our chins. We drank a nice '99 Brunello, a hot year, but you can't go wrong with Gianfranco Soldera, even if he was an asshole.

Then, as one should, we fucked in the glow of the fireplace, the lambent light turning even Casimir's white skin a toasty tiger. I found his mouth pressed against the vertical slit of my cunt a pretty sight until I came and was done. Casimir snuggled me and guided his pin-straight cock into me. I locked my legs around his pelvis and flipped him onto his back, straddling him. Leaning back, I rode him.

My left hand found the handle of the ice pick warm, weighty. I held it, appreciating its vintage heft, its history, and its design. I knew what to do. In an arc as perfect as a fifteen-year-old girl's breast, I plunged the ice pick deep into the right side of Casimir's pale throat. I felt it pierce his skin, his meat, and his cartilage. I felt it graze something hard, a cervical bone, likely. Casimir's eyes met mine, asking something. "Why," perhaps. I pulled the ice pick out, and crimson jets spurted rhythmic and sure. It was a metronome of blood, a ticking of the heart's time, told in rich red. I stabbed again. Casimir moved, darting away. I struck and hit his raised left hand; the point deflected away, bouncing off the hand and skittering across his face to his eye, where it lodged. I pulled the pick out again; it left the eye behind, drawing a slick slug trail of mucus. I stabbed at his heart and struck the sweet spot between his ribs. The pick stuck in his chest, quivering, like an arrow that has found its target.

I remember there was so little sound. Gurgling, mostly, some harsh rasping for breath. Perhaps I severed something in Casimir's vocal cords; they weren't working. I stood up, and he seemed so distant below me, huddled and bloodied on the floor. Blood jetted from his throat in rhythmic arterial arcs; each spurt came more slowly, each weaker than the one before, like an old clockwork toy slowing down, every surge another last tick of the works. Casimir turned over and began to crawl toward his pants, fumbling into his pockets, reaching for his phone. His hands were palsied. I watched him claw the phone from his jeans pocket. Casimir cradled the phone with his stuttering, weakened hands. He jabbed the screen with his forefinger, vainly trying to hit the emergency number icon at the bottom of the screen.

I kicked the phone out of his hands and across the room; it made a satisfying whoosh before thudding solidly against the wall. Casimir looked up at me; his whole body deflated, limp and lost. He paused in an exquisite stoppage of time, caught like a film still in the black frame of nothingness. And then, my breath caught in reverence, I watched as his eyes grew blank with ethereal suddenness. It's such an intimate thing, to witness another's death. Orgasms are a dime a dozen. Any old human woman can see a man orgasm. We so rarely get to see them die; it has been my greatest gift and my most divine privilege.

There was blood, a lot of blood, such great black-red sprays of blood in the firelight. It's shocking how much blood a body holds. I'd seen it before, but it never gets old.

I stepped and slipped. Blood underfoot. Blood trickling like chocolate sauce off my breasts, onto my belly, and down to the slit of my pudendum. Blood everywhere. I read somewhere that in filming *Psycho* Hitchcock used chocolate sauce to simulate blood, and looking at my delectable body, he made a good choice. I walked across the room and checked to make sure that Casimir was dead. Pressing fingers against his pulse points, I found nothing. Where Casimir had been there was naught.

Naked but for a pair of latex gloves, I wrapped up the remainder of the duck confit to bring with me; then I laid out layers of woolen clothes on a chair by the door. I checked my steps around the house, chucking anything that might have my prints into the center of the living room. I moved about the kitchen, cleaning up telling traces. When I felt sure I'd wiped, tossed, and cleaned all of my marks, I showered, taking my time, drying my hair.

Then I tossed all of Casimir's belongings on top of his cooling body, and I poured the rest of the mason jar of alcohol over the muddled mound of corpse, clothes, dishes, and pans. I scattered a few corks on top of the mess. At the door, I dressed, lit a match, and tossed it into the center of the room. A bright, clear flame flew with a whoosh, and I turned out the door, into the darkness. Paces down the walk, I could see the flames bright orange through the beachhouse's wide, clean panes of glass. I walked past a row of darkened, still houses down to the shore; the wind blew clean and hard, cutting through my canvas overcoat as I walked along the beach.

I walked for an hour or so in the black, the smell of the sea washing me, the stars peering like wallflowers from behind the curtains of cloud. A half hour later, fire trucks passed me, sand whirling like dervishes after their wheels, their sirens wailing banshee songs, their red lights blurring like two drunks talking.

I returned to Dunewood, to the house I'd borrowed from my friends, took another very luxurious shower, settled down on their ivory shabby chic couch, poured a nice glass of cognac, and watched a couple of episodes of television before falling asleep, delighted.

The house in Robbins Rest wasn't my house, you see. It wasn't even the house of my friends. It was just a house, a stranger's house, an empty house located apart from others, one with an easily picked lock and running electricity. A house closed for the season, empty of people and barren of company, and now it was burnt. I'm quite certain the owners had insurance. After all, they had a lovely Le Creuset cast-iron French oven.

That sort is always well insured.

2

Roast Parsnips

rison is boring. It's noisy, and it's bright. All around you, all the time, every day, there are people, unless you're in solitary, which I might enjoy if I knew I could leave when I wanted, which you cannot. Moreover, you aren't allowed pens or pencils or sometimes even books in solitary. I tolerate humanity's crush in order to be allowed to write. I behave beautifully so that I have paper, pens, and occasional access to a computer. I suffer for my art.

In my nun's narrow bed at night, I hear covers rustling. So much whispering, so much snoring, so many people breathing—I might as well be sleeping with all of them. These are not, almost to a one, people I want to spend time with, yet together we do time. Time binds us, time flattens us out, time makes us familiar. So much time, so many people. I've never liked people, and now I like them less. They're nearly all women, too; I've so little to play with. There are male guards—the less said about them, the better. I see them, the guards, terrifying the vulnerable inmates. They're bullies, these men living their fantasies of power, as if their squalid teenage dreams cracked open and spilled incarcerated candy at their feet.

Prison company is bad. Prison food is worse. Even when you game the system, the food is lamentable. My kingdom for a delicately roasted parsnip, a perfectly cooked rack of lamb, a slice of *coppa di cinghiale*, a glass of Montevertine Le Pergole Torte. I'd kill for some biodynamic Tuscan extra-virgin olive oil. This last is not an overstatement, nor is it a threat—not yet, anyway. It's also the only item on that list that I have any chance of getting here in the pen.

For the first time in more than a decade, I have a job—you can't freelance in prison. I work in the library. I am not yet allowed to help people find books. I'm not yet allowed to check books out or check them back in—these jobs come with nearly unfettered access to a computer, and they're positions of much envy. I stack books on a cart, I push the cart to the stacks, I find the books' rows, and I return them to their predetermined locations. It's dull work, humiliating and borderline pointless, but at least it's not physical. At the end of my working day, I've got energy to write. Rolling my cart under the numerical guidance of the Library of Congress, I mark my days by remembering meals, and they're not the meals you'd imagine. It's not a parade of gourmet dishes, baroque as popes and twice as rich. No fantasy ortolan, delicate songbird bones crunching as fat runs down my veiled chin. No Thomas Keller–orchestrated dinners, each plate a bar played in a grand, pure symphony that edges on Wagnerian excess. No savory, silky feast of the seven fishes; no effusive, bubbly banquet of El Bulli foams, extractions, and mousses.

No, the dishes my memory presents me with are stark as a wimple. A simple plate of cut tomatoes oozing their sun-warmed guts, drizzled with oil, and sprinkled with flaky diamond-white salt. A fat slice of fresh, hot bread spread with daisy-yellow butter. The crackling skin of a roast chicken spitting hot fat into my mouth. A bowl of berries daubed with obscenely thick cream. They're the foods, God help me, my mother would have served.

People tend to think that the most natural stories begin at their beginning and unwind through their middle to their completion, and sometimes they do. But that narrative structure is only as true as time, which is to say it's as much a construct as a house or a dress or a turducken. Stories are, like justice or a skyscraper, things that humans fabricate. I started this story, for example, somewhere near the end, but that doesn't make it any less true. It makes it artful, but not false. Let me pause to tell a story from when I was a little girl. It's also true. Everything here is true because, really, why would I lie.

When I was very young—long before I ever lost my virginity or even kissed a boy, around twelve, I think—I had a vision. I imagined throwing a lavish affair, a sort of punctuation mark on my adult life.

I saw myself inviting all my lovers, present and past, to a dinner party. I knew even as puberty was dawning, fluffy and pointed as a kitten, that my life would be rich with men. These men, I imagined, would be plentiful, interesting, attractive, and, above all, devout.

In my imagination, I'd send each of them an invitation. Something etched in black spiky ink on heavy stationery—weighty as *Schlag*, textured as flan, colored the delicate white of the fat marbling a prime cut of steak. Each man would RSVP yes, delightedly, each unknowing that the invitation was not for him alone, and each thrilled to his core to see me. I could not then imagine I'd ever have a lover who would not want to see me again. I still can't.

I envisioned a long dinner table, so much longer than it was wide, shiny and black as a beetle's carapace, lined with tall straight-backed chairs that were topped with long, spired skewers, like the spikes in an iron maiden. In my imagination, these men I loved would sit together, ranged along the two sides of the table, joined by their adoration for me, and united in their befuddlement. They wouldn't know one another. They wouldn't know why they were there, and I would sit at the head of the table, smiling.

In my jejune imagination, my dream lovers were uniform, each as beautiful, masculine, and replaceable as an Arrow shirt model. Really, what does a twelve-year-old know about men. To a girl, a man of thirty is impossibly old, if inconceivably desirable and infinitely replaceable. At twelve, my lust was little more than a vague mauve ache nestled in my cotton panties. I knew that lust was a dangerous thing, but I wanted these men to lust for me because, even though I didn't know the precise shape and weight of lust, I knew that lust was power—and I wanted power even then.

Thus my painfully specific imagined feast, the formal invitations, the long and slick black table, the two martial lines of men, the spiky dining chairs, the shiny cutlery, the glinting of glasses, the smell of roast meat, the quiet sound of polite if menacing conversation, the palpable bewilderment, and my sitting poised and plumped as a Persian cat at the table's head. Thus my fantasy of power. This from the fecund imagination of a twelve-year-old girl.

It's amazing I didn't turn out worse than I did.

It's not as dangerous as I thought it would be, prison. A couple of women have tested me, but being a tall, known murderess tends to keep potential harm at bay. Just after I first arrived, two women—what do they say?—*got all up* in my face. It was kind of adorable, really, their desperate grab for dominance. They cornered me as I was exiting the shower; I looked down at them, their faces hot with inarticulate want, and told them that I'd killed a man with a piece of fruit. I let that assertion sit, and I saw their limited wonder about their own personal and painful Achilles' heels. Then I swept out of the shower area, stunned silence in my wake. These women were merely petty felons clad in stolen dominance, you see, while I was a naked, dripping murderer. There's a lot to be said for intimidating intelligence and a dearth of conscience, and I possess both.

It didn't take long for the forensic psychology and criminal justice students to start fluttering to me, like common gray moths to a bonfire. Two weeks after I'd landed at Bedford Hills Correctional Facility, and I'd received my first interview request from a Ph.D. candidate. One request became two, then three, then more. Like hail dropping from the sky, eager students fell before me, jostling each other for my attention. It was delightful to be so avidly courted by so many keenly interested young things. I felt like the belle of the carceral ball.

I was given batteries of standardized tests. I acquiesced to MRIs and genetic testing. I was asked repeatedly about my childhood. I was plied with cans of mineral water and the finest snacks the vending machines could provide, and I gave my permission to have my psyche plumbed and prodded, plumped and pushed. The students were mostly thirty-year-olds, who, irrespective of gender, wore studious glasses and the kind of asexual, atonal clothing that functions like mental saltpeter. But I've always found that being the center of attention is an implicitly erotic state, and I spread my exotic wings under the students' bland collective gaze. The Hawthorne effect is real—as I was observed, my behavior changed, not always innocently.

For one thing, I knew that the students' interest in me was in direct proportion to how well I conformed to their prepackaged expectations, and I knew that the more I teased the edges of their working diagnoses, the longer I could keep them hanging on. I enjoyed my place in the limited limelight. I wasn't going to let my audience down, so I bubbled in the responses that would make me spicy to these students' lips. And above all, I knew what these darkly optimistic students were hoping to find.

It wasn't hard. I do have a long, florid history of using aliases. I do have a delicious record of nonconformity. I was convicted of violent crimes predicated upon a piquant mélange of impulsivity and preparedness. I genuinely lack remorse. And one of the reference books in the Bedford Hills library stacks happens to be the *DSM-IV*, out-of-date but extremely useful. Knowing what I knew, it was easy to lay the derangement on thick when I wanted and to drizzle it with delicacy when I determined that was the right approach. I can't, of course, tamper with the MRIs, but even neurologists admit that when it comes to mapping the human brain, we are Christopher Columbus: motivated by dubious ethics to search for a route to Asia and "discovering" these America-shaped continents by mistake. Brains are an imprecise science, in short. Easy to fake and even easier to deceive.

I am special, the students intimate. I am valuable, their breathlessness suggests. I am, as one excited student exclaimed, "A perfect specimen of a female Anti-Social Personality Disorder!"

To this, I laughed. I know what I am. It may not appear in the *DSM-5*, but just because you can't prescribe a pill for us doesn't mean we don't exist.

Indeed, I am the Bronze Copper of psychopaths, a big, beautiful auburn butterfly that flaps her darkling wings as she eats. I am rare, and sequestered in this endlessly gray penal institution, I am endangered. I first suspected I was a psychopath years ago with an armchair test of twenty-six questions, but even before I sat down with my computer and ticked "agree" for "I tell other people what they want to hear so that they will do what I want them to do" and "Love is overrated," I knew that I was different. I merely lacked a name for how.

One mark of psychopaths, or so I've learned, is that we calculate an action's personal benefits before we take it, and it benefits me to proclaim my psychopathy, both in prison and out of it. Here at Bedford Hills, my psychopathy earns me a wide berth. There in the world, my psychopathy sells better than sex—and sex plus psychopathy, well, that's a heady delight.

As a woman psychopath, the white tiger of human psychological deviance, I am a wonder, and I relish your awe.

For a long time, the scientists who study such things were reluctant to admit the existence of women psychopaths. Even with all the cliché evidence—the bad mothers who leave their children to cry in wet beds, the nurses who "help" their unwitting patients to die, the black widows with a wealth of dead husbands—people did not want to believe. Female psychopaths, researchers eventually realized, don't present like the males. To which I respond: No shit. We women have an emotional wiliness that shellacs us in a glossy patina of caring. We have been raised to take interest in promoting the healthy interior lives of other humans; preparation, I suppose, for taking on the emotional labor of motherhood—or marriage; either way, really. Few women come into maturity unscathed by the suffocating pink press of girlhood, and even psychopaths are touched by the long, frilly arm of feminine expectations. It's not that women psychopaths don't exist; it's that *we fake it better than men*.

Take a quick trip through history, and you see no shortage of flashy female psychopaths. Elizabeth Báthory, who killed between eighty and a few hundred people, mostly women, in the late sixteenth and early seventeenth centuries, before being walled inside a castle tower. Chile's La Quintrala, colonialism's poster girl, who slaughtered about forty indigenous people. Darya Saltykova, Muscovite, who dispatched a hundred or so serfs, mostly girls, in the eighteenth century. Delphine LaLaurie, who tortured and killed numerous slaves in her nineteenth-century New Orleans home. Women like these punctuate time with their bloody body count, yet people are still disinclined to believe. Even as Victorian women slayed whole families with heaping helpings of arsenic to reap health insurance monies; even as Aileen Wuornos shot her seven johns; and even as Stacey Castor's matricide got her fifteen minutes of fame on *20/20*, people didn't want to believe. Feminism comes to all things, it seems, but it comes to recognizing homicidal rage the slowest.

You who call women the fairer sex, you may repress and deny all you want, but some of us were born with a howling void where our souls should sway. I am a psychopath—and whatever their reasoning and whatever their diagnoses, the eager psychology and criminal justice students are right to study me. And if they're wrong, I still enjoy their attention, and I'll do what I must to encourage it.

Aside from the eager Ph.D. students—so well groomed and so poorly dressed, especially the men—I receive few visitors here in prison. My father comes; my sister has visited twice; my brother has sent his regards. Emma has applied to visit, but I won't allow it, for obvious reasons. I am impressed that she would consider leaving her apartment for the long, intricate trek to Bedford Hills.

(Though perhaps she knows I'd never approve the visit and she's merely applying to toy with me. That's not a possibility I'm willing to indulge, on the off chance that she appears some Sunday afternoon, dripping Vivienne Westwood and Guerlain Nahema. I don't even open Emma's letters.)

It's one small mercy that here in prison we don't have to see anyone we don't choose to see. In this way, prison is beautifully unlike real life. In real life, people from your past litter your life like cockroaches, popping out of crevices and scuttling across the dark. In the outside world, you can't escape fate's cruel crossing. You turn a corner, and there buying a hot dog is the editor of your college paper; you engage in conversation; you go out for lunch, and then to dinner, and then into bed, and then you love. Love is the languid sigh of death, and no one will ever convince me otherwise.

Prison may be the hell of other people, but at least it's not a hell of people you love.

3

French Fries

ust as most people don't wake up and become a murderer, most don't wake up and become a food critic, but I did. Embracing this particular skill set felt like slipping into a bespoke garment, something cut to flatter my exact, idiosyncratic body. And yet, however much I feel put on this planet to instruct people on how, what, and why they should eat, I am compelled to admit that my vocation as food critic wouldn't have been possible without men. I owe them so much.

In 1990, you had to squint to glimpse the Internet looming. In today's time of newspapers and magazines gurgling a nonstop deathrattle, it's hard to recall that, just a quarter century ago, print was basking in a halcyon moment. In '90s New York, it felt as if a new four-color magazine hatched everyday. It was a dizzying time of weighty glossies with oddly specific names like *Egg*, *Paper*, *George*, *Spy*, *Blurt*, and *Spin*. (These magazines, I believe, foretold the days of single-word restaurant names: Plum, Parm, Sauce, Supper, Den, Carnivore, and Home.) Ideas, print, writers, and money mushroomed with sweet yeastiness. One begat another, which begat another, which begat another, and before you knew it, you had a giant amorphous mass of words and people, pages and layouts, advertisers and editorials, subscriptions and readers, all demanding constant feeding.

During these *Twin Peaks*, *Pretty Woman*, "Ice Ice Baby" days and cocaine-fueled nights, ideas grew with fungal fecundity, and relationships were traded like currency. It was all about whom you knew, whom you blew, and whom you'd yet to screw. You just had to be at the right cocktail party, at the right gallery opening, at the right restaurant, in the right club's bathroom doing the right drug, on the right coast, in the right tight black skirt, thighs pressed to the right person, in order to find your name on a masthead of some slick publication.

And that was how I became the food critic for *Noir*.

I remember the exact night that birthed my career. It was at Beignet, where I found myself wedged on the restaurant's beige nubuck banquette next to Manhattan playboy Andrew Gotien. Over the thudding bass of C + C Music Factory and a sea of upended vodka shots, I shouted that the braised Malpeque in lemongrass crème tasted like a fifteen-year-old boy's fantasy of cunnilingus. I remember Andrew heard me and laughed as he slid his hand up my thigh. I remember going home with him. I vaguely remember some assertively athletic sex that ended in a misfire. I remember waking the next morning in Andrew's Tribeca loft, and I remember, as Andrew's sperm dried on my belly like donut glaze, he propped himself on one elbow, looking at me appraisingly.

"I want you to be the food critic for my new magazine," he said.

Noir, he said, would take a dark sideways look at culture, fashion, politics, art, and pretense. I'd be perfect for it.

"Of course," I said, drawing an idle doodle with his spunk. "You'll pay me $4,000 a column."

We sealed the deal with a sloppy kiss and a squelchy fuck.

I say I woke up and found myself a food critic, but it's equally true that my life's sinuous lines led me to my career. Looking back on it now, as I often do—prison really facilitates introspection—I feel as if I was raised to write about food. Just as dairy cows are raised to give milk, Nebbiolo vines are cultivated to make wine, or civet cats were created to defecate the world's best coffee, I was raised to give voice to food's consumption.

In retrospect, it seems fated to be, and, much to my distaste, it begins with my mother. You see, unlike most Americans born in the early '60s, I was reared on hand-crafted food. Like Daniel Boulud, I never ate store-bought bread unless I was at a restaurant—in fact, I never ate store-bought anything. My mother made her own bread, kneading it with measured sensuality, dough perpetually drying in the crescents under her fingernails. She grew her own tomatoes, then she canned them, and then she used those jarred tomatoes to make fragrant cassoulet, salty steam rising as from a bagnio. She drove to the dairy and carted home great pails of unpasteurized milk from which she then made her own butter, yogurt, and crème fraîche—creamy, blond cups of it. She'd pour it, unctuous and fragrant and drizzled with honey, over bursting berries, sun-warmed and brambly. My mother grew the berries and kept the bees, too.

She made it, she made it all, and she made it well. She stood with arms akimbo in her Connecticut garden; she strode her kitchen as a colossus. In our small world, she was the great, ever-giving Mother, maker of mysterious soups, magical stews, peerless fluffy loaves of bread, shiny fruit tarts glowing like family jewels, crispy-juicy brown hunks of roasted meat, vegetables cooked so crunchy-tender that your teeth wept, pottages of cream, sauces of jus, mysterious dishes of rice and herbs, salads that slayed you, all from produce grown in my mother's own meticulously kept garden, or from ingredients sourced with an alchemist's care. My mother was a witch in the kitchen and a Demeter in the garden. We hated her for it.

My father worked all day, churning out advertising copy with an electric mind that crackled and popped syntactic snaps. His kinetic brain prickled with quick, thick witticisms that sold stuff well and reliably. He worked long, late hours (time that, as it turned out, was punctuated with a series of mistresses, women whose identities blurred furry into a string of pronouns and epithets—*her, she, that one, that bitch, your whore*. I'd hear my parents argue in raw hushed tones, my mother making a show because propriety demanded it. In truth, she expected more integrity from the jars of preserves in her pantry). For a man given to 60-to-80-hour work weeks, my father's home was less his castle and more his weekend office.

My mother, who ruled our home with a floured fist, was nominally, philosophically, and aesthetically French. Her Francophilia inflected her speech, her cooking, and her red lipstick, which she wore even when tending her organic garden, her hair tied up in a careful bun, giant gloves on her hands, faded cotton jacket on her back, and Wellies on her feet. Her faux Frenchness enabled her to roast a chicken to succulence, then take that chicken and, with a shaman's magic, turn it into an evolving kaleidoscope of meals: roasted chicken became chicken in aspic, chicken sandwiches, chicken stock, chicken with dumplings. My mother made a roast chicken stretch forever, an unblinking eternity of chicken.

Taking her work as head nurturer seriously, my mother lived to feed her three children—my two younger siblings, one son and another daughter, and me—from her garden, her pantry, and her larder, places defined by my mother's necromantic abilities, Protestant determination, and single-minded snobbery. (Protestant, after all, because my mother was fake French. She was, like a gilded Louis XIV chair in a despot's palace, a knockoff.)

In contrast to my ever-present stay-at-home mom, my father was a presence in equal parts ephemeral and unchanging. He smelled like tobacco and brown liquor; his voice sounded like an emery board; he carried his slender body with a slight, resigned defeat, even as he made the kind of money and owned the kind of property and gave his Gen-X children the kind of education that defines privilege. My father was always precisely dressed— Brooks Brothers during the week, L.L.Bean on the weekends, and Ralph Lauren for special occasions—he complemented the wood-beam and cotton-duck farmhouse like he'd been purchased to match. Limited as my father's home life was, you could set your watch by his presence, even if that presence felt as solid, and as visually perfect, as a cinematic projection. Together, my parents constructed a Potemkin village for our nuclear family; it looked good from the outside.

But every family has secrets, and my family's was me.

Here's an interesting thing about privation—it causes hallucinations. For example, sleep deprivation often brings psychosis. The human brain can go only so long without deep REM rest, a break from our walking, talking, acting cognitive selves, before our brains do it for us, taking a deep dip into the waking dream state. Enough time awake, our skin begins to crawl with insects, centipedes and butterflies alighting, itching, fluttering, inching. Our ears ring with the voices of the dead or the detested. Our eyes see apparitional flashes of ghosties and beasties, exploding shafts of light and shifting landscapes; we can't trust our hands to hold that shuddering doorjamb. Our adrenaline spikes and our hearts beat a tachycardia tattoo. Our brains wrap nightmares around our sleepless flesh.

Food privation similarly sheathes you in a cocoon of yearning. I'm not saying that Bedford Hills starves its female populace—it doesn't. We eat. We eat puce goop and ecru glop and flat brown patties of unknown origin. We get peas tepid from the can, swimming in an oleaginous, salty bath. We get gluey, chewy bread spread with near-rancid margarine. Swallowing meals of government-issued apathy, we eat, three times a day. Sometimes, to slake our phantom appetites, we cobble together dishes from vending machines and commissary goods.

But most of all, we want. I want so hard and so viscerally that my brain wills food into being and floods my head with a tsunami of perfect ceviche from Playa del Carmen in Mexico, shrimp and tilapia basking in the spiky tang of sun-warmed limes, shivery slivers of papaya and guanabana cuddling with serrano and jalapeño. I'll reach to shelve a book, and I'll be slammed with olive oil cake, rough and crumbly, salty-sweet and scented with the fat bellies of green olives, chased with a mouthful of bittersweet espresso. I sit on my bed and pomegranates crush my lips, rack of lamb curls in my nostrils, hot black bread slathered with cultured butter fills my throat, and it chokes me. Ghost food wafting in crystalline recollection—a perfect besotted Manhattan, a half shell oyster shucked and glimmering with seawater, a bowl of minestrone curling with evergreen pesto, the first salty bite into a warm chocolate chip cookie—my mouth wets as my cunt once did. My jaws close on emptiness. Privation serves up these beggar's purses of imagination, and I could die with want.

At home with my family, I ate my mother's organic meals that gave meaning to her life. Out with my friends, though, I gorged on junk

33

food. Kick-lines of fries, umber and indefatigably crisp; volcanic apple pie nestled in crust bubbled like deep-fried bubonic plague; milkshakes tinged with an inescapable plastic sheen—junk food was my rebellion. I never smoked, to give you a point of reference. Both of my parents smoked. They wouldn't have cared if I balanced one of their Marlboros or Gitanes between my index and middle fingers, struck a match, and inhaled deeply after a dinner of trout almondine and haricots verts. In fact, they expected it. Junk food was my adolescent insurrection. It was my teenage dissent, my Che Guevara's beret, my black-gloved fist in the air, my vicious mohawk, snarling lip, and ripped leather jacket.

Too sweet, too salty, too plastic, and too glorious, junk food is a debt I owe my teenage girlfriends—but were they my friends? I don't know. They were the people I modeled myself after because fitting in was easier than sticking out. I wore what they wore. I watched what they watched. I listened to the music they liked, and I screamed at musicians' names because these girls screamed first. I swept my eyelashes with blue mascara because they painted theirs indigo. I peppered my speech with "like" and "went," using the former as a filler and the latter as a synonym for "said." Most excitingly, I ate what these girls ate because at home I never got to eat Whoppers or Whoopie Pies.

Friends or not, these girls let me explore the new appetites— junk food, junk sex, real power—that I couldn't access in the eternal childhood of my parents' home. But were they my friends. I don't know whether I am able to have friends; friends, for me, are usually people I like well enough to act as if our relationship isn't wholly transactional. I suppose Emma is my only real friend, though the jury is still out—the metaphorical jury, of course. The actual one handed down their decision on November 13, 2014, just a few days after Emma testified against me, but I digress.

I have reasons to feel forever grateful to my fake teenage girlfriends, for aside from teaching me about junk food, they taught me how to be feminine. Snuggled in their blossoming Love's Baby Soft–scented bosoms, I learned to approximate a female—how to talk, how to walk, how to dance, how to flip your hair. How to part your lips as for a kiss but not for a bite of food. How to end your declarative sentences in a question. How to twitch your hips as you left a room. Why you laugh when you feel like screaming. Over trays of Bonnie Bell Lip Smackers and mountains of cooling fries, I learned that being female is as prefab, thoughtless, soulless, and abjectly capitalist as a Big Mac. It's not important that it's real. It's only important that it's tasty.

I remember after-school hours speeding around Connecticut corners in cars, singing "Cold as Ice" and drawing out the last "I know" with our perfect mouths rounded like *Playboy* bunnies. We were just being girls as we squeezed around plastic tables to pick at our plastic food, batted our cerulean eyelashes at boys in the booth across the way, and pulled our lip gloss out of our collective purses and swiped them as one, a Lucite sheen sticky on our collective lips. We were girls being girls at the keg parties and house parties, eating frozen pizza, holding red plastic cups of bad beer or worse wine, convening for late-night McDonald's, and meeting for gropings in the dark with interchangeable boys-will-be-boys boys. Spending time with these scented, luscious girls, I felt I was stealing something precious. All these years later, a couple of bars of "Don't Fear the Reaper," and I'm instantaneously holding a plastic cup of tepid PBR, looking to make out with the nearest, stupidest lacrosse player.

Junk food was rebellion, rebellion was femininity, femininity was junk. Adolescence immersed me in an ouroboros of desires, and it was ecstasy. What choice did I have but to lose my virginity to a fry-cook.

He was nobody to me, just a guy bent over a grill, artfully flipping burgers, and that made him perfect. He caught me with his slick spatula dance, a quick wrist snap and a hip shimmy. To him it was a nothing move, something he'd done again and again, burger after anonymous burger, one dead cow piled upon another in a line of prefab patties. Cunt-struck, I watched him. His striped smock hitched above his hips, skinny and serpentine. I saw that snap-shimmy and imagined the furrow of his spine, the downy trail of hairs snaking below the waistband of his 501s. I imagined the feel of his sharp hips under my palms, I envisioned the weight of his body. I wanted to lose myself in his skin's dead-meat-grease stink.

He turned toward me, his back to the grill. His hair feathered around his paper cap, like a little boat riding atop a sea of waves, his face narrow with full lips the Disney red of Snow White's poisoned apple. I imagined his lips, a little chapped, and his tongue, a little thick. I imagined the slubbed silk of his skin and the pang as his dick pierced my inviolate pussy. I imagined the relief after my hymen broke, the sense that with this one tiny moment, a seismic thing had shifted, an act I could never take back. I could see myself as if it had already happened, born anew, driving away in my car, bleeding ejaculate into my panties, and tasting his salt on my hands. I ate my cheeseburger while listening to my friend chatter on about how, like, she went to DJ? And he was all, like, What's up? And she went, You know, nothing? And he went, Yeah, me too?

I listened and responded, my eyes on that feather-haired Fryolator boy. The girl across from me prattled on, and I watched the fry-cook. I willed him to look at me. To see me sitting in that blood-red plastic booth, naked and potent in my blooming desire. I knew if we made eye contact, he would fall into my hands like a ripe plum. I could already feel his hair gummy-slick under my fingers, I could already feel the clash of his teeth, the rough strawberry of his tongue. I imagined his car had a bench front seat wide enough to ranch cattle. I wanted to sprawl across that late-model Crown Vic, spread my legs, grab his narrow flanks in my hands, and swallow him whole.

I watched his nylon-clad back, his paper-boat hat clinging to his hair. With every nerve of my body, I commanded him to turn around and see me, turn around and see me, TURN AROUND AND SEE ME. And he did. Our eyes met. I smiled and put a french fry in my mouth. Chewing it, I stared at him. The moment hung. A machine buzzed, and he turned around. But I knew. I knew. He was mine. Whoever he was.

My girlfriend and I finished our food, and left together. Walking to the car, I listened to her yammer on about DJ and the way he, like, looks at her? And, like, the party that weekend? Did I think, like, her and DJ would totally make out? Yes, I said, I did. I was sure of it. I was positively expansive with possibility.

Two hours later I returned alone, parked my car in the back parking lot, and pushed play on *Talking Heads: 77*, whisper-singing the lyrics as I watched the back door. "Who Is It?" segued into "No Compassion," which segued into "The Book I Read." The door opened and my Fryolator boy walked out with a big bag of trash in either hand. He crossed in front of me as he stumped to the dumpster. I clicked on the interior light. Our eyes met across the black of the parking lot, our gaze suspended like an aerialist midflight. I clicked off the light.

When he came out again, I was waiting in the March chill, my fake-fur jacket lamb-like and approachable, my tight Calvin Klein jeans ending in four-inch Candie's, my body leaning against my sports car, one foot tucked up. He wore this lame leather jacket that was trying too hard. I bet his car had an eight-track. I hoped it did.

"Hi," I said.

He stopped, smiled. His grin was lopsided, but his teeth were pretty and white. From six feet away I could catch that burger scent, the finest that Jersey labs can craft.

"Hi." He said.

I walked up to him, looked in his eyes, took his hand, and, like an alien, told him to take me to his car. Joy of joys, it was an Impala. In its wide smoke-scented front seat, we grappled like raw students in a dojo. I inhaled his smell, drowning myself in it. I stripped off my clothes and urged him, hard and lean, into me.

"It's okay," I told him. "I'm on the Pill."

He stuck me. I yowled, then I luxuriated in the unfamiliar pain, a sensation that thrilled and frightened me. A miasma of beef tallow, dirty corn oil, and unwashed man surrounded us. To this day, I can't look at a Burger King cheeseburger wrapper without feeling my clit twitch. Such is the power of that particular madeleine.

I wish I knew that guy's name. I'd like to look him up.

4

Tofu

*L*ove them or hate them, people are the plumb line in a person's life, and, aside from my family, the person who centers my life is Emma Absinthe—yes, *that* Emma Absinthe. The agoraphobic painter Emma Absinthe, most famous for her series of oil self-portraits portraying herself as the great men of history. Emma Absinthe as Napoleon, one hand clutching a roasted chicken, the other on a sword hilt, grease shellacking her carnivore's lips. Emma Absinthe as Winston Churchill, fat cigar, impeccably tailored gray flannel, sly erection draped to the left. Emma Absinthe as George Washington crossing the Delaware, surrounding soldiers a battalion of lesser Emmas, the river faintly and ominously reminiscent of menstrual blood. Emma Absinthe as Socrates, folded linen, beetle brow, a flock of languorous Emma-boys lounging at her feet, and a cup of hemlock. Emma Absinthe as FDR, pince-nez, cigarillo, wicker pushchair, cross-dressing Eleanor behind her. You've seen the series because everyone has seen the series; the series is everywhere.

I knew Emma before anyone knew Emma. I knew Emma before Emma knew Emma. I even knew Emma before Emma *was* Emma, for when I first met Emma, she was merely Joanne Correa, a shy, milk-skinned, frizzy-haired girl who wore an endless progression of Gunne Sax by Jessica McClintock, dress after dress with pastel tiny-flower prints, a parade of dainty spaghetti straps, a procession of futzy leg-o'-mutton sleeves.

I hated Joanne from the first moment I saw her. We were freshmen at Pennistone College, the small, elite liberal arts school in Vermont near the New Hampshire border, an institution of higher learning that in 1980 had only recently opened its doors to women. The majority of the student body was privileged, intensely white, and frankly fussed that they hadn't been admitted to Yale, Brown, or even Dartmouth. The remaining students were like me; they enjoyed the optimistic statistics of there being three men to every woman on campus. Math can be so animating.

The luck of residential draw slammed Joanne and me together—fortunately, we shared a very big room, for our dislike was instantaneous, passionate, and mutual. It could hardly have been anything but. Joanne seemed specifically designed as an object of my loathing. Her little-mouse-on-the-prairie dresses, those eyelashes lacquered into Marcel Marceau points, her lilac-print matching duvet and curtains. Her excessive prissiness and her endless passion for cats. There were cats everywhere. Flattened on walls and plumped into cushions, pictured cats and printed cats, ceramic cats playing with string and cartoon cats smugly punning on Mao. So many cats.

The first day I walked into the dorm, a building of arterial-red brick and blinding, deep-pocketed white trim, I found Joanne awash in frills, perched on her pouf of a comforter, weeping into a stuffed cat. Her eye makeup had melted with her tears, running in great Rorschach circles around her eyes. She was the very picture of an adorable faux-Victorian waif, so dejected on her bed, like a little broken match girl or a flower-maker gone ulcerative from arsenic exposure. I wanted to put my hands around her slender white throat and shake her.

Joanne was just that delicate. While I had rushed my family out the door, Joanne wept over her parents' leaving. Her fat glycerine tears rolled, unappetizing as beads of tapioca. I put my box down on the empty bed, the one away from the window with the view of the trees, close to the window with the view of the parking lot.

"I'm Dorothy," I said. "I'd shake your hand, but you're all wet."

Joanne took a look at me and stifled a sob with her tufted cat. Our relationship did not improve. After winter break, I returned to find her side of the room empty, not a sole B. Kliban print, not a single crumb of her endless English muffins, the only food I ever saw Joanne eat. I heard from the RA that I had borrowed Joanne's eyeliner (and had sex on her bed) one too many times, driving her to flee to housing on the other side of Pennistone's campus, as far away from me as she could get. Occasionally, I'd catch sight of Joanne crossing campus in a seraphim wave of ruffles, but as the years wore on, the Joanne sightings grew fewer and further apart. It was as if Edward Gorey's hand was slowly erasing her from my life, recognizing her for the mistake she was. E is for Emma who'd never be born; J is for Joanne dead from my scorn.

On the whole, Pennistone was good for me. I read, I wrote, I learned, and I fucked—it was a classic liberal arts education. Of its approximately 3,500 undergrads, Pennistone men counted for just under 2,400; I slept with about fifty. You'd think that having sex with that many young men—a group whose predilection for gossip makes mahjong-playing retirees look like Cistercian monks—I'd have gotten a bad reputation. But I'd been careful. I protected my good name with excellent information, and I didn't fuck anyone I couldn't ruin. My philosophy has always been that if you look hard enough, you will find something wicked on nearly every man—everyone has at least one devastating piece of information. I enjoy research, and I found serious dirt, always with supporting evidence. But I didn't use this information to coerce anyone into my sheets—I didn't have to. No, I held on to the information until just before the amour's bitter end and then I'd hint at the dangerous dirt I'd dredged (I've always had impeccable timing). Let me put it this way: I was so careful and so thorough that ex-lovers would stand up for me, not because they liked me but because they feared me.

You can't be a woman without protection. Condoms fail. Pepper spray can be turned against you. Information almost never does.

To whit: Lyle had a hushed-up history of quasi-incestuous rendezvous with his two cousins, one female and one male, twins, possibly together. James had never, not once, handed in an original paper in his 3.5 years of higher education, and he'd never, not once, strayed from the Dean's List. Michael, center on the basketball team, had had the great fortune of twice playing second-string on teams where a mysterious and debilitating accident had befallen the first-string players; he replaced them. Jean-Georges wasn't actually French, nor was he actually Jean-Georges; it's amazing how far a family will go to cover up a spate of pubescent pyromania, given enough money, time, and loss of life. Armstrong's father was on the run from the SEC; rumors would later abound that Armstrong *père* was the model for Gordon Gecko. And as a side note, Armstrong should've thought twice before making that phone call to my RA on that Wednesday night—it wasn't as if he hadn't been warned.

It's a habit I've not given up. In an anonymous, undisclosed location, I have a file cabinet locked in a storage facility under an assumed name with the kind of information that could take down members of Congress, multinational corporations, and one very small duchy in Liechtenstein. You can be too rich and too thin, but you can never know too much.

I've always been amazed by how much information is available to you if you listen quietly, read carefully, and know how to pick locks. Dorm room doors are stupidly easy; you need only a credit card and a lissome wrist. The cars of the '70s and early '80s had ridiculous locks—a quick pop of a wire hanger would open most, and never underestimate the ability of a young woman with a distressed look on her pretty face to persuade a cop to help her. Residential doors were more challenging, ditto locked trunks, but hairpins, paper clips, and public libraries are remarkably helpful tools for the willing mind. Information is like a feral cat: what it wants most is to be free and to bite someone. Who am I to stand in the way of the call of the wild.

Thus, protected by knowledge and the Pill, I fucked my way through college. It was easy; it was fun; and it was educational, if not reliably pleasurable. Emotional attachment is for children, and sentimentality is for great meals you'll never eat again. I went to college for an education, and I got one.

By the time I donned Pennistone's scarlet-and-marigold graduation robes—such vulgar colors; yellow the shade of bile and red the hue of an overcooked rib roast—I'd accumulated a body of knowledge tailored for adult life. I could speak Italian passably well. I could argue the basic histories, literatures, and politics of major European nations. I could cook a passably decadent four-course meal using a hot plate and a toaster oven. I could deep-throat a seven-inch phallus. I could research and write a charming, sprightly, thousand-word article in record time. And I could investigate, seduce, and drop a man with elegance and ease. I could, in short, support, nourish, pleasure, and protect myself. I felt like a proud parent of a devious mind.

I graduated college in 1984, a year that failed spectacularly to live up to its Orwellian promise. I moved to Boston, and, based upon my portfolio of writings from the *Pennistone Cynic* and various other local publications, I got hired at the *Boston Phoenix*, an arty alt-weekly that, like so many others, eventually died a slow, heavy asphyxiation under the boot of the Internet. Funny how something as flimsy as a string of ones and zeros can be so massy. As democratic as the tax code, as voracious as a black hole, as weightless as a fart, the Internet has made writers out of everyone, and it has made publishing into a short-term con, but I digress.

For two weeks here in Bedford Hills, I couldn't write. Nothing so humdrum as writer's block—rarely does anything stand between me and full, easy expression—I couldn't write because I had no pens, no pencils, not even a crayon. An inmate that people call Deuce stabbed a guard. I don't know Deuce's real name, nor do I know how she became Deuce. She was inconsequential to me until her actions impacted my life. Deuce worked in the kitchen; she'd spent some number of stolen hours smelting a ballpoint into a shiv, melting the end in the gas burner, then rubbing the pen against a rough concrete corner until it held its edge. The word whispered across the line is that the guard—a squat, hairy comma of a man known to take liberties during pat-downs—grabbed Deuce in her crotch. Her response was to coolly slip her hand into the waistband of her sweatpants, spring her shiv, and, in one silky move, slip it knuckle deep into the guard's neck. It was, the whisper-line said, like watching a viper uncoil and sink her fangs into unsuspecting prey.

The guard's blood spurted in a high arc of droplets, ruby red on the institutional butterfat yellow of Bedford Hills's halls. Within seconds, some other guard had hit the alarms, and we inmates dropped to the floor, brooms, books, saucepans, and rakes beside us, like so many narcoleptic goats fainting in rigid, wary lines.

Our stuff was searched. Our things were rifled. People with pistols overturned our beds and pored through our cubbies. Our pens, our pencils—my pens, my pencils—were seized. Deuce was whisked away, disappeared into the bowels of Bedford Hills, although her belongings lingered for a day. Deuce was gone but not forgotten because, while Deuce was no more, we had to live with the consequence of her actions. Deuce couldn't cope with a homunculus pawing at her parts, so I couldn't write. Such is communal life and carceral justice.

I was forced to store up my stories like nuts in the cheeks of a squirrel. Two weeks passed before the guards let us have short, choppy pencils, like the kind that come with Yahtzee games or IKEA shopping baskets. When the pens returned in another six weeks, it was as if no one could remember why they'd been taken away in the first place.

Writers say this kind of thing all the time, but to me writing is like drinking water or eating food. Writing sustains me. I don't know who I am if I don't write. More important, you don't know who I am. If I don't tell my story, it's as if I've died. I'm in prison for life, and I'm not going to die early.

It was 1986, and I had been living in Boston for almost two years, when, crossing Harvard Square to buy some linens at Conran's, I saw a small, fierce woman dressed in all anarchist black. She rode a bulldozer, perched high above a knee-high forest of egg-white vulvar ceramic vases. She had shut down a portion of Harvard Square, and a small crowd of students, professors, and errant Bostonians had formed a semicircle around the ceramic forest. The tiny virago leaned precariously from the cage of the bulldozer, her body on the verge of toppling out. She held a bullhorn close to her lips and murmured a stream of feminist epithets in a rhythmic, shamanistic drone, sounding like a Filene's Basement Patti Smith channeling Andrea Dworkin. It was hard to hear her patter—her voice rose and dipped illogically like a poorly designed roller-coaster—but so many dust-heap feminism phrases fell, thudding with the threat of wooden nickels.

The woman abruptly dropped her bullhorn and ducked into the cab of the bulldozer. The engine flared. The gears ground. The machine lurched forward, crushing the white vulvar vases, mashing them into pointy white shards, and grinding the shards into dust. Backward and forward went the bulldozer with stuttering movements, herky-jerky and ill-conceived as the woman's speech. I was fascinated by its palsied grace.

Soon all the vases were reduced to fine white dust layering the cobblestones. So much white dust and so many pieces scattered like cremains. As the small, fierce woman was picking up her bullhorn to begin another unintelligible screed, the Cambridge police swooped in to arrest her, plucking her from the bulldozer's cage with cartoonish ease. The cops frog-marched the woman to the cruiser, and she lifted her head to look at me. We made eye contact. It was that visual electric snap that rarely happens with strangers, that shock of inexplicable recognition, that fast catch and firm latch that happens when a cerebral switch is flicked.

Usually these moments come and go, ephemeral. They get filed in the uncanny corner cabinet with déjà vu and validated premonitions, then they're forgotten. But this was no stranger, I realized, looking into those blue octopus eyes. This was my college roommate, Joanne Correa, formerly frilly, now feminist punk and wildly more fascinating for it.

I decided to go to the jail and bail out Joanne. It was the least I could do, after stealing her navy eyeliner and setting fire to her pink tufted cat that first semester of freshman year. It was no grand act of charity. I just paid the fine, a few hundred dollars, and she was free.

"I forgot how short you were," I said as Joanne walked through the police precinct's tall wooden doors. Just below my chin, Joanne's hair, a fuzzy aureole the color and shape of a benign white dwarf, exploded around her head.

"Thanks for the bail," she said and faltered. She looked around and hoisted her purse farther up her shoulder. It was one of those green canvas gas-mask holders from World War Whatever that the kids those days carried to affect affectlessness. Joanne looked around, lost. I was afraid she was going to cry. I hate crying. So pointless, and so damp.

Joanne's back tightened under her black canvas jacket. "Thanks," she said again.

"Hey, Joanne," I said. "I liked the bulldozer. Very impressive."

"It's not Joanne anymore. It's Tender. Tender deBris." And she walked down the steps, away from me.

I looked at her walking away and considered taking her to lunch, but she had the look of someone going through a "meat is murder" phase. Intrigued as I was, I couldn't stomach the idea of sitting in a café that smelled like unwashed anarchist listening to Tender née Joanne talk about feminine energy while a plate of tofu scramble slowly congealed in front of me. There are things that simply won't do, and anything that tries to make tofu something other than what it is—an unappetizing excuse for protein with the texture of boiled pencil eraser and the flavor of brown paper towels wetted with weak tea—is one of them.

I let Tender go on her way, but even with the name change, Joanne wasn't hard to track down. Of course I found her. How could I not.

I wasn't writing about food for the weekly the *Boston Phoenix*. Not food, not yet. I was a reluctant reporter of "lifestyles." When I think about those meaningless lifestyle columns, I hear humanity's death knell. All those words written on color-coordinating small appliances with your biorhythms, all those column inches devoted to finding inner bliss through low-impact aerobics, all those hours going clackety-clack on the keyboard while trying to stave off homicide with another thousand-word piece on the Scarsdale diet. (You have to respect Jean Harris, though you can hardly give her points for killing her ex-lover with a common handgun. Any moron with a clean record and a government ID can buy a handgun, but how many can engineer a perfectly timed bee sting?)

I hated the lifestyle section. *Lifestyle* means nothing; it's the part of the paper dedicated to making its reading public feel pointlessly bad about themselves—and then convincing readers that the solution to their existential woe is buying the selfsame stuff that made them feel bad. The lifestyle section exists to prescribe a standard of living to which ordinary people should aspire and ultimately fail. The only people to whom a lifestyle comes naturally are the very rich or the exceptionally famous. Everyone else is just trying to hardscrabble an existence about which they don't feel an unendurable level of shame.

Still, I enjoyed writing, and I loved the access that writing professionally gave me. For example, working at the *Phoenix* allowed me to interview Nina Hagen in Boston's two-block Little Germany. We ate schnitzel and drank yeasty beer, at least I did. Nina is a vegetarian, regrettably. Later that night, I sat in the second row of Hagen's show at the Beacon and enjoyed the sight of her bass player's right testicle, which had escaped the confines of his tight carpaccio-hued short-shorts. The next morning, I woke swaddled in clammy white sheets at some hotel, wrapped in the bass player's dreadlocks and wafting with the mushroom smell of scrotum and the fetid green-tea stink of pot.

Make no mistake: the *Phoenix* got me laid. Never underestimate the seductive power of a reporter's notebook and red-tipped nails grasping an elegant black pen. Lifestyles-section sex is the only thing that makes me wish that, rather than covering floor coverings, Ric Ocasek's wives, and Cabbage Patch Kids, I'd covered politics. Who doesn't want closer access to the Kennedys, if only for the post-cocktail hour lubrications, midnight lucubration, and later revelations.

Using my *Phoenix* resources, I found Emma, then Tender, formerly Joanne—her unlisted number posed no difficulty to me. She was remarkably easy to find, and as soon as I found her phone number, I called Emma, née Tender, née Joanne. We had coffee, and then we had margaritas, and then we collapsed in her bed, surrounded by sketches of vulvas. We laughed, we talked, we drank. We grew. We changed. We got closer. All these years after finding Emma, much to my anguish, I have yet to lose her. My relationship with Emma might be my greatest accomplishment—it's certainly my greatest wound. But maybe that's just nostalgia finally hitting my cold, fortressed heart. Prison will do that to a person, even a psychopath like me.

Jolly Time

*T*he mid '80s in Boston meant cheap bands and cheaper alcohol, dance moves that were all elbows and knees, done in stirrup pants and acid-colored dresses, in rubber bracelets and in lace. It meant hairstyles that required sticky handfuls of "product." It meant plates of sushi, new to American palates, bright slabs of pastel fish and the strange protocol of sitting obeisant on your knees at tables atop tatami mats. It meant leaving bars at two A.M., because Boston has never shed its puritanical past. (Boston is, parenthetically, the least sexy city I've ever known. I suspect Bostonians drink to make them think they might want to have sex, and the city closes its bars early to ensure that they still can.) It also meant knowing many, many gay men, many of whom would not live to grow older than thirty.

The mid '80s in Boston meant going home with men to discover they wore bikini underwear the same exact purple as grape Bubble Yum, and it meant not being certain if this was attractive or repellant. Living in Boston, as a woman between the ages of twenty-two and twenty-six, meant fucking men mired in their post-college morass of cartoons, bong hits, piles of laundry, and towers of takeout containers. These men held maturity at arm's length, deferring it with a slouch-pelvised, shrugging commitment to slacking. So many hopeless, hapless Bostonian men. The best thing about sleeping around in Boston was that I could focus on my work and didn't have to spend much time researching first; the city is big enough to find numerous partners, none of whom knew anyone else in my life. That's not to say I didn't do research on them; it's merely to say that I didn't have to. It was optional, not obligatory, and any dirt I discovered I saved for myself. Sometimes it's just nice to know what you can know. Other times it's nice to use what you know. In any case, though I didn't necessarily need to add to my files, I often did. Almost out of nostalgia's sake—almost, but not quite.

Being in Boston in the '80s also meant sleeping with women. Maybe it's being six feet tall, maybe it's my forthright air, but I've been hit on by women for almost as long as I've been hit on by men. However, apart from that slender waist of time in Boston, I never looked twice at girls. I gave it a go; you know, when in Rome and all that—Boston was positively seething with lesbians—I don't like to be left free of a fad. For a time, I took up with a lovely little alabaster-skinned redhead. We seduced each other in this nautical-themed bar with netting hung from timbers, ships' buoys on the wall, and tables shaped like captains' wheels. We had sex to Sade's *Diamond Life* because it was 1985, and it seemed like the thing to do. In 69, all red bushes and red locks, we looked like a strawberry-swirl ice cream. It was worth it for the visual alone. But both of us were dabbling Sapphics, and we dilettante-drifted, she with her freckles and bud-like nipples, and I with my unquenched yen for men.

Next, I dallied with a buxom bottle blonde who lived in Allston and went by the name Trashette. She was clued into the Boston arts scene—I think I met her through Emma, but I could be wrong. Trashette lived in a collective in an old firehouse that they were interminably renovating. Trashette, whose real name was Marie, played the '50s housewife to the group. She loved to make retro dishes like bacon-wrapped water chestnuts and tuna casserole with a cream-soup base and those little dehydrated onions sprinkled on top. Her space in the collective was assertively atomic kitsch; every item could have leapt out of an episode of *The Andy Griffith Show* or *Father Knows Best*. It was a kind of tyranny, Trashette's fierce adherence to her girdle-and-bouffant aesthetic, but she did make a dynamite pineapple upside-down cake.

The last woman I dabble-diddled was a Latina microbiologist from Harvard. She was very efficient, almost curt, all tight hospital corners and pressed jeans. Elena had kissed a man, but from the moment I laid eyes on her compact, neat body, I knew she was a lesbian. Elena was, in fact, the first and only woman I ever mind-fully pursued. There's a perverse pleasure in bringing someone to a truth about herself that she has long repressed. We met at a ski lodge in Vermont, separately on vacation in the same location. The first night, I drew her away from her friends, and she sat beside me, the length of her thigh pressed against mine, heat passing like some shining flame between our limbs. The second night, I kissed her goodbye in front of her inn room's door. The third, I didn't have to. She spent the night tangled in my bed, enjoying the first orgasms she'd ever experienced with another person. Raised a strict Catholic, she'd never known man nor woman, until I ruptured her hymen with my fingers and licked them clean.

Elena and I returned to Boston, and I took great pride in making her swerve from her regimented schedule that had afforded Elena her perfect academic record. Worn-out from fucking, she began calling in late into her lab job and sleeping through classes; we fucked so much, so long, and so often, we passed a yeast infection back and forth like a joint. We fell wildly, passionately in love for a number of weeks, and then, in a snap, it was gone—for me, at least. Elena had some trouble letting go, but I helped her relinquish her white-knuckled hold by moving to a new apartment with no forwarding address.

These four Boston years, working and playing hard in a go-go '80s style, I was no gourmand. I subsisted primarily on a diet of Diet Coke and microwave popcorn. I was busy and the *Phoenix* didn't pay. I lived hand to mouth, and neither my pay nor my free time allowed much space for the thoughtful purchase and careful preparation of food. I had too much to do—and too many to do—to think about cooking.

The first time my mother stepped into my Kenmore apartment, she opened the door to my refrigerator. In the fridge's white glow sat two six-packs of Diet Coke and an impressive array of condiments. There might have been a few stalks of wilted celery.

"Dorothy," she said, pressing her lips into a fine crimson line, "where is your *food*?" I smiled and waved my hand at the shelves of Jolly Time popcorn, boxes blaring yellow and red, the bright colors of lipids and blood. My mother sighed, and before she left for Connecticut, she filled my fridge with produce and meats, and my shelves with dried beans, jars of tomatoes, and boxes of rice. The former rotted, for the most part, while the latter accumulated a layer of dust.

Boston was, in short, a twentysomething's idyll. However, my time in Beantown was not perfect. My apartment was small and dark and given to sudden infestations of pests in the summer and clanking noises in the winter. It always smelled faintly of lobster pot, no matter which incense I burned or how often I rubbed the countertops with lemon. But it was thrilling to pay for my own life with money I made myself, even if I made that money by informing the good people of Boston that their lives were not as fabulous as those of Steven Tyler, Cyrinda Foxe, or Aimee Mann.

But then I got a phone call, and things changed, as they inevitably do.

It was, I think, April of 1988. The air had begun to warm with the scent of flowers and dirt. The birds were chattering. The leaves misted the skyline with green. I was in the midst of taking my summer clothes out of boxes and putting my winter clothes away when the phone rang.

"Dorothy, it's your mother." As if I didn't recognize her voice.

"Hi, Mom."

"Dorothy, your father and I are wondering whether you've plans for next weekend. We were hoping to have you and your sister and brother to the house." My sister, eighteen months younger, had graduated from Duke the year before; she chose to stay in North Carolina, where she was slogging away at a nonprofit. I couldn't understand why you'd go to Duke to be philanthropic, but that's my sister. My brother was still in college, a junior at Brown; he hadn't come out yet, but we all knew it was just a matter of time. Or maybe just I knew. More than once, I considered just letting that gay cat out of the rainbow bag, but even a psychopath like me has some compunction when it comes to the mental health of her baby brother. Besides, it wasn't as if I'd take any pleasure in telling his news.

My family was not the kind of family given to spontaneous acts of unity. Calling the three of us offspring to Connecticut signaled a major upheaval. I wondered if my mother had gotten her fill of my father's understated philandering. This felt unlikely. My mother didn't like to admit defeat. I wondered whether my father had decided that, now that my siblings and I were tottering toward adulthood, he could divorce my mother with propriety, if not elegance. This was not outside the realm of possibility.

I had, of course, investigated my father. I'd begun while I was still in high school. Over time, I unearthed the names and addresses of three of his paramours, all women he seemed to have met through work connections. (I'd unearthed other women he'd enjoyed, but these scraps of skirt didn't warrant full files.) The first I'd found was an executive assistant to a marketing honcho at a large German car corporation; their dalliance had lasted some time—throughout my last two years of high school and my first year of college. At first, it seemed as if it were a happy situation. As the months wore on, I realized that, rather than enjoying a peaceable fling, my father was feasting on melodrama. He seemed to mistake passion for love, and insanity for passion. This is never a good thing to learn about one's father.

As I saw my father's mistress grow more and more needy, making outrageous demands and late-night phone calls, I recognized something fundamental about my parents' relationship. I realized that had my mother never given rein to her rare but scarlet-tipped flights of rage, he'd have left her long ago. Some men need to witness female anger to believe in that woman's love. Some women need to get angry to experience that love. Some people grow together like horrible species of lichen. My parents, I learned, were precisely this kind of symbiotic organism.

Eventually, I put an end to the relationship between my father and his marketing assistant mistress. Don't get me wrong—she still lives and breathes, as far as I know. A sternly worded, uncomfortably specific letter written in my mother's hand on her monogrammed stationery landed on the desk of the assistant's boss. This missive made very short work of that affair—and the assistant's job.

My father didn't wait long to acquire a new lover. Unlike the executive assistant, this new woman was independent, candid, busy, and, judging from the subtext of some of her notes, more than a little kinky. From afar, I admired her, and if my father hadn't been so enthralled by her—he called her "feline," a tribute to her up-tipped eyes and disdainful spirit—I would have been entirely fine with their affair. Alas, he lost his head. It was alarming.

I didn't want my mother to lose my father to another woman, particularly one that I knew would drop him like a dirty stocking the moment he was single. Her independence made it difficult for me to find any information wedge for leverage. It also made me admire her a little. I like to think of this woman, whom I watched through a telephoto lens, as a distant role model. She seemed to be that rare woman who had it all, or at least everything that I wanted: financial success, personal freedom, the slavish adoration of a man, and unshakeable self-esteem. Then, struck by the emotional epiphany that he held a losing hand in this relationship, my father called it off. It was a Pyrrhic victory for unhappy marriages everywhere.

My father's final mistress, and from what I could tell still his current amour, is a freelance stop-motion animator. This animator sits in the sweet spot. She is neither too crazy nor too sane. She is neither too independent nor too attached, neither too successful nor too ambitious. Not too hot and not too cold, not too soft and not too hard; not too big and not too small, she is the baby bear's chair, porridge, and bed. My father snuggles in her mediocrity, and I feel fine about it.

I also tried to dig up dirt on my mother. Either her life was as boring as her Burpee seed catalog, or she was superb at burying the bodies. In any case, I found nothing on her. I was bitterly disappointed, though I'm not sure in whom.

So it was April 1988 when, after my mother called her family meeting, we convened in our living room. My mother sat in her chair, rigid as a bold lie. My dad stood behind his big leather club chair, leaning on it nervously, his fingers spidering on its surface. My sister, my brother, and I ranged along the overstuffed couch, its down cushions holding us like a hug. To a one, our bodies were taut scribbles of dread. My father seemed to quiver, running at a higher frequency than usual. My mother thrummed a low bass-line. My sister, empathetic soul that she is, oscillated with nerves. My brother, who clearly had smoked a hit or two off a joint in the barn before joining us, looked at once jittery and calm, but he had his own secrets to keep.

My father looked at us and cleared his throat. "Kids," my dad said, "you probably wonder why we asked you to join us—"

"Are you getting divorced?" my sister asked, her voice tense.

"Good gracious, no," my mother said. "Nothing like that." Her hand made a spasmodic move toward her purse, but stopped short, as if she'd touched something hot.

"Your mother and I have always loved each other very much," my father said. "We'd never—"

"—Don't be silly," my mother interrupted, her objection knitting with my father's. His fingers twitched. Her hand lurched. Their eyes met; their speech stopped. "I'd never allow a divorce. I love your father."

A pause wedged itself between them, uncomfortable as a sweaty stranger on a bus. They made eye contact. Almost in sync, they took a breath. My father's fingers spasmed toward the bare end table, and stopped short.

"I get it," I said. "Which one of you?"

"Which one of us what, Dorothy?" My father asked, his voice frayed like a knot.

"Which one of you has cancer?"

My brother looked at me; my sister blurted a short chain of vowels, sucking up the air in the room.

"I do," my mother said. "Lung. It's stage 4. Inoperable. *C'est la vie.*" She pressed her crimson lips together and raised a perfect eyebrow. "I really would enjoy a Gauloises, but I suppose I've already enjoyed enough for a lifetime." She exhaled sharply, and her face softened, my mother accepting her mortality in a single breath.

And that was the beginning of her end. The spring turned to summer; the days grew hot and languid. At first my mother tried to garden and to cook, but it was no good. She'd begin to knead her bread and lose energy before the dough grew elastic. She touched her berries and she felt no future. She stopped going outside, she grew still, she flattened. She removed herself from the world, and the world moved on.

Beyond my mother's bedroom window, her garden went slowly to seed. The asparagus blew to big, filigreed flowers. The birds ate her berries, the cutworms decapitated her broccoli, the deer nibbled her roses to nubbins. Forgotten tomatoes ruptured on the vine, eggplant and zucchini engorged to the size of small groundhogs, corn wizened on the cornstalk. It was a slow erosion, an anti-Eden, and though the rest of us did the best we could to slow the deterioration, the truth was that we were paralyzed by not caring very much. We simply didn't have green thumbs, and even if we did, our mother was dying. How could we care when the green beans grew large and furry as miners' mustaches. Every day the garden ran more to riot; every day my mother diminished. Run to its inevitable end, fecundity will always turn to decay.

My sister was the first to move home, returning from Greensboro in June. She came to cook for my father; she came trying to please my mother, who as she edged closer to death grew no more human, which is, if I think about it, perhaps the most logical response. My brother rejoined the family in July. By the end of the summer, my mother had given up hope, and my father had no choice but to hold her hand as she let go her life, a little bit day by day. She briefly went into the hospital, but she refused to stay. She didn't want more pain; she didn't want to prolong her days or forestall the inevitable black. Back in my apartment in Kenmore, I imagined her looking at her X-rays, tracing with her elegant crimson nail the great black roses of cancer blooming in her lungs. I suspect she moved home to grant them room to flourish, to nurse them into spectacular arrangement, to turn her body into the fallow ground for her cancer, the last thing she could cultivate like a blue-ribbon expert.

When my mom moved home to hospice care, I too returned, quitting my job and packing up my Kenmore apartment. The *Phoenix* told me they wanted me back, but I'd had my fill of Boston and its early nights, its Brooks Brothers boys, its New Wave dudes, and its semeny chowder. My family expected me to return home to Connecticut and watch my mother die. I would fulfill their expectations. I can't say I wasn't curious about death.

What can be said about cancer that hasn't already been said. It's a rotting death, and it reduces people with wants and drives and desires and thoughts and quirks to puling, puking, pained animals. There is no grace in cancer. Slowly, one by one, my mother's habits fell away. Confined to her bed, she was unable to cook, to garden, to harass farmers for their finest milks and thickest creams, to jar her preserves or bury her fists in the fragrant warm flesh of bread dough; she let go of one bit of living, and then she let go of another. First, she stopped dressing. She would do it tomorrow, she said, when she felt better. Clothes, she said, were too weighty a burden for her skin to bear. She'd spend her days in her bed, at first sitting up and reading but then mostly dozing, her nurses rotating like sandwiches at the automat, each one seamlessly able to take the place of the other, tending to my mother's meds and smells and effluvium. She'd look out at the garden, and we knew she was having a good day when she had the energy to castigate us for not weeding it, for not picking berries and putting up the gem-colored jams. She wore endless pajamas and bed jackets, frilly quilted bits of fluff that tied like a baby's bib underneath her chin.

Then she stopped putting on makeup, doing away with her daily application of foundation, concealer, blush, eyeliner, mascara, and lip liner. She kept just her Dior Rouge 999 lipstick, because she was not herself, she'd always said, without it. My mother's greyhound body became skeletal under the bedclothes. The skin on her hands looked almost translucent in the morning light, and her hair, previously lustrous, black, and thick—she was only fifty-two, after all; she'd not even finished menopause before the diagnosis—looked like an orange eraser had tried to rub her locks off her head, leaving a halo of gray, wispy tufts. One morning she refused her lipstick, and my sister and I looked at each other, knowing the end was visible in our mother's pale lips. They were the color of earthworms, her lips.

By the time the frost came, my mother had ceased sitting up in bed. She lay flat as postage, inert and breathy voiced. She slept a lot, while my father paced in soft-soled shoes. Always a kinetic man, he couldn't sit still and watch his wife die. He wore a circle in the floor of her room with his quiet shuffling. I felt more for him than for her; she had morphine. He only had scotch and guilt—and plenty of both.

My mother died on the day before Halloween. In Connecticut, we call this day All Saints' Eve, but it goes by other names in other places. It doesn't matter; language always fails, especially in death. Days before she died, my mother called me to her side. Her eyes were bright, and she took my hand in hers. It felt like paper wrapped around sticks.

"Dorothy," she said and patted my hand. "You were never my favorite." You'd expect that to hurt, but it didn't. She wasn't my favorite either. She closed her eyes. I kissed her forehead. She hadn't given up her perfume; she smelled like Chanel No. 5 and necrosis. A couple of days later, she was dead.

The days after my mother died passed in a rush. So much to do, so little will to do it, so many people and so many caring casseroles, one more florid than the next. I sat through the funeral in a miasma of disconnect. I didn't care. It was over. I wanted to be anywhere but there.

I remember when I was a very little girl, my mother sat me down at her vanity. She showed me her cosmetics: concealer, foundation, blush, liquid eyeliner, eyebrow color, eye shadow, mascara, powder, lip liner and lipstick. Magic golden tubes, magic glass vials, each smelling of bosoms, fragranced with adult possibility. One by one, she showed the little metal or glass containers to me, held them under my nose, dabbed a little of each on my cheek, my eyelid, my lips.

"This," she said, "is what a woman wears instead of armor. You put on the right makeup, and you look invincible. You feel like a warrior. You will still be a woman, but you will wear this on the outside so that on the inside, you will stand tall as a man. Do you understand?"

I told her I did.

"Your place is wherever you want it to be, Dorothy. You can work at home, like Mommy, or you can work outside, like Daddy. No matter what you do, be excellent at it, and always look your best." She paused. "That way the bastards won't ever get you down." She looked at herself in the mirror, and our eyes met in her reflection.

"No bastards," I said.

"That's right, my darling." Her lips red, eternally red, infinitely red, an everlasting crimson circle. "No bastards."

From my mother, I learned that beauty was armor. From my teenage friends, I learned that femininity was junk. They were both right.

After my mother died, my father sold the Connecticut house and he moved to the city, buying an apartment on the Upper West Side. I also moved to New York City, landing in the East Village, where, in 1989, twenty-seven-year-olds with aspirations to coolness chose to pay too much money for their apartments. On East 7th Street between 1st and 2nd Avenues, I found a tiny railroad one-bedroom apartment, a fifth-floor walk-up, and I was delighted. My bathroom window looked out on a small courtyard, and I had a loft-bed perched above my closet, a futon couch in the living room, an exposed brick wall, and a wee Juliet balcony.

My mother's death put around $60,000 in my bank account, giving me the freedom to find work without worry, to indulge in dinners at Odeon and fifteen-dollar margaritas at El Teddy's, to take cabs home from Tunnel at four in the morning, to buy short, tight dresses from Patricia Field, to fly to Florence and to fuck Marco in a ridiculous rococo Florence hotel room, and, for a limited time, to be as generally fabulous as I wanted. There's much to be said for being young, beautiful, and independently wealthy, however ephemeral these qualities may be.

By early summer of 1989, I landed at *Gotham Ace*, a weekly that was trying to wedge itself into the niche between *The Village Voice* and *New York Magazine*. I wrote the same kind of pieces I'd been writing for the *Phoenix*, lifestyle fluff and star profiles, but I got to do it in a real city with real food, real dirt, real nightlife, and real men.

New York City may have a commercial skin, but it's built on a skeleton of sex and magic. The bridges hang like jewels around the throat of the night, and the rivers unspool in endless runners of oily gray silk charmeuse. In the soulless corporate canyons of Midtown, the buildings point accusatory fingers at the uncaring sky. The streets flow with an endless human wash, so many people running like dumbstruck salmon, looking for love, looking for money, looking for a place to eat, wanting for fame, hoping for a place to sleep, hoping for a person to sleep with, praying for meaning in the dark before dawn. It's easy to get lost in the magic that is Manhattan, not only because you're one in a million but also because the city pulls you tight in its steely embrace. Expletives fly like art, traffic blares loud and comforting, bodegas welcome you with anonymous yellow light and the salt-vinegar-and-sugar smell of steam tables. Everywhere you go there is something wonderful, if only you open your heart, your mind, your wallet, or your thighs.

Like Venice, New York City is an improbable bunch of rivaling islands, held together by historic bridges, a common language, and a well-earned understanding of superiority. Rome may dwell in the land of cock—and it does, the phallus dominates that city's skyline; Roman men strut with unquestioned self-confidence, their limbs decked in crimson, in mustard, in peacock blues and greens, each demanding your gaze—but as much as the long penile lines of the skyscraper may define New York City, it's a place that doesn't care who fucks whom, as long as you do it. Fucking, metaphorical or literal, is New York City's soul. Fucking with, fucking up, fucking over, fucking around, fucking right: New York Fucking City has earned its name. It makes perfect sense that I felt at home on its streets. The catcalls of its men were a comfort.

The year I moved to New York, I pried Emma from Boston to spend New Year's Eve in Manhattan. "You need to meet a proper city," I told her, "one whose bars don't close until four." We scaled the wrought-iron gates to the Central Park Zoo, and wandering the somnolent grounds in the dusky chill, we swigged Krug from the bottle and toasted to Gus the Neurotic Polar Bear (what other kind would live on Fifth Avenue?) until two security guards made us leave. We hopped the subway and took the train to Houston Street. Passing the Duck Man, the SoHo fixture who nightly pushed a shopping cart of plush Donald Duck knockoffs, we waved, and we weaved our way to I Tre Merli, a very loud and rather awful but terribly chic restaurant on West Broadway. Emma wore a long black vintage tutu over fishnets and John Fluevog boots; I had on a black Lycra catsuit. We made a spectacle of ourselves, drunk and young and gleaming with promise and promiscuity. A table of older men next to us chatted us up, plying us with the lemon vodka shots that were all the rage.

Midnight came and went; the men paid for our meal and swept us up in a limo that vomited us out on Mulberry Street. We entered a nondescript door and found ourselves in a seedy wood-paneled room bedecked with pictures of the Pope and burly men in bad suits, a Mafia club. We drank brown liquor and snorted cocaine; we mercilessly teased these connected men to their great joy and greater discomfort; and a couple of hours later, we stumbled out into the fractal Manhattan dawn.

In the cab back to my apartment, Emma and I raised phantom glasses to the buildings blurring in our taxi's windows, bright in the whitened night, like the lights of a sinking luxury liner. We toasted to love, we toasted to friendship, we toasted to cock, we toasted to my dead mother, and we toasted to our lives, shiny and slick and feral in the sleepless city.

It took Emma nine years to join me in my glorious New York City, but I was glad when she did. I found it pleasing to have a friend.

6

Lampredotto

*T*he plastic cups and utensils here in Bedford Hills leave a flat aftertaste, an echo of regret that rings anew at every meal. Sip of enervated coffee, spiral of contrition; mouthful of clammy gray oatmeal, swallow of remorse. A year into my sentence and I remain unsure what I regret. In my heart and in my guts, I know that if I had the chance, I'd kill them again. Maybe I regret not killing more, or killing better, perpetrating more, better murders with higher style and slyer humor. Murder in the vein of Schiaparelli's Skeleton Dress. Murder as homage to Louise Bourgeois's *Maman*. Murder with the final beauty of Zaha Hadid's Bridge Pavilion in Spain. Murders kissed with an artistic certainty, uniting us in our collective will to cross to our filigreed, immutable end.

Of all my men, Marco is the most important, though it might be more accurate to say that he was the most lasting. What is importance, anyway, but the weight of experience. Marco and I have the most history; our lives are the most inextricably bound. Marco and I grew together like wisteria vine on a building that, as the vine's many tendrils burrow into the brick, causes the structure to crumble. The inescapable, imperceptible power of time reduces even mountains to molehills. Marco is the man I've known the most, the longest, and the best; we shaped each other during our lives, and we shape each other even after death.

Marco and I met in Siena in 1983 during my junior college semester abroad. Though Marco had graduated the Università degli Studi di Siena with a Scienze Biologiche degree, he lingered like a mysterious stain. He traveled with a complement of testosterone-charged men, all decked out in the swinging velvet crush and smudgy eyeliner of the New Romantic, slaves to the glittery, fashionable charms of Bowie, Roxy Music, and Adam Ant. Marco and his friends were the best post-punk that *la bella figura* could bring in their tight black trousers, frock coats, and ruffled white shirts.

Life with Marco was delectable. I liked having a slightly older Italian boy to drink wine with and fuck on long, languid afternoons. He had a Vespa, of course, and I loved careening around on the back of it, helmet on head, cigarette on my lips, Marco's narrow hips scissored between my long thighs. I enjoyed having a man with whom I could visit other cities—Firenze and its salty joy of *lampredotto* sandwiches, sleepy Montalcino and its Brunello and *pinci*, Radda and its Chianti and its *pici*. And to be candid, most of all I liked having an agreeable Italian man on my arm when I didn't want to be bothered by other Italian men.

You've seen "American Girl in Italy," that famous Ruth Orkin black-and-white shot of the tall brunette sashaying past a pack of braying Italians, louche and lounging in suits. It's a cliché because it's true; you couldn't walk down an Italian street without men slavering like dogs at veal bones. Though it was often uncomfortable to be a lone woman in Italy, it was sometimes even more uncomfortable to be in a group of women, especially a group of two or three American girls, or two or three non-Italian Europeans—in those days, Italian men weren't adept at telling an American from a German from a Brit from a Swede, particularly if we were all speaking English. You and your friends would be in line at the pizzeria to get a bite after class, standing at the bar in a café to drink espresso, or standing in the piazza and deciding where you were going for dinner, and one or five Italian boys would glom on to your group like remora on sharks, unclear even to themselves what they hoped to accomplish.

I found Italy an interesting place to be a young American woman. I rather enjoyed being objectified. I like it when men look at me as if they want to devour me. I find it deeply entertaining. It becomes annoying only when they start talking, as if I'd have any interest in anything that comes out of their mouths.

I remember this one man in Siena. Every Tuesday and Thursday, he would follow me from literature class to the *pensione* where I lived.

I didn't have class these afternoons, and I cherished this time by myself. (One thing about Italy: the natives don't trust people who like to be alone. Italians abide by the saying, *"Chi mangia solo crepa solo"*—he who eats alone dies alone. I myself adore eating alone. Like my hero M.F.K. Fisher, I love sitting at a restaurant table and chewing each bite thoughtfully and completely, lavishing every morsel with my undivided attention. Italians consider this kind of solitary endeavor an aberration; it horrifies them. Forgive the meandering. Sometimes it's hard to keep a tale on the straight and narrow.)

The man who followed me would watch me exit through the school's stone archway, and he would peel himself from the side of the wall like a shadow. He would walk beside or behind me, talking in my ear. "Signorina, why do you-a notta talk to me? You are so beautiful. Like the—what do you call it, the America mountains—the R-r-rockies? You are Americana, *si*? Please talk to me, say-a one word to die me happy."

Tuesday after Thursday, week after week, as long as the weather was dry, the same ritual. This man would lie in wait, smoking; he'd see me and separate from the wall; and he'd follow me, whispering Iago-like in my ear. Twice a week, week after week, I would hold my chin up and walk. There was no need to let him know that I could talk to him in his mother tongue, and there was no need to tell Marco about my shadow man, this lanky black-haired shade who trailed me like creepy clockwork. Had I told Marco, he and his gang of roustabout romantics would likely have beaten him to pulp. One of the wonderful things about true Italian men is that their default setting is about a cunt hair away from physical violence where their heterosexual bonds are concerned. I do enjoy men with a whiff of menace.

But I didn't tell Marco, and I hardly spoke to my shadow. I let him slink beside me, sputtering nonsense seductions. After about a month, he started using his hands as well as his voice, briefly touching my elbow, my shoulder, my hip—tiny, tentative taps, as if he were checking whether a pan was hot. After a month, he grew bolder, physically barring my entrance into my *pensione*, where my little old *nonna pensione* owner would often be taking her siesta, her snoring audible. Speech led to touch with this strangely obsessed Italian man, touch led to grabbing, and grabbing led to boldness. One day he pushed past me as I unlocked the *pensione*'s door and made it to the top of my stairs. Only my shutting the door in his face stayed him.

And then one Thursday afternoon, I wasn't fast enough. It was winter, late November or early December, and the lanky shade slithered past me into my room. He grabbed my shoulders and pinned me against the wall, pressing my face against a crack that, when I lay in bed, looked like a rabbit. This close, though, the rabbit was just a crack, a curving, thin fault in the plaster, abstract and disembodied. My face mashed against the wall and his elbow jammed against my spine, I heard the THWCKK of leather whipping through a buckle, the ZZHPP of a zipper unzipping. I felt my skirt lift and my tights and panties pulled roughly to my knees. A sharp elbow dug into my shoulder; my knees buckled from the pressure, and my face slid down the cool plaster wall.

I felt his fingers spread my labia and the sharp jab of his cock entering my pussy. I didn't speak. I barely breathed. I'm being raped, I thought. Fascinating. I heard the shudder of his breath, felt him spasm against and inside me. Then he stopped, and so fast that it almost felt like a hallucination, he was gone. I straightened my clothes and cleaned my mascara from the plaster wall. I never saw him again. My shadow was no more. He evaporated into the medieval gloom that shrouds Italian towns.

Of course, I got tested for venereal diseases. It was hard work to find an Italian doctor to take my unmarried, American blood and run the tests—so provincial, Italian doctors. I chose a doctor on the wealthy side of town, feigned ignorance of the language, popped a cheap wedding ring on my finger before my visit, and cushioned my request for an STI panel with a breathy sob story about discovering my new husband with a blond "cover" at a nearby hotel. It worked. Everything was blissfully negative. Whatever depravities my rapine shadow was guilty of, spreading syphilis and gonorrhea wasn't among them. Naturally, I was on the Pill. I knew from a young age that motherhood was a cage I never wanted to inhabit. Children make me turn on the oven and reach for the rosemary.

Life was merry in Siena; Marco was a lovely companion during my time abroad. He was jovial and gluttonous, two qualities I appreciate in a man. His friends were pleasant enough, and they appreciated our reciprocal relationship: I'd introduce them to fast foreign girls and they'd suffer my presence. My ability to converse in their native language helped—Italians have little patience with Americans and our boorish adherence to English. Marco and I had a grand time. I always enjoyed fucking him.

There was one trouble, however. Unlike my experience with the Pennistone boys, I failed to find any compromising information on Marco. Part of it was that I didn't know the system well enough. Part of it was that Italy has never been known for its systems. The fact that something as nefarious and weird as the Mafia can replace government in a sizable portion of the country (and the fact that someone as nefarious and weird as Berlusconi can gain and hold power) suggests Italy's ability to function without much of a system. In this, America is not like Italy. Americans adore systems. We want a system that obscures the system so that we feel comforted by there being both a system and a conspiracy system behind the system. We Americans are absolute fiends for rules. Italians are not.

It was thus difficult to find dirt on Marco, and it was hard for me to relax into the relationship. For these reasons, the only man other than Marco that I fucked that extended year abroad in Siena was my creeping shadow. I was sure that Marco was dallying with others (and I'm now certain that his occasional trips out of town were to court the woman who would become his embittered Versace-wearing *donna*). But I couldn't catch him at it. I knew that Marco wasn't smarter than me; I just couldn't prove his stupidity. It was frustrating.

But something about Marco's malingering in Siena smelled noxious. While it wasn't that out of character for young Italian men to be unemployed and practicing *l'arte di non fare niente*—the art of doing nothing—Marco's *dolce far niente* was colored by his disquiet over it. I'd sometimes catch him staring with a cat-startled look on his face. We'd be lying in postcoital lassitude, sharing a cigarette, and, defenses down, Marco would freeze and prickle. He'd give me a rueful smile and brush my hair, as if I liked to be touched after sex, and he'd murmur something about my beauty. It read like a script—his vulnerability, his body's emotional betrayal, and his deflection on to me. He wore time like a man who feared it would fray and tear. He may have aspired to the relaxed carelessness of the *ciondolone*, the idler, but Marco was idle only in appearance. At his soul, he was angst-ridden as Kierkegaard pondering his deathbed.

I had to find out why, and I knew if I was vigilant that I would. Marco's secret began to coalesce with his absolute refusal to visit Rome, which I found inconceivable. Italians love Rome. A trip to Rome is less a holiday and more a pilgrimage that ends with excellent offal and artichokes. Italians rarely turn down the chance to show off the Eternal City, especially when it's just a short train ride away. An Italian in Siena refusing to take his foreign girlfriend to Rome would be like a Bostonian refusing to show New York City to an Italian: inconceivable.

I, of course, love Rome. Aside from New York City, Rome is the only place that I could imagine myself living. Rome wants to lie back and let you stroke it, lick it, and devour it whole. Rome makes my head swim with its beauty, the sheer weight of its history, its crazy quilt of architectural movements, and its breathtaking men. The men in Rome saunter like they have great towering monuments between their legs. I find it difficult not to go entirely bent-kneed and supplicant, mouth open and teeth delicately bared, so great is the power of Rome.

But Marco, usually so generous and agreeable in indulging my whims, presented me with stony-faced rejection whenever I raised the topic of visiting the Eternal City.

"*Mai*," Marco would say. Never. And then he'd change the subject.

And that was what it took. That refusal. That word. That adamantine tone. I knew that there had to be a reason why Marco, a man who'd drop everything to take a four-hour train ride to Genova to see a secret Stranglers show at the Milk Club, was so implacable about visiting Rome. I began searching for a missed connection, and it took months, but eventually I found one.

It was a business card. Small and unremarkable, found stuck to the bottom of a recently emptied wastebasket. Just a business card for a Roman *macelleria*, a butcher shop. This plain, utilitarian, stark piece of paper white as a winter landscape slashed with the black of wet trees. One side was in Italian, MACELLERIA IACHINO GIANCARLO, VIA DEL FORTE BRAVETTA 164, ROMA and the name DAVIDE MARCO IACHINO. The other side was in Hebrew, a language I don't read.

My head spun. I knew Marco's last name to be Iocco, a name that acts like Smith or Jones in America, inscrutable in terms of place or origin. I held the card in my hand, turning it over and over. Could it be that Iachino was Marco's actual last name? In Italy, Iachino is like Goldberg or Silverstein in America; it's a name that immediately marks you as Jewish. Was Marco Iocco really Davide Iachino? This, I thought, was at least the warm bullet casing, if not the smoking gun.

I began searching Marco's room, rifling through his sheets and under his mattress, tap-tap-tapping on his desk drawers, shaking his books, and turning over the prints on the wall. And finally, finally, secreted away under a loose board beneath his bed, I found his passport. Marco was not Marco. Marco was Davide, and Davide was a Jewish butcher in Rome. Intriguing.

It explained a lot, actually. Why Marco took an almost orgiastic delight in consuming *gamberi crudi*, raw shrimp, and Aquacotta della Maremma, the seafood stew that's served along the Tuscan coast, rich with bivalves, mollusks, and crustaceans. Why he ate cinghiale, speck, lardo, guanciale, and pancetta at restaurants every chance he got—but why there was never any pork, not even a paper-wrapped pile of thinly sliced prosciutto, the quintessential Italian staple, in his refrigerator. Why some Saturday mornings, particularly those that punctuated debauched weeks, Marco was nowhere to be found, and not even his band of floppy-haired velvet-coated *amici* knew where he went. But most of all, it explained why Marco wouldn't go to Rome with me.

Rome may be one of the world's great cities, but it's not New York. It's a small town by comparison, and it would take only one person who knew Marco to see me with him for his whole congregation—

his whole community—to know his secret, hidden life. His family knew he was living here in Siena, but they didn't know the full extent of Marco's activities, and if they had an inkling, they likely looked at Marco's Siena time as his rumspringa, an adolescent interlude that would end when Marco assumed his adult responsibilities. Marco, it seemed increasingly clear to me, was biding his time before taking over the bloody family business.

To be a shochet, a kosher butcher, was, I soon learned, a serious occupation. Not just anyone could train to become a shochet; you had to be pious, sincere, and committed. You also had to be an Orthodox Jew, at least in Italy. Learning shechita, the Jewish dietary rules for ritual slaughter and butchery, takes many months; some people study for as long as a year, and understandably so—it is a complex process. The shochet has to slice through the animal's esophagus, trachea, jugular, and carotid in one unflinching stroke. The animal has to be exsanguinated and porged, or removed of veins, nerves, caul fat, and sinews; after, it has to be koshered, a process involving copious running water and salt. It is intense, precise, finicky, bloody work, and I could not fathom Marco—with his white skin, tousled hair, and kohl-lined doe eyes—doing any of it.

I pondered what to do with this knowledge now that I had it. Marco's band of eyeliner boys had no idea that Marco's New Romantic velvets shrouded a secret Semitic identity. Marco's group bonded with the casual racism so endemic to Italian culture, making jokes about Jews and indulging in the kind of armchair anti-Semitism that is the heritage of a formerly fascist country. After all, Italy's famous *Manifesto della razza,* or Manifesto of Race, the 1938 document that stripped Italian Jews of their citizenship, wasn't yet fifty years old when I was living in Siena. You need generations to cruise past that kind of racist thinking, and Italy had hardly seen one changing of the guard.

Marco may have been a louche layabout, but he worked hard to hide his history from his circle of friends, and from me. Not that I would have cared, though I admit I had wondered why Marco was circumcised. I felt disappointment the first time Marco's pegged trousers hit the floor. I hadn't yet been with a man with a foreskin, and I wanted to see what all the fuss was about. One hears things, and one hopes that other countries will gift you with at least a little exoticism. Certainly, Marco wasn't the first Jew I'd ever fucked. Pennistone, for all its WASPish, clench-jawed elitism abounded with Jews, and my Connecticut day school was stuffed with them. In fact, the first person who ever used his mouth to give me an orgasm was Jewish; he was also almost kicked out of school when someone tipped off the principal that he had a fat wad of marijuana in his locker. Only his mother's money and a generous donation to some school building fund saved him, I heard, though he did have to spend some time in rehab and he did get a suspension. Had he never breathed a word to his friends about that kegger and that blowjob, nothing would have come between him and his beloved bong, but I digress.

While I could not have cared less that Marco was Jewish, I was delighted to finally find his dirt. I knew Marco's real name, his family's business, what he was hiding, and whom he feared would find out. It was a wealth of information, and I had multiple ways I could use it. It put a spring in my step, a smile on my face, and a slick of wetness between my thighs. Power is the ultimate aphrodisiac.

In the end, I chose to do nothing with what I knew, not immediately—not for a year. I bided my time and I treasured my find. I stored the business card carefully in a book that I knew Marco would never touch (Alice Walker's *The Color Purple*), and I kept quiet. I took so long to unearth this precious dirt that I had only six more weeks to spend with Marco before I was scheduled to meet up with my family for an obligatory turn around Europe. It wasn't something I was looking forward to—at twenty, I'd already had a lifetime of watching my mother go glassy-eyed with the joy of being in Paris, and left to my own devious devices, I'd rather have plundered the boys of Capri—but my parents had stipulated my presence at a Daniels family vacation before they'd fund my stay in Siena.

After my classes finished, Marco and I made a mad dash to the Maremma coast, where we tanned on the beach and picnicked in the *pineta*, and enjoyed very quiet, very unobtrusive sex in some stranger's cabana. Taking Trenitalia, we looped Italy, pretending we were married and spending a weekend in a hotel room in Verona, where we saw Puccini's *Madama Butterfly* at the Verona Arena, and held our breaths as Raina Kabaivanska sang "Come una mosca." I recall that we had the most sublime *risotto con capretto*—the steaming rice suspended in a savory sauce, so light that the tiny bits of goat, bones intact, seemed to float above it, like Jesus walking on water—at a café that has been open since before Puccini was born. From Verona, we crossed Italy to the Riviera, and we hiked through Cinque Terre, the Ligurian Sea hundreds of feet below us ruffling like cobalt silk caressed by invisible fingers, both of us clutching the iron chains bolted into the rock face, our feet on paths no wider than our hands. We made the most of those weeks, and I never, not once, raised the specter of forbidden Rome.

I returned to my senior year at Pennistone, and I became Arts Editor of the paper; I wrote some cover stories for *The Green*, the weekly in Burlington, Vermont; and I got my first piece published in the *Phoenix*. I thought of Marco often, frequently while fucking other boys. I decided that, after graduation, I would take a trip to Rome.

After my plane landed at Fiumicino, I waited for the jet lag to cool its engines and return me to my original upright position. I was going to be in Rome for ten days; there was no immediate reason to rush anything. I wandered through the Palatine Hill and got swimmy-headed with Stendhal syndrome in front of the Temple of Caesar. I may be a titanium-clad bitch, but I am undone by the swirl of Rome's ancient air, the press of its ancient rocks, and the knowledge that these stones, right here, were touched by Marcus Antonius, by Cato, by Octavian, by Nero himself. The College of the Vestals, standing serene and decapitated in its terrible stone row, makes me quiver. To give up sex for thirty years is one thing, but the vestal virgins wielded serious Roman weight; power almost always compensates for other losses, and the vestals had much. To have and to hold the written wills of powerful men is to have a mother lode of information. Able to vote, able to own property, and serving as confidants of the powerful, these virgins were no one's bitch. The fact that few married after their service was finished is telling; why abdicate power when you have become accustomed to the joy of it.

I walked Rome from snout to tail, traversed the line from the Circus Maximus to the Villa Borghese, from Vatican City to the Catacombs of St. Sebastian, from Trastevere to Castro Pretorio. I walked and I toured and I wore my Walkman, carrying extra batteries and pretending to be just another American girl who didn't understand a goddamn word of Italian, unless it served me. I didn't want anything or anyone between me and my getting pelvic with this glorious rotting city.

To this end, I had lied to my parents. I had invented a friend, Amy, who was traveling with me, but whom I was meeting in Rome as her semester abroad ended. I concocted conversations, forged letters, and imagined scheduling; I made Amy so convincing that my parents were relieved that I had a good friend waiting for me. Imagined Amy aside, I was gloriously alone; I had a hotel room to myself, and ten lone days in Rome. Best of all, I felt secure in the knowledge that I was going to scare the absolute fuck out of my former lover the moment he saw me walk through his butcher shop door.

Part of my wandering for four days before I visited Marco was my desire to get to know Rome on my own terms. Part of it was the jet lag. And part of it was that I met an adorable banker from Bern at the Spanish Steps, and I spent twenty-four hours in his fine hotel room, fucking him tongueless. So anal, and I mean that in the best of ways. You can't fault a Swiss for his punctual proclivities.

But the greatest portion of my delay was that I was enjoying imagining how Marco would react when he saw me. Of all the kosher butcher shops in all the towns in all the world, I had to walk into his. I imagined Marco wrapped in the ubiquitous white apron, a large glass-faced case of meats between us. Marco looking up at me; it taking a moment for my face to register; his cleaver clattering to the floor. I imagined the blood draining from his face, his knees weak, his pulse thumping. I imagined his struggle for composure, and his loss of it. I imagined him stuttering and trying to formulate some kind of sentence as he tried to work the mental math of my being there, in his shop, in the Jewish ghetto, in Rome. I imagined him failing. And then I imagined fucking him. I always did enjoy fucking Marco.

This is more or less how it transpired. He didn't drop his cleaver; he wasn't holding one. He did stagger a bit, and that pleased me inordinately. He was, in fact, wearing a large white apron, a neat black beard, and a small gold band. Marco, it transpired, was married. This development was thrilling. Mistresses have much power and so little responsibility; it's hard not to respond to the pure erotics of the situation.

Marco came from behind the counter, he held out his arms—and he dropped them, pressing them against his sides like a penguin, restraining himself. He couldn't hug me. Not only could it betray the secret of our carnal past, but as an Orthodox Jew, Marco couldn't touch women who weren't family. He struggled to control his speech, sputtering; I stayed cool and supremely confident. Speaking in English, I said I'd seen him through the shop window and felt compelled to say hello—it had been so long since Siena and the university, I said. I told him he looked well. I let him know where I was staying and how long I'd be in Rome. He didn't say much. His face turned white, then red, and finally settled into pink. I had unsettled him, and I was delighted.

Two hours later, Marco was in my crimson-covered bed at the Hotel Campo de' Fiori. *"Mia cara, ti ho perso così,"* he said, *"odori come i fiori che crescono dalla figa di Venere. Come mi manchi leccarti, gustarti, il mio sogno Americano."* My darling, I missed you so. You smell like flowers growing from Venus's pussy. How I miss licking you, tasting you, my American dream.

Looking in Marco's eyes, I pulled his left hand to my mouth, pressed his finger to my lips, and pushed his ring finger down my throat far enough to make me gag. Coating his finger with spit, I worked the ring slowly off his finger with my teeth. When it was free, I spat it at his chest. It hit and bounced to the floor, where it lay for the next eight hours.

The first time I saw Marco in Rome was also the next to last. Which is not to say that I never saw Marco—I did, often. For almost thirty years, we would meet anywhere but Rome. Frequently, we met in Toscana; once we shared a Bolgheri inn room that was precisely the assertive pink of my interior labia; another time, we pushed together a pair of beds, narrow as a nun's thighs and just as tight, at Terme San Filippo. The hotel held all the sensuality of an OB-GYN office, and the air wafted with the hellish sulfur smell of the mineral waters. The food was medicinal and the wine list prescriptive; still, we had delightful sex. Another time, we stayed at this wonderful former monastery turned aristocratic seat turned B&B in Chianti; the establishment had a grappa room, something I found very civilized. Once we stayed in a friend's seventeenth-century villa in Montalcino; we accidentally set fire to the compost pile, missing the embers in the ashes, and spent a precious hour and a half carrying buckets of water back and forth to quench the flames.

All told, we met about once a year, sometimes skipping years, rarely meeting more often, for almost thirty years. Marco's and my get-togethers had a *Same Time, Next Year* kind of vibe, except they took place in a cavalcade of hotel rooms and with far less sentiment. Sometimes I would come to Italy and Marco wouldn't be able to get away from his *donna*; other times he wouldn't want to. Over the years, Marco and his bleached-blond wife had five children, and with each succeeding birth, I felt more pride in my cherry, show-room-quality genitalia.

When I met Marco that first time in Rome, he'd been married only a few months. The marriage, he said, was a largely strategic union, joining his family, butchers from antediluvian times in the Ghetto di Roma, and her family, who owned a slaughterhouse in a small town near Firenze. The marriage meant that his family's butcher shop had unfettered, direct access to a supplier; they would get the best meat at the best prices, and under Marco's guidance, the company fattened.

Learning about Marco's fledgling meat empire, I understood why Marco took his degree in biology; he followed it with an advanced degree in animal sciences, and, with this knowledge, he'd go full organic, or "bio," as it's called in Italian, making his company a boutique-driven purveyor of dead animals. Dario Cecchini in Panzano aside, Macelleria Iachino was the slow-food-movement meat poster child, if there were such a thing. Even people who didn't care for kosher meat—so bloodless as to taste fatigued, kosher meat has little to recommend it—would visit Macelleria Iachino; such was the power of Marco's animal husbandry. I was proud of his business acumen; I like successful men. They smell like money, confidence, and expensive hand lotion.

When he was with me, Marco generally reverted to his genial, jovial, gluttonous self. He ate everything. He fucked me silly. He sang snippets of songs by the Psychedelic Furs. He was a reminder, every day I saw him and in every way he touched me, of our shared youth. That golden time when we smoked as if we were immortal, danced as if we were graceful, and fucked as if we would never have another opportunity.

The main thing that youth has going for it is porpoise-tight skin. Raw, wide-eyed newness is meaningless. Nostalgia for knowing nothing is asinine; you can't recapture it and you don't want to relive it. Better to sing a song of experience with your burning tiger's heart.

7

Truffles

ecember 12, 2000, was a very good day. I had a ticket in my
hand to visit Italy for truffles. One does that. One goes to
Italy for white truffles, as one goes to Nova Scotia for Fourchu
lobster, as one goes to Ginza for Fugu-chiri, as one goes to Paris for
macarons, as one goes to the Iowa State Fair for deep-fried butter.
If one must.

Ostensibly, I was going to Italy for the truffles—white, mostly,
but I'm not opposed to black. *Tartufo bianco*—white gold, twee food
writers call it—melts with delicacy on your tongue; it's earth made
ephemeral, ephemera made earthy. It's why God made Barolo,
really, for there are few entities made for each other so completely
as truffles and Barolo. While the black truffle has its delights—it has
muscle, heft; it needs heat to open it, to pry its tiny knees apart and
entice it to offer up its sex-tasting funk—the white truffle is the ne
plus ultra of *funghi*. Italians love few things as much as they love
their mushrooms, and they love little more than they love their
tartufo bianco. Truffles, Italian truffles, are a course in erotics for your
mouth. I don't trust anyone who doesn't adore them.

In the winter of 1998, about eight years after Andrew hired me
to write for *Noir*, it folded. However, I was fortunate to sidestep the
magazine's demise. I'd caught burblings of *Noir*'s closing, and in
1997, I'd jumped from Andrew's bed and masthead to Gil Ramsey's
Eat & Drink. At Gil's magazine (and also in his bed), I had free rein,
able to pursue my own flights of food fancy with a breathtaking
budget and a remarkably lavish lifestyle.

Thus it was in December 2000, *Eat & Drink* was sending me to
Italy to hunt for truffles. Looking back, as I am wont to do during
these mind-numbing incarcerated days and restless imprisoned
nights, I wonder if I hadn't been called to Italy by a higher power. I

don't believe that everything happens for a reason—things happen because we make them happen—but sometimes the mystic reaches its long fingers through the ether and taps us on the breastplate. Truffles or fate, Italy beckoned that December, and I was thrilled.

Some people prefer truffles from Languedoc or Provence. I prefer mine from Alba. I could justify my preference; I could say pointed things about terroir and minerality, about the proximity of cypress trees and Nebbiolo vines to truffle-hosting oaks; I could sing an aria about microclimates, sun-slant, and tubers. I could talk a silky swath about tradition and the Italian Lagotto Romagnolo, an unparalleled hunting dog, and the gleaming bond between truffle hunter and hound. I could, but I won't, because my preference is purely chauvinistic. I prefer Italian truffles because I prefer Italy. I prefer Italian wine, Italian food, Italian opera, Italian culture, the insane troll logic of Italian bureaucracy, and Italian men. I admit that French women's fashion is better—with the exception of Gucci, Italian women's fashion is boring, really. The boots are good, I'll grant them that.

I am visceral and I am lazy. I like my truffles like I like my men: Italian. And if in Europe and if I'm in a pinch, Spanish. I have nothing against American men (and much in favor of them), but America doesn't produce white truffles, at least not any worth eating. Don't believe the lies. Don't believe those lies, anyway. Believe others, if it makes you feel safe. Safety, too, is a lie.

That winter, Marco was sadly eschewing all pleasures of the flesh beyond the borders of his marital bed. It was a tedious thing he did from time to time—grow conventional, make nice to his screeching *donna* with the bottle-blond locks and the veiny hands, heavy with jewels wedged on starving fingers. In any case, Marco was regrettably unavailable. *"Mia cara, mi dispiace ma non posso vederti. Il mio cuore appartiene a mia moglie, siamo due fatto uno, come cigni, come lupi, come tortore,"* he wrote to me. He was sorry. It wasn't possible. He and his ropy Borghese *donna* were two made one, he said, like swans, like wolves, like turtledoves. "Like black vultures," I wanted to add, but why bother. Soon enough, Marco would drift away and return to his natural bonobo ways. I had only to bide my time.

I fortunately had a backup plan in Giovanni, a man who was different from Marco in almost every way but his passport and his names' ending in vowels. Giovanni was slender, almost emaciated. He could have body doubled for Gandhi, had Gandhi looked stereotypically Italian. His legs were thin, his arms were thin, his chest was thin, his knees were knobby as a whippet's. My thighs nearly matched the circumference of Giovanni's waist. His wrists bobbled with bones like small bags of marbles. He had fantastic hair, though, rich and lustrous, and long. The hair on his chest grew in these pin-straight follicles approaching two knuckles in length. Likewise the hair that nestled his penis; giving him a blowjob was like pawing through an Easter basket to find the last candy eggs.

(Side note: *cazzo* is Italian for "cock," but it really means so much more than that. It's a word that's larger on the inside than its five letters would lead you to believe. *Cazzo* carries a fine, long, winding caravan of epithetic meanings: cock, dick, prick, shit, penis, pecker, and fuck. For example, you might in exasperation exclaim, *"Che cazzo stai dicendo?"* Which, literally translated, means, "What the cock are you saying?" but more meaningfully translates to "What the fuck are you saying?" However, if you're a woman talking to your girlfriend, she might ask of your new lover, *"Ha un bel cazzo?"* an inquiry regarding the fitness of your new lover's genitals. *Cazzo* is an elastic word, one whose growth verges on tumescence.)

To be honest, Giovanni's *cazzo* was *bello* enough, I suppose. It landed slightly on the niggardly side, a metonym for the man. Generosity was not Giovanni's strong suit. Aside from his hair, he was skin and he was bones. Were Giovanni a fowl, you'd stew him and use him to make stock.

I had met Giovanni two years before on a train going from Venice to Genova, where he lived. I'd taken an apartment in Chiavari for the summer. I'd wanted a break from New York to work on my first book, *Ravenous: The Guide to Eating Gloriously*, so I traded apartments with a man who lived near the beach in that Italian Riviera town. It's a strange place, Chiavari, equal parts Mussolini-era stacked white apartments and crumbling fin de siècle villas, with a dash of Roman-era aesthetics as seasoning. But Chiavari is on the Mediterranean, and it's easy to get anywhere you want to go, and it's close to Portofino. Plus, it's home to Osteria Luchin, home of divine *farinata*. This specific *farinata*, a thin, wood-oven-baked bread with a pleasing, crisp crust and an elastic center, stands as the apotheosis of chickpeas, which are ground for the flour. Sometimes on rainy days, I taste it, a phantom *farinata* accompanied by a ghostly minestrone; it's a wish my unconscious makes, a prison tease.

Seated across from one another on the train, Giovanni and I chatted; he was surprised I spoke Italian. Giovanni's body was slight as a political prisoner's, but his eyes were a severe blue. Bright, charismatic eyes and these long eyelashes like thickets on either side. In short time, my skirt was hiked up over my ass and we were unsteadily studying each other's face in the train's bathroom mirror as he fucked me from behind, out of time with the rocketing of the train.

Among many other bothersome qualities, Giovanni was a mystic. Everything happened for a reason in Giovanni's dragonfly-pocked world. Everything could be believed. Everything was energy. Everything was imbued with woo. Everything was there, radiant and untrammeled and lying in wait for ripe understanding. Giovanni was ever credulous, as long as the tenet to be believed blazed with the otherworld.

There's a strong strain of the mystic in Italy. It might be the sheer improbability of Italy's existence, a peninsula that juts like Europe's tasty cock into the briny twat of multiple oceans. The mountains that run their course up and down and side to side. The volcanoes that burble and threaten and occasionally belch acrid smoke. The steroid hills of Tuscany and Piedmont that pop like acne out of the plains. The quick vertigo of cliffs tumbling into the Ligurian Sea. The crystalline light of Venice, and the dowager's string of jewels that makes up that sinking, fetid city. If any of this is possible—and all of it is, all of it lives in the weird, cheek-by-jowl, *e così* resignation of Italy, a country that is still, for better or worse, not much more than a collection of nation-states on speaking terms—then why not reincarnation. Why not believe in the energy of stones. Or the power of shamans, or the importance of balanced shakras, or that sickness comes from baring your wind points.

Giovanni. Say the name and it's a push-me-pull-you contraction, like the ululation of a sea anemone or an orgasm. Say his name and the mouth kisses twice, the second time more lasciviously, as it should. Humbert Humbert had his tongue-tripping Lolita, but I would take my Giovanni (and I would leave him, and he me; it was a complicated relationship and so rarely fun).

Giovanni. I killed him, and ate his liver.

It was an accident, of course. Well, the killing was accidental; the eating was deliberate. I cooked Giovanni's liver in the Tuscan way: I made a paté using a recipe calling for *fegato di cinghiale*, liver of wild boar, spread it on crostini, and relished it with a good Chianti and a kiss of irony. The paté was surprisingly tasty, sapid yet nuanced, though I did have to cheat and use a touch of chicken fat to make it creamy. But given Giovanni's decades-long adherence to veganism and a lifestyle so ascetic it anesthetized his desires, what else could I do. It was the cleanest human liver ever likely to cross my path. I could hardly waste it.

Truffles brought me to Italy in December 2000 because everyone loves truffles. Truffles were becoming all the rage, and *Eat & Drink* had to have truffles. At the turn into the new millennium, truffles were ubiquitous—truffle salt and truffle oil and microscopic filings of shaven truffles. If you've a fat wallet, a broad palate, and a pica-driven yen, truffles are your fix, the methadone to your dirt-eating ecstasy. But at the bottom of it, you should know this: you wanted to eat truffles because someone like me told you to eat them. Without me and people like me, food commoners would be like Sims characters, turning endless, aimless circles, appetites spinning them into unrequited nothingness.

Working with *Eat & Drink*'s big, beautiful, bloated budget, I found a *trifulau*, a truffle hunter. A gnarled olive tree of a man, Salvatore, the *trifulau*, was a superannuated uncle of a Barolo producer I knew (not biblically—I didn't like his scent). This uncle was a very successful truffle hunter, one of the legends in the region. And even though the *trifulau* held his hunting secrets close as a drug dealer, I'd managed enough money to convince him to take us on a hunt.

It's more or less a charming myth that truffle hunters use pigs. Pigs are big and obstinate; it's hard to shove a pig into the back of the car at the end of a hunt. The uncle had once used pigs to hunt, way back when this wizened tree was a mere green sapling, but now he used dogs. He had three, all in different stages of training, all mixed hounds with pink sensitive noses and limpid eyes. Truffle hunters had switched to dogs for the simple reason that dogs rarely weigh more than the human holding the leash and thus they can be restrained when they try to eat the truffle, which dogs tend not to do. Stupid dogs, placated with a desiccated biscuit and the tossing of a ball. Pigs can't be bought with charades; they shuffle and snuffle and eat that fungus whole.

There were four of us who met at six A.M. that chilly December morning, and for Salvatore, this was a very late start. He customarily began hunting in the tiny hours of the morning, the club hours, when, hazy with dance beats and flirting and drugs, you fumble your way with someone strange to your bed, or you to his. Grappa aside, truffle hunters tend to be an abstemious bunch. They go out with their dogs in the dark of dawn or in the gloom of twilight, for to hunt during daylight is to risk other hunters stealing your secret spots. But it's tough to get good photographs in the dark, and, soothed by the salve of *Eat & Drink*'s copious lire, Salvatore had kindly agreed to lead us in the daylight hours. He wasn't happy about it, but he didn't have to be happy; he only had to be rustic and photogenic and capable of finding us some fucking truffles, or at least faking it for the camera.

Fog snuggled the ground like a fat gray cat. Driving through those swirling Piemontese hills, our little Fiat's headlights pushed weakly against the fog's wispy fur, lighting a few feet at a time until we reached the farm where my photographer, Giovanni, and I met the uncle *trifulau*. Of this *ménage a quatre*, my photographer, Matteo, and I were hungover, but the others had the audacity to be clear headed: the uncle too ancient to drink and Giovanni too pure.

Truffle hunting, it turns out, is exactly as tedious as you'd imagine. So much tromping over tufted grassy hillocks. So many trees, so many fallen leaves, so many loose rocks, so much boredom, so many moments of waiting for something, anything, to happen. The sheer slow-wittedness of walking with a dog as your guide is like being suspended inside a koan: what is the sound of one mind snapping? From time to time, Stella, the dog, would stop and bury her nose in the dirt, her blunt hound tail quivering in the air like an antenna. She'd dig, and Salvatore would call her off, palm her a dog biscuit, and, with his ancient truffle hoe, carefully part the ground, gently feel for the fungus, and gingerly twist until it pulled free. Then, he'd studiously fill the hole. Like a surgeon, Salvatore knit the wound back together, nurturing next year's growth.

Three times the truffle was no bigger than a gumball, yet when Salvatore held it up, tiny and crenulated as a fetus's brain, the white truffle's honied funk filled the air. Even tiny, these truffles were potent. The long-ago lore is that *trifulau* used sows to hunt because truffles smell like male pigs' pheromones. All these sows hoping to fuck and finding a tiny, tasty morsel in its stead, a metaphor for modern women's twee passion for cakepops. Me, I'll take the truffle.

Eventually, we gave up. We had to stage finding a generously photogenic *tartufo bianco*. We had prepared for such a scenario—there's a reason why, ounce per ounce, white truffles are almost as expensive as printer ink: they're rare. You can cultivate black truffles, after a fashion, but science has yet to nail nature's alchemy for white. For this reason, and for the growing love of the Japanese and the Americans, white truffles are very dear, indeed. We unwrapped a golf-ball-sized *tartufo bianco*, and handed it to Salvatore, who first appraised it with a jeweler's eye, gave a grudging consent, and then gently placed it in the dirt.

Matteo took several shots of Stella finding the *funghi* and Salvatore unearthing it—sorry to be a truffle truther, but we faked it. The sun almost high in the sky, we pronounced the hunt to be finished, and we all piled back in our cars, happy to be clear of one another. We waved goodbye to Salvatore and the cheerful dog, and then Matteo, Giovanni, and I went to this trattoria outside of La Morra that I love.

It's tiny, just six or seven tables, and they're almost always filled with winemakers. Winemakers brook no bullshit with their food. If you're in wine country, find out where the winemakers eat and go there.

The next day, Giovanni was displeased. There was little pleasing Giovanni, something that might have been explained by his fruitarian existence. We fought, he behind the wheel, I riding shotgun. We'd driven about an hour away from the La Morra *agriturismo* to go to a restaurant I'd heard about. I was delighted. *Tartrà piemontese*, delicate little custardy quiche-like entities filled with truffles; *sanguinaccio*, the Piemontese answer to blood sausages, so thick with copper that the flavor hung in your throat; *insalata di carne cruda*, a kind of Italian steak tartare, topped with shaved truffles; and *brasato al Barolo*, beef stew that died and went to Barolo heaven. It was glorious. I could roll naked through those dishes.

Giovanni, however, was upset because the proprietor had refused to make his *bagna càuda* without anchovies. He was in a pet, having to sate himself on white bean salad and risotto reluctantly made with vegetable broth, poor vegan fool. He was nearly vibrating with rage, while I was mildly drunk and fatted as a Japanese cow happily awaiting her next massage before slaughter.

"You," he said, "you are too interested in words. What are words? Pfft," he said, and his mouth turned down as his shoulders moved in parabolic arcs. His body looked like a series of parentheses.

"Yes," I said. "I'm a writer. Words would be important to me."

"Words! What is important, it is here." He thumped himself on the chest. "Words are nothing. They are like this." He puffed his cheeks full and blew the air out at me. "I know everything I need to know by looking into your tiger eyes."

Yes, well, I thought, then why the fuck are we having this discussion. The ice-blue light of the Fiat's dashboard cast a spectral glow on Giovanni's bony wrists.

"My tiger eyes," I said.

He glanced at me. "They used to be wolf's eyes, but now they're tiger." The eye of the tiger, the thrill of the fight. The car cut around a curve and the trees seemed close enough to brush. He stared at the road. I stared at the road. We stared at the road together, and then the wheels went bump over something.

It wasn't a big bump, just a modest bump, but a bump all the same.

"*Che cazzo,*" Giovanni said. He pulled to the side of the road, as far as he could on that narrow Piemontese shoulder. He clicked on the hazard light, glared at me, and opened the door to inspect the cryptic bump.

I tried to open my door, but the car was wedged against a guardrail. The door opened about four inches, then a wide girth of steel stopped it, and a good thing, too, because even by the light of the moon and the weak light of the Fiat, I could see that it was a deep drop, down, down, down into the Piemontese black.

I heard Giovanni muttering, and in the rearview mirror, I could see him standing with pelvis thrust forward, his posture of consternation. I slipped over the gearbox and got into the driver's seat. I saw the key in the ignition.

I was tired, frankly. Tired of arguing and tired of trying to defend myself to a man I wasn't even sure I enjoyed. Tired of trying to unscramble his inscrutable Italian idioms and his impossible new-age beliefs. Tired of tiger eyes and stinky feet and tired of the knowledge that Giovanni was a man who liked women best when they didn't like him. I was tired, too, of disliking him.

I closed the door, clasped the seat belt over me, turned the key, and left him in the middle of the road with the undisclosed bump.

Driving felt cathartic. I opened the window and let the cold air run like river water. I drove and imagined finding a little taverna where I could get a proper grappa. I could use a drink. I looked at the sky and the tree branches flickering past like Morse code and the twin beams of my headlights that verged together like fate to make this cone of silence and peace.

And then, I felt bad—guilt or something like it. I had left my lover in the dark with a bump. The road was narrow; beyond my headlights and below the canopy of the trees, the night was ocean dark. I slowed the car. I stopped. I made a ragged three-point turn, and I drove back toward Giovanni, scanning the night for him and the bump. My bowels contracted in anticipation of his fury. It was not altogether unpleasant.

The return seemed longer; perhaps I was going slower. Gripping the steering wheel, my knuckles turned the white-blue of raw tripe in the light of the Fiat's dash. The car caromed around a corner. Giovanni's slender form was silhouetted against the revenant trees. And something happened. I felt for the brake with my foot. I fumbled. My foot slipped. It pushed the gas pedal. The car leapt forward. The fender on the driver's side struck Giovanni, who pirouetted like a toreador, and, airborne, flipped over the car and landed behind. I could, I think, hear a splat. Maybe I imagined it, the splat. There was a noise. There had to have been a noise. I'm sure I heard a noise.

This Giovanni splat was more meaningful than the earlier modest bump, the bump in the night that brought me here, parked once again on the slim shoulder of the road. I reversed the car, driving a few feet backward, the Fiat's headlights now illuminating Giovanni, who hung on the guardrail, suspended, teetering on the edge of the Piemontese abyss.

He did not look good. Giovanni glistened, for one thing. People ought not to glisten, not darkly in the night, not like that. For another, Giovanni's insides were out, and much of his outsides were gone, trailing down a length of pipe—a long metal rod, rebar, I remember some man calling it—sunk into the ground alongside the guardrails. The rebar stuck straight up as a monolith, stood rampant as a needle, gleaming with a dull metallic evil in the light of the pale moon. Impaled, Giovanni hung on the rebar, glistering ominously.

Dying, Giovanni had become the scarecrow that he'd always threatened to be in life. Judging from the glistening and the juicy viscera, he'd not had an easy time of it.

Seeping in great blooming stains, the blood looked grape-skin black. It all was so broken, so limp, so vulnerable, and so tender, like *conigli* at the butcher shop. Great reams of intestines, a vague almost hallucinatory wash of purple in this half-light, tumbled higgledy-piggledy, like streamers. There, though, that orb. That fat, succulent bit right there. That bulbous piece that popped like a fat tomato, squidging with pressure from the ribs. *That*, I thought, *that* orb was a liver.

I once had thought I had loved Giovanni. We'd whispered declarations of love in multiple tongues, had laid them like the petals of roses on each other's flesh. We'd stared into each other's eyes and felt the hot rush and push of blood and hormones. We'd fumbled for each other in the dark, and we'd found that fumbling fleeting sweet. We'd loved, or it *seemed* we had. Once the affection is gone, I always have a hard time recollecting it; it comes to me in phantasmagoric slivers in the quicksilver small hours of the night. Once the affection is gone, it slips from my memory like the face of a dead relative.

I looked at his body, pierced like a medieval saint's, and I remembered. We'd loved, Giovanni and I. Giovanni's head lay back as if in a postcoital swoon. His eyes were open, and for one last time, I stared into them. At last I knew what I would do.

I walked back to the Fiat, rummaged through my purse, and found my wine key and the nylon bag that all Italians carry with them for trips to the market. I flicked open the foil cutter on the corkscrew and walked back to the body that lay limp and perfect, glinting still in the silent night.

The blade was tiny. It took some patience and more time than I strictly wanted to give, but I worked the blade through the gristly bits that held the liver to the body. The liver was hard, slippery, and hot, though cooling quickly in the night air. Finally, the liver sprang free into my fingers. I wrapped it in my nylon bag. I returned to the car and found a bottle of Pellegrino in the back, and I poured it over one hand, then the other, trying to wash the gore off my hands in the lights of the Fiat. I found a second bottle of Pellegrino and an old shirt stuck in the back seat. I wiped first my hands and then the Fiat's fender, and I hoped that no one would stop me as I drove back to the *agriturismo*.

When I got back to the farmhouse, I threw the bloodied shirt into the fire in my room. I brought the liver to the farmer's wife, saying that I'd received a boar's liver as a gift. She cleaned it for me and put it in her refrigerator. I kept it on ice as I drove back the next morning to Giovanni's apartment in Chiavari, where I cooked it and ate it and found it delectable.

8

Rump Roast

*T*he human body holds 66 pounds of comestible meat, on average, more than you might expect, given how much of humans is inedible. More interesting to my thinking is how many different human parts are ingested by different peoples. Some argue in favor of the obvious cuts—the buttocks, the loins, the tender bits around the ribs, the savory marrow, steaks round as speed-skater's thighs, the succulent brain. Others go somewhat more outré: the palm of the hand, the cheeks, the upper arm. To eat a human heart seems cliché, almost tautological in its weighted emotional shape. I could see the beauty in consuming the blood, perhaps in a nice sausage, but most argue that the blood is too problematic, too potentially contaminated; I suspect it's merely too gross. Universally, people seem to avoid eating the eyeballs and the penis; the former is bitter and the latter, chewy.

Do a little research and you'll find there's a surprising amount of available information on the cooking and eating of people, so much, in fact, that one could begin to believe it's entirely normal. Of course, in some cultures, it is. Ours is not one of them—no Western European culture openly embraces the eating of people (we will do it on the downlow, though; medicinal cannibalism lives into the twenty-first century). Even in the South Pacific, the cannibal capital of the world, not many cultures continue to practice traditions of cannibalism. It has been bludgeoned out of them, with religion, with laws, and with sticks. No, there aren't many people on this wet blue planet that do condone the eating of humans, and those who do are hardly held up as a beacon of culinary inspiration.

Cannibalism, tellingly, isn't illegal in many countries. It's perfectly legal, for example, across most of the United States of America— Idaho's felony law prohibiting cannibalism is an anomaly. Kill and eat a human, and the authorities will charge you with murder, of course; merely eat a human, and you may be hit with the charge of desecrating a corpse; in most states, it's a misdemeanor. I'm not telling you this to imply you should eat a human; I'm telling you this merely to show you that you *could* eat a human. If your tastes run that way, that is.

I killed Giovanni in 2000, and I got away with it. The *polizia* called me several days after I had returned to New York, which was two days after I had hit Giovanni and one day after I'd turned his liver into a nice paté and spread it on good Tuscan toast. After the *polizia* had found his body, they wanted to talk to me; I was, after all, the person who had most recently seen him alive. Giovanni Traverso, an officer explained in a voice careful and measured as a metronome, had been hit by a car with great force; his body had flown and been impaled; he lay there for hours, until he was found by a local farmer, who had summoned the *polizia*. Judging from the state of Signor Traverso's body, the police suspected that he had, in part, been eaten by *cinghiale*, which populated the woods.

I murmured, *"Come terribile."* How awful. And then I shuddered a wee, stifled sob into the receiver.

"Per favore, signora," said the *poliziotto* on the other end of the phone, a voice heavy and reassuring as a bowl of *pappa al pomodoro*. "We know it's very difficult, but we need to know if you have any idea how Signor Traverso came to have his *incidente*, how he might have been hit by the car."

I told him it was very difficult indeed. I asked for a moment to compose myself. I'd had several days to come up with a plausible story about why Giovanni was walking on that narrow Piemonte road in the dark, how it might have been conceivable a car would have cause to hit him, why I might have been entirely innocent in this whole regrettable situation. None of my stories were very good; all fit like couture garments—too extravagant, too improbable, too embroidered. I went with the truth, or a version of it.

"We had a fight. Giovanni was so angry with me," I said, dropping my voice to a whisper. "He stopped the car in the middle of the road and he yelled at me. He said—he said—he said—he *hated* me. He called me names. Terrible, terrible names. He got out of the car and threw the keys at me." Tears crept into my voice; I didn't know I was capable of them, but I sometimes surprise myself. "I didn't know what else to do—he scared me so. I turned the key in the ignition, I began driving, and I just kept driving. I drove back to the *agriturismo*, expecting he'd show up. But he didn't." I paused.

"Please, signora, continue," the avuncular *poliziotto* said kindly.

"The next day I drove back to Giovanni's apartment in Genoa. When he didn't appear, I assumed he was so angry that he was avoiding me. I decided to leave his car and go home. I changed my ticket and flew back to New York City early. I didn't hear from him. I thought he was angry—not *dead*." I let my tears flow. The *poliziotto* waited patiently. He told me to please calm down, maybe drink a little wine, to call a friend, to eat something. He told me he was sorry for my loss and he was sorry to be the bearer of such terrible news. He inquired if this number was the best to reach me, and I told him it was, asking him to call me if he heard anything about Giovanni. He thanked me and that was that. I never heard another thing about Giovanni Traverso. He was a luscious memory I held in my head. I could take his memory out of safekeeping and stroke it when I needed it. Giovanni was right where I needed him to be.

Why, you might wonder, am I telling you this. Is it not, you might ask, a legal confession. Could it not, you may ponder, get me in trouble. To this I say, Trouble: I'm in it. Like prison, I'm never getting out of trouble. The only thing I can do is make my trouble your joy—because here's the thing about reading my memoir: it will make you feel good about yourself. You feel morally superior even as you identify with me. You slip into the supple skin of a cannibal for nearly three hundred pages, and enjoy it; then you can slough it off, go about your happy, moral business, and feel like you are a better person.

One murder, then another, then another, then another. In my history, murder comes in easy links. Bodies fell, connected like sausages, like syntax, like film stills. View each in focus, move them quickly, and you see a facsimile of motion. Look at them one at a time, and there's the comfortable fiction of stasis. Neither movement nor stasis is more true—like a photo of mountains snapped from a car rocketing down a highway, both movement and stillness are equally true. Life erupts with contradictions, and we contain multitudes—in my case, quite literally, as I've eaten them.

In prison for the rest of my life, I sit surrounded by and surrounding these bodies, navel gazing at Giovanni, at Andrew, at Gil, at Marco. I write as if I am moving through a petrified forest, the sole living being for miles. But in truth, for all my torpidity, I know there is movement beyond me. I can't see the wind wearing down the mountain one micron at a time, but that doesn't mean it's not happening. Outside the walls of Bedford Hills, people move and they change. They live and they eat, and they visit new restaurants and cut off ties with decades-old friends. They find strangers and have sex with them; they walk the streets and they find new lines in their face and they shop and they dance and they go to sleep in big, wide, clean beds. Outside the electrified perimeter of the prison, life goes on. I don't want to be forgotten. Kill one man and you're an oddity. Kill a few and you're a legend.

If getting away with Giovanni's murder was a piece of cake, getting away with Andrew's was the whole dessert tray. Really, no one should be this easy to kill, especially in such a complicated manner. The bare facts are these: I laced Andrew's drink with Xanax; kenneled his dachshunds in the run outside; dismantled the carbon monoxide detector; blew out the pilot lights in the stove, the oven, and the water heater; and let the carbon monoxide do its work. It was all surprisingly easy, even with Andrew's labyrinthine home security system—all you needed to know for the home security code was Andrew's IQ, 142, and his penis length, 7.5—men can be so predictable. Early the next morning, I returned to find Andrew a rosy shade of dead, opened the windows, aired out the house, sliced off two nice chunks of Andrew's choir boy buttocks, released the hounds, and let time, canine hunger, and nature take their inevitable courses.

It pained me to leave so much of Andrew behind, but, really, there was nothing to be done about it. Just as I had neither the opportunity nor the vision to butcher Giovanni, I was still lacking both when it became poor Andrew's time. I was so inexperienced, you see, still inching my way into the dark end of the pool. In fact, I am a little impressed with myself for killing Andrew at all. It's quite one thing to let one's foot slip on the accelerator; it's quite another to hatch a murderous plan and see it through to its sanguine conclusion. Even walking up to Andrew's door and ringing his doorbell, I hadn't fully believed I would go through with it. Crafting a plan to kill your former lover with carbon monoxide, to slice the meat off his buttocks, and to use his happy, peanut-brained dachshunds as a cover-up is not even in the same congressional district as actually killing him, slicing him, and eating him. The plan is so much mental masturbation. Enacting it, though, that's better than most sex. Still, it hurt to leave so much of Andrew on the floor, where only his dogs and the police could appreciate him.

South Sea cultures refer to human meat as "long pig," and many accounts of cannibalism claim that human flesh is reminiscent of pork. Armchair cannibal William Buehler Seabrook, however, maintained that human meat tasted not like pork but like veal. Seabrook might have been full of shit. A reporter of the derring-do school of journalism specific to the Roaring Twenties, Seabrook claimed to have spent time with the Guere, a cannibalistic tribe in West Africa. His book, *The Magic Island,* glories in the joys of dining on human flesh, of which, he said, the company of the West African tribesmen availed him. Poppycock, it turns out. The Guere smelled a gastronomic bounder when Seabrook's scent hit their collective nostrils, and they called foul. Long after publishing his book, Seabrook unveiled the lie, saying that, while he had eaten human meat, the African tribe hadn't shared any of theirs. Rather, he had bought his portion from a morally ambiguous morgue worker at the Sorbonne. Seabrook took home a few choice pieces, cooked them for himself in a variety of uninspiring ways, and waxed poetic about the vealiness of it all.

Human meat, in my experience, has a texture that's most like bear, which I have eaten a few times, both privately and at special wild game dinners at the Metropolitan Club. In the mouth, bear feels at once denser than beef and more ethereal; it's the Amarone of meats, able to embody in equal parts the earthbound and the celestial. That said, it's difficult to extricate the eating of bear from the knowledge that what you're eating is bear. If you're a modern person inured to peering through cellophane at anonymous meat, you can't put an ursine morsel in your mouth without thinking, "Bear!" Likewise human meat, and thus my conflating of the two.

At its most essential, human meat makes me think of magic. I can't flatten the experience of eating human meat into pork, to veal, or to beef, something common sold at the Piggly Wiggly. In my experience, eating a human is like eating unicorn, or Pegasus, or griffin. It's a flavor that best belongs in a bestiary, if bestiaries had butcher shops. To eat human is to dine on a chimerical hybrid, a marvelous, mythical meat that has the sensuality of lamb combined with the poignancy of wild game and the naïf quality of pork. To eat people is to get the taste of a Titan. It's infinite immortalization. It makes a god out of a woman.

But then, I am an excellent cook.

You may wonder why I bothered killing Andrew at all. By the time I sliced off his buttocks, tied the meat in petite rolls, and roasted them, he had been out of my life for more than a decade. *Noir* had folded in 1998, and I'd abandoned the ship long before it went down—I am neither captain nor rat. Fleeing to Gil's *Eat & Drink* in 1997, I left Andrew to be surrounded by his flamboyance of flamingo-legged girls with lofty asses in tiny black skirts. I timed my exit perfectly. In 1997, diners were discovering the joys of the tasting menu and Thomas Keller's French Laundry; they were flocking to

Nobu, where they'd crane their necks and search for sightings of Robert DeNiro, because nothing accessorizes raw fish quite like the shattered gleam of celebrity—and I was delighted to document it all for Gil's *Eat & Drink*. After all, by 1997, I had long ago stopped fucking Andrew, or perhaps he had stopped fucking me. Sometimes it's hard to recall who didn't do what to whom first.

I had moved on, in short. Then late one afternoon in March 2008, eight years after I'd tasted Giovanni, I started thinking of Andrew. I thought about our late-night dinners at Odeon, packing ourselves into the bathroom stall, where I would bend over and let Andrew lay a rail of cocaine on the curve of my ass, snort it loudly, lick my skin, and fuck me until someone knocked so loudly we couldn't ignore it. I remembered how, before the *Noir* office had opened, Andrew had ordered an entire meal from the River Café, and we sat on *Noir*'s fresh carpet, inhaling the acrid odor of the rug as it off-gassed. We ate Ossetra caviar, chateaubriand, and foie gras with our fingers, swigging Dom from perfectly chilled bottles—at *Noir*, office furniture was secondary to an impeccably stocked wine fridge.

How strange it was that, more than a decade after I left *Noir*, I sat by myself in my apartment, thinking of Andrew. His sleek cotton button-down shirts and his suits, wool so fine my hand slid along his shoulders as if pulled by magnets. Andrew's long, strong cyclist's legs and his pointed tongue. The way he never let his early British childhood leave his voice or his word choice, and my annoyance when he asked me to ring him at his flat. The way Andrew moved, as if he were not dripping with but rather made of money. It's a marvel that *Noir* failed, given Andrew's unending reservoir of cold, hard international currency. I imagine he merely lost interest in it, or as one ego-driven magazine died after another, perhaps he feared it was no longer chic to be a publisher. Perhaps he couldn't compete with Oprah. But who can.

I wondered how Andrew had changed. I wondered whether he still smelled of cedar and wood smoke. I thought of the time we had shared in bed and out of it. I thought of the plates we'd broken and the baker's dozen of luxe shirts I'd cut into tiny fluttering strips after I caught him *in flagrante delicto* with my assistant.

Which was, I recalled, sitting in my living room, what caused our split, my leaving Andrew's *Noir* for Gil's *Eat & Drink*, and my calling in that one teensy little favor with that IRS secretary to the deputy commissioner regarding some of Andrew's less savory tax havens. Still, that was more than a decade ago. How long could Andrew hold a grudge, and, really, there was no way that he would know that the IRS investigation had any connection to me or to the time I saw Andrew pull his hand, lacquered in vaginal juices, from between the legs of my assistant. Even if he did make that connection, what did he expect—it was my office, and she was my assistant.

I sat in springtime's thin, lavender-yellow light and thought about Andrew. The more I thought about him, the more I wanted to see him. As any modern woman would, I Googled my ex-lover. Within a few keystrokes, I discovered that Andrew had sold the Tribeca loft in 1998, and he was currently living in a brownstone, which he owned, in Park Slope. I also learned that he had married my assistant—and divorced her. In the interim, she had birthed a pair of children, Ryan and Mackenzie, twins, born in 2001. It was all horribly predictable.

I decided it was best not to call Andrew, not immediately anyway. Instead, I took the F train to visit his neighborhood. It was tree-lined, with quiet sidewalks broad enough for the double-wide luxury pram that Andrew and his former wife, my ex-assistant, had un-doubtedly pushed together—until they didn't. It was strange to think of Andrew living here in Brooklyn, so far from the action, from the bright lights and the big city and the rampant opportunity to seduce flocks of models.

I tried to justify the man as I remembered him with the street I saw before me. I tried to tuck Andrew neatly into the row of brown-stones and their wide staircases, to slide him into the lives lived here, lives of people bound by law and dumb genetic luck. Lives of people who reproduce wee, hopeful versions of themselves. Lives of people who proudly watch these replicants grow verbal, and then turn defiant and cynical, guarded and cold, or servile and cowed. Lives of people who together bought things—great things like buildings and cars, small things like gemstones and socks, medium-sized things like couches and armoires—and after eating together and sitting in chairs together and sleeping together and rising together and doing all the banal breakfast things that culture tells people they should do with others, wake one morning to discover that none of it fits.

I tried to imagine Andrew living here on this street. I tried, and I failed. I couldn't imagine him coming home, taking off his work-a-daddy jacket, hanging it in the closet, and putting his keys into the pottery bowl handmade by an unseen indigenous person, a bowl that sat on a sideboard handcrafted from repurposed library shelving, a sideboard that sat atop an antique hand-knotted rug, a rug that was all the more collectable for its worn bits. I couldn't imagine him checking his face in the antique looking-glass that hung in the foyer as he left for the day, his inability to sustain this prolix fiction growing more visible in the apprehensive lines around his mouth and the sparseness of his hair. I couldn't imagine Andrew settling down. I couldn't imagine him settling. I couldn't imagine him here, and yet.

As if my imagining summoned Andrew into being, there he was, in the aging flesh, walking toward me. His hair was, indeed, thinner, and his face was, in fact, more lined. But it was unmistakably Andrew loping toward me, still fit and fine and wearing black like a proper Manhattan libertine. First, he was surprised to see me; then he looked happy. He hugged me. We chatted, the March wind slapping our cheeks. He invited me into his home, and I dropped my gloves into the pottery bowl atop the sideboard. The bowl was gray and charmingly lumpy; I was wrong about the sideboard—it was blond Scandinavian wood, mid-century and nearly incandescent with cost.

Thus I reentered Andrew's life, almost as if I'd never left it. Before the sun rose the next day, I had cooked for him (a simple salad of greens and blood oranges, risotto with peas and porcini, sausages with braised fennel), we polished off a nice bottle of Anselme Selosse Champagne, and we had fucked, to mutual delight.

Talking to Andrew, I discovered that my assistant, while only marginally adept at her job, was spectacularly good at being the kind of woman who makes otherwise intelligent men lose their absolute shit. I always marvel at this sort of woman, the sort who accepts total, monogamous devotion like it's her birthright. To my experience, there's nothing that unites these women—they can be smart as pinstripes or dumb as fake fur, they can have the classic beauty of a perfectly ripe Honeycrisp apple or the compelling plainness of pie. They tend to be skinny; perhaps their performance of appetite suggests comfort with deprivation. Maybe they dupe men into thinking that they, like air plants, don't need nourishment to survive.

I suspect what makes these women irresistible is this: the women who impassion men are those who can maintain that tension between being not in love and succumbing to it. In my experience, this delicate space is where men are most keen. On either side of this emotional divide, they may fall away, succumbing to boredom on one side and fear on the other. Women who sustain that emotional tension perform the emotional equivalent of edging an orgasm. My fondness for gratification has always been my downfall.

Plied with Champagne and fellatio, Andrew started talking. My assistant, it turned out, had possessed a preternatural vagina. His hunger for her in the early days could not—would not—be slaked. Their affair had started on some long night of closing some long issue when she bent over to pick up a pen that Andrew had dropped and allowed him a view of her labial charms. My former assistant, it turned out, did not believe in undergarments, despite their verifiable existence. The early days, Andrew waxed, were wondrous. One lingering ecstatic moment of unimaginable pleasure. He plundered her body that she gave up in tidbits, sweetmeats, and morsels; she hand-fed Andrew's libido with a breathtaking level of foreknowledge. For every pleasure she gave him, she took an emotional step back, requiring him to lean farther out, to extend his hand as if wooing a shy forest creature, and to hope with his breath bated that this time, *this time*, she would feed, petal-pink lips coyly nibbling from his open palm.

Eventually, she did. They married, a fairy-tale wedding in the Hamptons with a Vera Wang gown and a Bora Bora to Pago Pago honeymoon. And then reality slowly came creeping in on hausfrau-slippered feet. My assistant, it turned out, was not a goddess; her vagina was just a vagina; the wild forest creature was just another housecat. You wake up with someone one too many mornings and you realize that any magic you'd seen was magic you'd made. The twins (one boy, one girl, I forget which is which) were great, really great, he said. He loved being a father, he really did. But the marriage fell apart. He had kept the brownstone in the divorce only through some fast financial footwork on the part of his lawyer and his accountant; his ex-wife now lived about ten blocks away, closer to Ryan and Mackenzie's school. He saw the twins on Wednesdays and alternate weekends, and, anyway, he said, he had the dachshunds, Rags and Riches, for company.

His head lying on my left breast, Andrew sighed deeply. "It's really nice to see you." He snuggled his face into my bosom and sighed again. "It feels like the last decade was a dream." He nosed closer to my heart.

He needed to die.

Starvation is the most easily understood reason for cannibalism. Pressed close to death, even a vegan will make a meal of man meat. Our survival instinct is too strong to not eat the food put in front of us; this is what makes those rare individuals who hunger-strike so admirable. Faced with the very real threat of starvation, the sweating majority of us will reach for the meat, regardless of its emotional or moral cost. For this reason, while we may pleasure-shudder in the careful consideration of cannibalism, or while we may armchair quarterback the survivor's guide to being stranded in the Andes, when faced with the reality, we will chew and swallow our loved ones. It's better to live with guilt and remorse than it is to die—just look at how many of us cheat on our partners, our taxes, our diets, our dissertations. And that's not even with our backs pressed cold against a dead glacier wall. It's surprisingly easy to overcome moral qualms, if you give in to the appetite.

Whereas survival cannibalism gets a discomfited pass, the other major kind of cannibalism does not, yet it's the reason for the majority of cannibalistic acts. This reason is symbolic. In the anthropological trade, it's called cannibalistic essentialism: the idea that ingestion of human flesh imparts a crucial element. Sometimes it's strength, sometimes it's honor, sometimes it's fecundity, sometimes it's something inexpressible in English, but from New Zealand's Maori to the Congo to the Amazon Basin, many cultures have practiced symbolic cannibalism. Anthropologists like to break essentialism down into two more discrete subsets, materialist and idealist, but, really, only pedants give a warm fuck. You eat a person because the flesh holds a secret meaning, and to eat it is the straightest line between the abstract and the embodiment.

Eat your dead companion, and you live on with the knowledge. Eat your dead to honor or triumph over them, and you're nourished with metaphor. But it's all so much intellectual fapping. We as an English-speaking people can't *not* eat our dead—our language loves a cannibal. We don't just win at sports, we kill the other team; we demolish them; we devour our opponents. To express our appreciation for a baby's cuteness, we say we could eat her up. When we have sex, we ravish our lovers, nibble their ears, lick their vulvas, or swallow their cocks. Gleeful, we banquet on flesh.

If ritual cannibalism is metaphor, then metaphoric cannibals abound. Look at your Eucharist. As Christians sip that wine and let that wafer dissolve on their tongues, these words roll around in their heads: "This is my body; this is my blood." Cannibalism is so deeply ingrained in our culture that a good portion of us engage in the sacred act once a week. Turn up your nose at people like me, people who accept as actual what you all comfort yourselves with at a linguistic remove, but you're no different. The blood is the life, and human history is littered with people who eat people, the pluckiest people in the world.

In sum, you and I are the same. You may not admit it aloud, but I know you will read this book and wonder how your lover would taste sautéed with shallots and mushrooms and deglazed with a little red wine. You read, and you wonder, and you know the answer would be *delicious*. Roll that word around in your mouth and feel the tang of its call.

The issue with killing Andrew was figuring out how not to leave a trace. I couldn't count on vehicular manslaughter and incompetent rural policing to provide adequate cover. I couldn't slip him poison, because I wanted to eat him. I couldn't think of a way to lure him into a secluded area that wouldn't create a digital trail leading straight to my computer or a physical trail leading to my door. I couldn't shoot him because, first, it's just so indelicate, and, second, guns are to cops as the Mister Softee jingle is to children. The biggest issue, as I saw it, was the fact that I had reappeared in Andrew's life after a decade-plus absence. If I became at all visible to the police, any NYC cop worth his weight in crullers would immediately point his finger at me, the spurned woman who popped up like a whack-a-mole from Andrew's past. From the moment the knowledge that Andrew Must Die glimmered in my brain, I also knew I didn't want to be caught. I needed to devise a plan that would cover up my tracks like footprints in fast-falling snow.

The first thing I did after I left Andrew's apartment was to buy a prepaid cell phone. When he asked for my number, I gave Andrew the number of my old, defunct landline; later, I called him from the burner, as the cop shows call these phones, telling him I realized my mistake. I explained it away with the excitement, the confusion, the orgasmic joy of seeing him again. Burner in place, Andrew had a dedicated phone, one I used for him and him alone.

I got his schedule under the pretense of planning a trip somewhere special. It wasn't difficult to persuade Andrew to give it to me in all its twin-addled, single-dad permutations. The rest of the information I gathered from his iPhone and his computer. Really, people's passwords are too easy. Andrew's iPhone passcode was his kids' birth month and day (0714, Bastille Day, if you're of a historical mind). I quickly confirmed he'd continued his tradition of using Bowie lyrics as his computer passwords. It took me three tries to discover that "thinwhiteduke" unlocked his computer, two to get into his Gmail with "g0ldenyears," and three to find that "G0ld-whopwhop" granted me access to his bank account. I'd have gotten the last two on the first try but for the fact that "ohs" had been replaced with zeros. This is what happens when you've sung the same song in the shower for fifteen years. No wonder my assistant left him.

With this knowledge, I could easily access every scrap of information that Andrew wouldn't want his psychopath ex-girlfriend to have. I knew his bank balance and his bill payments—and how much Andrew's super-rich status had thinned to relative leanness. Andrew's economic decline seemed to be the effects of paying a simply breathtaking amount in monthly alimony, raising two children in the style to which they'd early grown accustomed, and some abominable financial decisions. Andrew's bottom line, it turned out, was not very nimble. It was also fairly clear that as much as Andrew claimed to be a private equity manager, he mostly went to the office to watch Netflix and porn (he seemed to have a thing for cuckold videos, but then most straight men do), take long lunches, and occasionally dabble desultorily in the stock market. Clearly, Andrew missed *Noir*, but who didn't have a raging nostalgic hard-on for the years of Clinton excess, Damien Hirst, and chefs whose goal was to build the plate higher.

Andrew, for all his Thomas Pink shirts and Oliver Spencer suits, was holding on by a silken thread. Which was all the better for my planning, to be perfectly frank, and, really, when am I not. I picked a long weekend when the kids were with their mother out of the country—the Bahamas, I believe. It was perfect; all I had to do to execute my plan was time everything impeccably. To an amateur cook, timing is the biggest challenge. Your reward for your hard kitchen work is the blissful, sated faces of your dinner guests, but you'll have failed if the Beef Wellington is a perfect medium rare and your roasted new potatoes are hard as marble. Timing is, as they say, everything; knowledge is power; and *To Serve Man* is a cookbook. My timing is as reliable as a Swiss train schedule.

I'm not only timely; I'm protean. As a food critic, I'm accustomed to being incognito. I'm tall, about six feet, and I've got flame-red hair, disadvantages for a food critic who needs to visit without detection. I have developed workarounds that rely on one principle: essentially solipsistic, people don't want to remember you. Humans are far more interested in themselves than they are in anyone else. You have to make over yourself with the kind of body that makes strangers' eyes glaze. In the service of being actively uninteresting, I own a whole closet of baggy, unremarkable clothes that hang on me like I'm a mannequin for Eileen Fisher or Eddie Bauer. Do I like these clothes? No, I do not, but when I put on a pair of mom pants and a tan cardigan, eight out of ten eyes will slide off me as if I were a nonstick ceramic skillet, and the last two will linger for a moment before finding something better to look at. To food critics, this knowledge is deeply useful. I understand the power of dress to disguise me, and if necessary, I have wigs.

I arrived at Andrew's midday on a Friday, dressed in a menswear topcoat and slacks, a fedora on my head, my hair tucked tight underneath. From a distance, I looked like a man. After slipping inside the brownstone, I kept myself hidden from the neighbors. When the deliveryman arrived with the groceries, Andrew met him. As I made dinner, I liberally dosed Andrew's dishes with Xanax and Ambien. By the time we showered together, he was so loose he couldn't get hard, a predicament that I should have considered earlier. I'd have liked to have sex with Andrew one last time. He had an exquisite penis.

I hardly had a chance to guide Andrew to the downstairs bedroom before he fell asleep. With a kind of martial quickness, I cleaned up after myself, wiping surfaces of my fingerprints, making it look as if Andrew had cooked for one. I kenneled the dogs outside, blew out the pilot lights, deactivated the carbon monoxide detector, disarmed the alarm, and slipped quietly down the street by 9:00 P.M., not so late that anyone would have thought it unusual for a guest to leave Andrew's, yet not so early that the Brooklyn street was crowded. I took myself to my favorite hotel bar for a drink, met a lovely Australian gentleman and taught him a few wonderful things to do with a finely knotted string of vintage pearls. After that, I went home and slept like the proverbial dead.

The next day, I let myself into Andrew's brownstone with his keys. I opened all the windows and sat in the backyard with the two dachshunds. They were overjoyed to see me, nuzzling their little Moroccan olive noses into my hands and pockets, flapping their velveteen ears everywhere. Mostly, they were hungry, but their hunger would have to wait. One thing about Rags and Riches: they were surprisingly quiet little chaps. Maybe it was that they were full-sized doxies, but while most of those ankle-biting dogs express themselves in a cacophony of sharp yipping, these two gave a couple barks and were silent. They nestled on my lap and stared at me with their tranquil brown eyes, and stroking their fur, I felt suffused with something like kindness. I gave them water, but I didn't feed them. I needed them hungry.

After about forty minutes, I went back inside, lit the pilot lights, closed a few windows, and went to the bedroom. Andrew looked as if he were joyfully asleep on his stomach, exactly as I wanted him. Here's a fun fact about carbon monoxide: slaughterhouses pump it into meat to make it look redder, juicier, more sanguine. Corpses dead from carbon monoxide poisoning aren't a livid shade of lavender; they appear rosy-cheeked as toddlers in the morning. Incarnadine and inert, Andrew looked like such a dear, lying face-down and dead on that bed.

The night before, I had laid down a plastic tarp before Andrew staggered in and passed out. (I can't imagine how anyone made murder in days before polymers—but then it was a more innocent time, a time before Luminol and DNA testing.) I took a large, sharp knife out of my purse, and with three plastic bags next to me, I readied to slice into Andrew's well-muscled buttocks. They were round as twin Hostess CupCakes, perfect melon spheres, just a lovely pair of butt cheeks. I paused before slicing, remembering all the many times I'd held his ass in my hands to pull his hips faster and farther at my pelvis. Tracing my finger down the cleft between his buttocks, I recollected all the times I would take Andrew fresh from the shower, bend him over a pillow, and plant my mouth on his rectum with a wet, open-lipped kiss. Rich, well-bred men have the best hygiene. "Eat the rich," they say, and in this they are not wrong.

I kissed Andrew at the base of his coccyx, then grasping the knife in one gloved hand and his right butt cheek in the other, I sliced a nice thick piece of meat. I did it again on the right side, dropping each piece into a plastic bag and sealing it. There wasn't much blood, but then Andrew's heart had long ago stopped pumping. I carefully pulled the plastic tarp out from under Andrew, rolled it up, and put it in the third bag. Wandering through the brownstone, I shut all the windows and triple-checked my tracks, ensuring that I left nothing behind.

Then, I let in the dogs, carrying them to Andrew's bed. As I left the room, I saw one of them, Riches, I think, licking the blood from Andrew's hip.

Good doggie, I thought and let the door click behind me.

Banana Bread

I took Andrew's rump roast home. I skinned it, trussed it, rubbed it with olive oil, red wine, thyme, lemon, garlic, and salt, and let it sit for a few hours. Then I seared it and popped it in the oven to roast until lovely and brown without and a bloody cherry red within. I made a delicious Bordeaux reduction sauce, and I served the roast with crisped tiny Yukon Gold potatoes, caramelized shallots, and sautéed asparagus. The meat was quite tasty, chewier than beef, certainly, but with an earthy thrum, a kind of truffled bass note, and the piquancy that comes only from the deepest flavor of nostalgia. I felt content.

While the rump roast was marinating, I took a walking tour of lower Manhattan with the leftover skin and the dedicated Andrew cell phone, which I'd bundled in a new dishrag, placed in a paper bag, and bludgeoned to bits with a hammer. I scattered the pieces of the phone all over the Lower East Side, and I dropped the orts of Andrew's skin in dumpsters behind various restaurants in Little Italy and Chinatown. As a measure of extreme precaution, I also donated the menswear coat I'd worn to a Goodwill on 8th Avenue in Chelsea. And that, with regard to Andrew Gotien's untimely death (ultimately ruled inconclusive), was more or less that. A few days later, I read his obituary in the *New York Times*. As it turns out, Mackenzie is the boy and Ryan is the girl. Andrew's life insurance was admirable, and the twins' college is funded with a trust. What else do you need.

Thus I became a serial killer. People believe that you have to kill three or more victims over a span of time and space to qualify as a serial killer, but people are wrong. In 2008 the FBI revised its serial killer criteria; where a person once had to have perpetrated a trio of murders to earn the status of serial killer, now one needs kill only two persons at two events separated by a period of time to qualify. I feel the FBI has set a low bar, but there it is. Locked in a cell, surrounded by women dressed in multifarious shades of gray and one shade of blanched orange, I am just a killer among killers—and among arsonists, thieves, drug dealers, hackers, and con artists, including one insufferable woman about my age convicted of insider trading. How many I've killed doesn't matter to anyone but my beloved behavioral science Ph.D. students, to you, and to my victims, I suppose.

Serial killing is, of course, discrete from being a mass murderer or a spree killer, this last term no longer used in law enforcement—sad, really; the word "spree" holds such whimsy. Distinct from serial killing's necessity of gaps in time and event, a mass murder requires you to kill two or more people at the same time, in the same event. Lizzie Borden (who was acquitted) was very likely a mass murderer. (While I believe we need more jump-rope rhymes inspired by female murderers, this one is factually incorrect. Lizzie did not give her father forty whacks, nor did she give her mother forty-one. She gave him around ten and her around twenty. Childhood: so hyperbolic.)

I could never be a mass murderer. Mass murder is gauche. Mass murder is to serial killing as McDonald's is to Peter Luger. Both establishments serve chopped beef, but one is indiscriminate to the point of ubiquity whereas the other is carnal dining at its bespoke finest. It's not merely a question of quantity. A mass murderer is blind to attachment; a serial killer, however, holds a close relationship with his or her victims. Even the D.C. snipers, John Allen Muhammad and his henchman, Lee Boyd Malvo, shared a relationship with their victims. Perhaps their relationship was not precisely with their immediate dead or wounded—they killed from a distant remove—but they did terrify an entire city. In this way, the entire D.C. metro area was their casualty. Mass murderers make homicidal psychopaths look bad, in my opinion. At least we serial killers employ art in our abandon.

When I killed Giovanni in December 2000, I did so in a headlong, confused rush. No planning, all visceral action—my foot on the gas pedal, a big crunch, and a swift shift from buoyant life to gut-slick death. Neither he nor I had a microsecond to consider the ramifications of the car's fender ramming him. It was the very epitome of rash action, the embodiment of wish fulfillment, a Freudian slip taken to its terminal extreme. Afterward, I felt a keen buzz, like the susurrations of a crush. But I also felt intensely anxious, taut and tight with the realization of what I had done. It wasn't guilt, not really, not as I fumble to understand what "guilt" means. It was more the pervasive fear that I'd be found out—or possibly the fear that I wouldn't. An inarticulate wonder that I'd come to inhabit the amorphous amoral space of having killed a man and being entirely okay with it.

The buzz faded first and fastest. In time, the anxiety faded. The memory bleached. And after a couple of years, I felt like I'd successfully navigated a potentially embarrassing unrequited love. I lived my life, Giovanni had left it, and all was fine, really. I didn't miss him, but then I never liked him all that much. I loved him, I suppose, but it was the love of an itchy sweater that looks too good on you to throw it away. Every time you slip into that sweater, you know you're going to get compliments and admiring glances, and every moment you're alone, you're going to scratch your flesh raw.

Killing Andrew in the spring of 2008 was different. His murder wasn't merely premeditated—it was planned with the exquisite care of a banquet for a head of state, and I took pride in the knowledge that I'd done it right. So many things could've gone wrong. Nothing did. It pained me that I'd performed beautifully yet no one but me would fully appreciate the act's crystalline perfection. I toyed with the idea of attending Andrew's funeral services—they were open to everyone—but I didn't. Why tempt the fates, or my desiring tongue. Most of all, I didn't want to see my former assistant, Andrew's ex-wife, or, for that matter, his spawn. I didn't feel bad about Andrew's death, exactly, but if I did feel something, it was attached to how I'd left those two children fatherless. I am fond of my father. He has always smelled of bay rum aftershave and tobacco. It's nice.

And unlike Giovanni, I liked Andrew. I enjoyed spending time with him. We had history; he had given me my first job in food writing, spotting in me a nascent skill set that I myself didn't know I had. I respect men who teach me something new about myself. They fall so far and few between. The days after Andrew died, I surfed a billowing crest of satisfaction. A gilt cloud held me aloft; everything glittered with the serendipitous new. Even the dreary early April weather didn't dismay me; I'd done something wonderful. From concept to execution, Andrew's rump roast was an unparalleled success. Only the fact that I couldn't share my joy marred its beauty.

Yet feelings of unease began to susurrate. Andrew could, after all, only die once. I wanted to spend time with him again and I wanted to kill him again; I wanted both, and I wanted them at once, and neither was possible. Were I able, I would gladly have brought Andrew back to life to kill and eat him, over and over. Multiple lives are wasted on cats.

I threw myself into my work, writing a piece on recession food for *Eat & Drink*, where I was now a contributing editor. After more than a decade, Gil had finally been pushed out of his role as publisher, forced out by a move of the board, so my interaction with him was now entirely libidinal. It's strange, really, when I consider my years with Gil. We were never exactly a couple—I clearly held no misgivings about fucking my bosses—yet for all the intimate, oily time that Gil and I spent in each other's company, we never considered ourselves a unit.

Gil, I remember him, that sweet-headed, lumbering lout. Such a contrast to Andrew's chrome-and-black-lacquer urbanity, Gil was an appetizing potpie of a man, all overstuffed Americana and bountiful appetite. He'd moved to New York from some tiny town in Nebraska, made lascivious money off the stock market in the '80s, and in the '90s parlayed that cash into salacious money during the tech boom. Gil had suddenly felt the need to start a magazine, and his magazine, *Eat & Drink*, contrary to all expectations, succeeded.

Indeed, it was so successful that eventually a large magazine conglomerate snapped it up. Gil remained as executive publisher as long as he could; he loved that magazine, the adorable lunk.

Eat & Drink had begun as a simple paean to simple pleasures, but rare is the gourmand who's content to rest at modest fare—even *Joy of Cooking* progressed from meatloaf to paté. Likewise, *Eat & Drink* changed because Gil's tastes changed. I helped change Gil's tastes, and I began with *spaghetti bottarga di tonno e ricci di mare*, pasta with cured fish roe and sea urchin. Gil loved to lick pussy; he'd spend long hours with his nose deep in my cunt, his tongue lapping like a dehydrated cat, his mouth thick. His cunnilingus was a five-armed starfish of a love, stuck and sucking, beautiful in its stupid devotion. *Spaghetti bottarga* was the perfect dish to seduce him into finer food.

Gil looked the part of the absolute upright bourgeois man-child. Blond and ruddy, Gil's looks spoke volumes about his English roots. You could easily imagine him striding out of a Hogarth etching. He had cornflower-blue eyes and tiny teeth like the nibs on an immature piece of corn. His hair brushed back from his head in a yellow-gold pelt; as he aged, faint lines of gray appeared like ghosts in a wheat field. Gil's waist was as generous as his appetites and as warm as his humor. His wasn't the kind of body I'd imagine myself enjoying when I was alone on a long winter's night, but it was a nice body, and an appreciative one. Gil moaned when I kissed him, like a dog when you rubbed his belly.

For all his bourgeois luster, Gil was a well-hidden libertine. He had a roster of vanilla women, a couple he even married, with whom he enjoyed workaday missionary sex sanctioned by the *New York Times* and the *Atlantic* (there is no prudery quite like the purse-lipped prudery of liberal publications). But Gil was like a perverted superhero. Mild-mannered Clark Kent by day, he hung like a bat by night, but for all of his juggling of lives, Gil never felt pained by it. He embraced all his erotic aspects with all the emotional torture of a golden retriever, which is to say none at all.

Emma has long said that men's erotic development stops at its first attachment. "It's the fixation principle," she says. Like a fly stuck in amber or a cherry blossom suspended in a raindrop cake, Emma says, men glom on to one specific image, construct, or fantasy, and they never sail past it. They may develop other interests, other obsessions, and new fantasies, and they may also embroider upon their existing ones, but at the end of the night, men never relinquish that first fascination. My father, for example had a thing for Leslie Caron, whom my mother faintly resembled, for he never got over seeing *An American in Paris* at a very imprintable age. We would know he was sad when we heard the overture to *Gigi* coming from the speakers in the den. To my dad, an ideal woman was sprightly, clean limbed, and French; my mother embodied all of these qualities when he met her at the age of seventeen. She outgrew all but the Frenchness. Emma may be right about men.

I suspect that it was Gil's stumbling across *Story of O* in his parents' bedroom at thirteen that sent him on his merry spiral into kink. Between his summers spent on the family sloop and reading Pauline Réage at a formative age, Gil developed a deep-seated love of rope and a desire to make girls cry and come. Later the same year, Gil's older brothers would sneak him into a drive-in porn theater somewhere on the Massachusetts coastline. Gil hid in the trunk, and when the screen lit up with that green wash, his brothers pulled the seat forward, letting loose unsuspecting Gil. He sprung like a young deer to find himself trapped in the skin flick *Behind the Green Door*. Caged in that Impala, imprisoned by the fear of his brothers' disdain and his brothers' friends' jeering, Gil sat through the entire movie, from skittering camera work to torrid kidnapping to theatrical orgy to heartfelt rescue at the end. Gil was not unlike Gloria, played by a creamy-skinned Marilyn Chambers: first terrified, then transfixed, finally ecstatic.

Gil moved fluidly from perversion to vanilla, accepting with good-hearted equanimity all the various pleasures of the flesh from missionary sex to anal. He was a rare good egg, my dear Gil. He was like Mister Rogers, if Mister Rogers hadn't trained as a preacher and owned a full complement of ball gags and spreader bars, all covered in fine English leather.

Gil, a good man, wasn't the only man. During the time span of our dalliance, I enjoyed many. Some were firefly fleeting in the warm belly of a July night—a tinkling cocktail party, twinkling lights, bare shoulders, sun-warmed flesh, the moist air salt-laden, wrapping you in an embrace even before you touched. Some were quicksilver flashes on trips, metallic clanking trysts thrusting like pistons and groaning with stress. Some slipped like silver slivers in hotels, motels, inns, and *pensioni*, fleshy shivers in crisp sheets, kicking the martial corners asunder. Some, very few, occurred in my apartment, the unfamiliar masculine funk of forest floor, bleach, and spunk overstaying its welcome. The toilet seat left up, jarringly.

And there was one, just one, who held my heart in his large hands. He lasted for a bit, but no more of him just yet.

The hollow in my life left by Andrew's death caused me, as complicated feelings sometimes do, to work harder. By the fall of 2008, I pushed myself deeper into my role at *Eat & Drink*, and I plowed through my edits for my second book, *Voracious: The What, When, Where, How, and Who of American Food*. In retrospect, there are better times than a major economic collapse to write a guide to topflight American restaurants. *Voracious* has a thick section on value meals— it's hard to discount the beauty of Florent or Vesuvio Bakery, now both closed, both casualties of the recession that caused rents in desirable locations to skyrocket—but the meat of the book came from restaurants where diners paid an obscene amount to eat hedonistic food, with attendant repressed shame serving as seasoning.

American restaurants turn on a dime. For every hoary Fraunces Tavern or venerable Union Oyster House, there are countless restaurants that close their doors within a year. In any thousand New York City restaurants, for example, eight hundred are dead within five years. New Yorkers' obsession with shiny objects might make those urban magpies flock to new, dazzling, star-studded restaurants, but there are only so many magpies in the city. Often, restaurant owners simply don't care much about quality—the ego wants what the ego wants, as long as there's enough money, coke, and young flesh in tight trousers or skirts—so restaurants will continue to operate on the sheer power of investor cash. Restaurants, in short, open and close like eyes in the City That Never Sleeps. It's not easy to run a successful restaurant, not in New York, not in San Francisco, not in Cleveland, Burlington, Portland, or Marfa.

I felt pressure to turn *Voracious* around quickly. There's no good in buying a guide to restaurants whose doors are locked. I needed to write a book that cherry-picked the best, most stable restaurants and food "experiences," and I needed to write it quickly. I culled from old *Eat & Drink* columns, but I broadened the scope beyond New York and LA to tempt the broad, tasteless belly of America to buy it. It was all a game, really, but just because it was a game didn't mean I wasn't going to play to win.

I took six weeks and crisscrossed America by plane, New York City to Seattle, Spokane to Missoula, Sacramento to Las Vegas, Tucson to Denver, Austin to Minneapolis, Chicago to New Orleans, and back up the East Coast. I felt like I was lacing America's corset, tightening it with gourmet restaurants, specialty butchers, regional burgers, molecular gastronomists, and locavore demagogues. I tried, in the interest of being an ethical critic, to pick only restaurants I'd visited before—it's unfair to judge a restaurant from a single visit. Even Daniel Humm can have a bad night, though at this point he's so cushioned by his plush team of handpicked staff that, were he to suffer a tough one, his long fall would land soft. I traveled and I ate and I visited and I chatted and I drank, and I hid my hair under a barrage of hats and my body under caftans of greige.

These travels consumed time, and the work nourished my loss. As I moved from one aggressively eggshell hotel to another, the Andrew-hollow filled almost imperceptibly at first, but by the time I finished my great American tour and could tuck into the long days of slogging through notes, composing fresh entries, and reworking columns, I was living in comfortable quiet with Andrew's absent presence. We were like an old married couple, Andrew and I, companionable in long silences and happy to be in each other's company. Except, of course, that he was dead and I had eaten him.

I took a leave of absence from *Eat & Drink* to finish the book, about ten weeks in total. It's hard, I find, to do the boots-on-the-ground work of being a restaurant writer while finishing a book. Columns require me to visit a restaurant no fewer than three times, always with different people, always under a name that is not mine and dressed in a style that blurs the edges of my identity, trying a number of dishes that overlap like a Venn diagram in those three or four visits, keeping notes straight, and then sitting down to write the cogent 300-, 600-, or 1,000-word review.

When people open their paper or their magazine (or, these days, load it into their browser window) to read the review of the latest marquee restaurant, they don't see the work that underpins that sleek skin of words. People think it's easy to be a restaurant critic; they think, Oh, how glamorous! How thrilling! How delightful it is to get paid to eat! And, you know, sometimes it is. Sometimes—rarely, but it does happen—you receive the golden Wonka ticket for a sublime experience. You get to roll creamy, piquant, savory, unctuous artistry around in your mouth and feel your tongue pulsate like the tender beating heart of a songbird. Sometimes—rarely—you stumble into sheer perfection. Sometimes, meals are transcendent. And in those times, you feel unaccountably blessed, like a whore whose john is good-looking, clean, gifted, and possessed of a sensibility that weds generosity with egalitarianism.

Most of the time, however, you eat meticulously composed dishes that taste of ego and pretension, and, if you eat enough of them, you will gag. People, by and large, are idiots. What separates the food critic from the dilettante diner is not merely a superior palate. There are legions of excellent palates walking and talking on the streets of New York. It's not even being an excellent writer; the world teems with people who can craft prose as liquid as silk and twice as strong. No, what makes a great food critic—and make no mistake, I am a great food critic, one of the greatest, and, I should add, a great food writer; Gael Greene, Ruth Reichl, Sam Sifton, R. W. Apple, and the rest can collectively kiss my delectable ass—is twofold: the willingness to slog through the hard work of conscientiously tasting dishes, and the ability to take those somatic experiences and translate them into transparent prose. By their natural temperaments, these two skill sets do not hold hands. The physical realm longs to remain ineffable, while the linguistic wishes to be clear and utterable. But if you're able to wed the fleshy and the linguistic, you have the makings of a great critic of food. We are a rare breed. Worship us.

In the ten weeks away from *Eat & Drink*, I finished a fairly polished draft of *Voracious* and turned it in to my publisher. I adore the satisfaction of sending a manuscript off—joy kissed with a soupçon of anxiety. Your responsibilities are mostly finished, and while you still have a tiny hand in your offspring's success, you invest in the hope that it does the work you intend it to do. Naturally, I thought *Voracious* a very good book.

The October day I met my *Eat & Drink* editor, Chloe James, to talk about returning from my sabbatical, the sky was that specific shade of translucent blue that's reserved for optimism and irony. I arrived at the office punctually for our ten o'clock meeting. Chloe sat behind her desk, her nails clacking on her keys like cheap high heels. She looked up and gestured for me to sit in the chair opposite hers.

Chloe and I made small talk, that linguistic waltz that polite people do as a prelude to saying the things that actually matter. She congratulated me on finishing the manuscript. I thanked her for the time. She told me that she was glad the magazine could accommodate my request. She paused, her smile flickering into a grimace.

"Dorothy," Chloe said. "As you know, 2008 has been tough for publishing."

"Two thousand eight has been tough for everyone, Chloe." I said.

I was not exaggerating. Brutal for most Americans, the 2008 recession had hit print media especially hard. In the first ten months of 2008, more than 45,000 writers and editors had lost their jobs through layoffs or closings, and during the course of my ten-week sabbatical, I'd heard about three acquaintances who had lost cushy roles at *Rolling Stone*, the *New York Times Magazine*, and *Elle*.

One of them had found work as an editor at a website that was, as far as I could tell, composed almost exclusively of pictures of cats saying ungrammatical things in capital letters. The other two were thinking about moving back to their family's Midwest hometowns. The open-thighed wet welcome New York media had given writers just a decade earlier had snapped closed, for New York media was a grim, unyielding bitch in 2008.

Chloe swallowed and said, "We're doing a little restructuring here at *Eat & Drink*." Chloe's left thumb compulsively pushed her wedding ring against her finger joint, then ran along the edges of her nails. I noticed Chloe's manicure lacked its usual luster.

I watched Chloe's hands perform discomfort; I saw her body taut as a bowstring. I thought of the strange desolation of *Eat & Drink*'s offices, the empty desks and dusty cubicles dotting the open plan office. A thrill of fear trilled from my crotch to my heart.

"Dorothy, I'm terribly sorry, but *Eat & Drink* is changing its model. We can't keep you on the masthead."

Chloe's words summoned the vision of an old newspaper, its creamy whiteness closely packed with spidery black ink. Letters marching in serif font like sensitive insect feet, headlines dark and heavy as a Victorian funeral.

"Publishing's changing, and, frankly, *Eat & Drink* simply can't afford writers like you." Chloe looked at me, a discordant, beseeching expression. Chloe paused, expecting me to say something. I kept my mouth shut, a narrow line, impassive as a window ledge. I waited for Chloe to jump.

"We're terminating your contract," Chloe said.

I stared. Chloe blinked.

"Dorothy," Chloe sighed, resignation creeping into her voice, "your contribution to this magazine has been substantial, and we value your work." Chloe's thumb spasmodically worked her wedding ring. She opened her mouth, closed it. "I'm sorry, Dorothy, but we've decided to take the magazine in a new direction."

Chloe's eyebrows climbed toward her hairline, a quizzical look, my invitation to respond, to object, to wail, to lash out, to break down, as Chloe broke up my eleven-year relationship with *Eat & Drink*.

I said nothing.

Chloe blinked, fumbled her papers. "The magazine business is changing. We have to change with it. Online short-form, more photography, video. It's nothing personal." She tossed a tiny, brittle smile.

I broke my silence. "Chloe, you're firing me. I can't think of anything more personal."

Chloe looked at her desk, her hands fumbling across it, composure cracking. "Here is your severance package." Chloe pushed a crimson folder at me. "You'll find it quite generous."

I picked up the folder. I imagined hurling it at Chloe's white, soft throat. I imagined the folder slicing her skin and thudding to a quivering stop, embedded like a dagger in her carotid artery. I wondered if her blood would match the scarlet of the paper.

Chloe looked at me, her shoulders slumped but her eyebrow cocked. "You'll land on your feet, Dorothy. I'm sure of it."

I paused, trying to think of something cutting to say. Finding nothing, I turned on my heel, and strode out the door. It was, until my arrest, the most humiliating moment of my life.

I had quit jobs, but I had never been fired. Like anyone who has ever freelanced, I'd had that experience when work relationships fade away with attrition, both parties silently agreeing that working together is simply not worth the hassle. I had pitched and I had been rejected, but any writer will say the same. I even failed to sell my first book proposal—an ill-conceived coffee-table book of the history of coffee. But I had never, not ever, been fired.

This sort of experience is difficult for ordinary people, but I found it unendurable. I went a little mad. I holed up in my apartment for a week, baking banana bread compulsively and drinking all the wine in my wine fridge. For eight days, I didn't get out of loungewear. When I wasn't baking, I flopped from horizontal surface to horizontal surface, carrying a bottle of wine, a loaf of banana bread, and a notebook with me. I scribbled plans and made notes, trying to find a way to grind *Eat & Drink* into sausage. It wasn't enough to get Chloe fired, though that idea definitely appealed to me; I wanted to see that magazine burn. I thought of every tactic

I could, turning advertisers away, IRS investigation, protracted litigation—something that would roast *Eat & Drink* so thoroughly it would be served in a body bag. But all the scribbling and all the charting came down to nothing but the empty ravings of a drunk, embittered woman, shaking her fist in the air and raging at nothing.

I look back at that impotent time and I think, This is how ordinary people must feel every day. You poor, pitiful fools.

In the end, it was Emma, the agoraphobe, who pushed me to move on. She read about my firing on some food-gossip site and called me.

"You're better than this. Do the goddamn work, Dolls," she said on the phone.

I told her I was obsolete, an anachronism. I was the rotary phone of the publishing world; I was a floppy disk, an IBM Selectric.

"Dolls." Emma interrupted, "just put one word after another and do the work."

It was a farce, I said, an airless, gutless, disembodied joke. The Internet was a rank, foul, fetid entity, and I was being swallowed by a weightless monster of binary code. My life was over.

"Fuck that pretentious, shitty magazine in its pee hole and do your goddamn work."

I was nothing, I said. I should get a job in advertising.

"Be a fucking writer, Dorothy. Do that thing you know how to do," she said and paused. "And, Dolls, bring me a loaf of that banana bread."

My friend was right. I was better than *Eat & Drink*, better than Chloe James, better than the magazine industry that ate my insides and spat me out, as if my work were gristle.

I bathed and dressed and brought Emma her banana bread, and then I got back to work. I was hungry. I was bored. I needed something to make me feel real. And I knew exactly where I'd find it.

10
Torta ai Fichi e Limone

*I*n the years since I had bailed Emma out of that Boston jail—a rare altruistic act that sprang from a motivation I still don't understand—we wended our way to friendship. We took to our mutual affection like a pair of feral animals stuck on a raft in the middle of a wide and frightening sea. Neither of us trusted the other, yet we recognized kinship in each other's alien sensibilities, and we saw the value of coming together, adrift as we were in a hostile world. What began as a curious détente had over time morphed into wary caring and then to devotion. Emma and I loved each other with the ferocity borne of a twisted shared history. I have no other explanation for our relationship.

After her unremarkable Pennistone years, Emma grew into being an exquisitely skilled, absurdly successful, and intensely reclusive adult. It was a flowering that stemmed from a rocky origin: her first panic attack. Shortly after her Boston arrest, Emma waited at the Pleasant Street Station on the MBTA Green Line and felt the earth shudder a seismic tremor under her feet. A Titan's hand gripped her rib cage. Her breakfast swirled and flipped in her tiny guts. Stars blinked in her eyes; invisible seashells clapped her ears, submerging her in a white roar. Emma fell to her knees, ripping her fishnets and her dignity.

Emma took one look at that chest-clenching, panting, and pained experience and she made a life where she wouldn't have to leave her apartment. The day of her first panic attack, she quit her job at a tony Back Bay framing establishment and secured employment as a phone sex operator. She sent one of her lovers to buy her a phone and a headset at RadioShack. She then gathered her vulvar ceramic vases, her EDP Wasp synthesizer, her megaphone, and her blue plastic kiddie pool (but not the case of canned frijoles negro), and she dumped them in the trash. Emma bid adieu to her dreams of being the next big thing in spoken word poetry and Karen Finley–style performance art and repudiated all creative outlets that required physical presence. In their place, Emma started painting. Tender deBris is dead! Long live Emma Absinthe!

Crowned with her headset, her brush a scepter in her hand, Emma was king of her domain. She was in control of her breath, her work, and her life. Most important, she could multitask. As a phone sex operator, she'd slip into a character—film noir dominatrix, doe-eyed college girl, Southern-fried frisky housewife—and she'd spin sweaty, semeny yarns that developed a cult following of horny men who, credit cards on file and dicks in hot hands, would cream themselves to her dulcet tones. In those days, the mid-to-late '80s, phone sex operators got a flat fee of $5 per call, no matter how long the conversation lasted. Emma saw her job as a kind of game: get the guy off as quickly as possible with maximum enjoyment. She had the preternatural ability to discern a man's most purple desires from a few words and to tailor a story to fit his dirtiest, most inexpressible longing. The company Emma worked for loved her because she was reliable and available; the squelchy-dicked men loved her because she wove fantasies that spoke to their tenebrous sweet spots; and Emma loved it because she could draw and paint as much as she wanted from the safety of her apartment while making pots of money.

As the phone sex model changed from paying by the call to paying by the minute, Emma shifted with it. For all her Jessica-McClintock-furbelow past and Goth-inflected sartorial present, Emma was motivated by capitalism. Making money now meant keeping men hanging on the telephone, so Emma rewrote her script. She still divined the man's murky desires and dragged them to conversational light, but now she amplified them, extended them, turned them luxurious, rococo. She kept those men squelching away on the other end of the phone for an obscene length of time. Men spent the kind of money on Emma's voice that they would on a firm-fleshed and mucous-membraned woman. It was a marvel, really.

As she talked, Emma painted, and she became hard, glittering, diamond-like. She drew and she painted, and somehow, without leaving her apartment, she found lovers who would bring her the things she needed to live her frugal, productive life. Having the appetite of an aerialist, Emma hardly ate. Her rent was low; she lived in a tiny two-room apartment over a Chinese restaurant, waking and painting and talking and fucking her string of lovers, male and female, to the scent of moo shu pork, egg rolls, and General Tso's chicken. This probably aided Emma in not eating. And, of course, Emma rarely went anywhere, which is a thrifty way to live.

Within a few years, Emma had built a body of work strong enough to get a show at a small gallery in Back Bay. She'd finagled her connections to get some dealer to visit, view, and fall in love with her first set of self-portraits, a show she called "Juvenile Deliquescence," a series of paintings of Emma as the titular heroines in the recognizable style of famous children's book illustrations. Emma as Dorothy from Kansas, Emma as the Lorax, Emma as Alice holding a querulous flamingo, Emma as the baby bear finding Goldilocks asleep in her bed. But in each of the paintings, painstakingly done in the style of the original, Emma painted herself as an adult woman, her face showing that exquisite torment that could only be orgasm.

It was the economic boom time of the first Clinton administration, and Emma's cheerfully subversive work sold like tech stocks. So many people had so much money, and they were not chary about spending it. It was win-win-web for Emma: the tech explosion that brought her sacks of cash came from the people who gave us dial-up modems and the internet, which made Emma's increasingly agoraphobic life ever easier. Each new year saw new ephemeral inventions, new ways of being, and a new understanding of what it meant to be human, and each new thing increased the possibility that Emma would, indeed, never have to leave her apartment or interact in person with anyone.

About the time that Clinton was finding novel uses for Monica Lewinsky's vagina, Emma used the 'Net to find and secure a loft in Hell's Kitchen. I think, though I could be wrong, that, previous to testifying at my trial, the last time she left her home was when she moved into this Hell's Kitchen loft in 1997. For example, when a fire broke out in an upstairs apartment, Emma climbed onto her fire escape, lit a cigarette, and moved to the ledge as the firefighters tromped down the stairs. That was about as far as she could travel into the frightening, crepuscular world that lay beyond the safety of her doors.

Happily holed up in her home, Emma cultivated the life of a latter-day Emily Dickinson. People tend to think of Dickinson as a hermit, but she wasn't. She was like a spider: a master manipulator who used her cloistered charm to bring people close. As Dickinson's local fame grew, people came to visit her and hear her read her poetry. She would sit in a room at the top of her Amherst home, her ghost voice calling down to her guests. As time passed, Dickinson wore white, wrote orgiastic odes to death, and grew slowly ever more disembodied—pure voice, an apparitional presence that drew the living with their sad, moribund meat-suits to prostrate themselves at her words. Like Dickinson, Emma made others come to her, and in her studio she held court while others kissed her ring and scurried to curry favor.

The internet enabled Emma. Anything she didn't have, she could order in, and the more money she made, the more she could do from the sanctity of her loft. You see, Emma is a rarity; she is a woman artist who is her own cottage industry, supporting a staff of helpy helpertons that enable her ceaseless capitalist creations. These people do the work of Emma Absinthe Enterprises: the public relations, the organization, the curating, the myth-building, the shipping, the receiving, and the thousand other sundry things that keep Emma famous and expensive. As Emma's enterprise grew, she rented the loft below her studio to house her costume-makers and her prop builders, her Gal Friday's office and her Gal Friday's computer, her flat files and her mock-ups, her canvases waiting to be stretched and her canvases prepped with gesso and linseed oil. Emma has, I think, visited this secondary loft thrice—once for ten days when she repainted the walls and sanded the floors of her living loft; the other two times occurred as she got ready for that temporary move. Emma, disembodied and regal, relies on Skype, computer cameras, and the fanatical devotion she inspires in the people around her. She is very rarely disappointed.

Thus it is that the woman I'd bailed out of jail three decades ago is also the person whom *Art in America* called "arguably the greatest American Realism painter working today," a coup, I pointed out to Emma, because nowhere in that clause did the words "female," "woman," or "feminine" appear. Emma has, improbably, become my best friend, my closest ally, and the only human who knew me almost as well as I knew myself. Naturally, it would be she who saved me from myself until she didn't.

Two weeks after *Eat & Drink* fired me, after my banana bread bender, after Emma told me to get off my ass, I returned to work. I first tended to my book. I had edits to make, drafts to review, desires to stoke. Then, in the interest of my career and to quell boredom, I decided I would remake myself as a food writer, and not be solely a food critic. After nearly two decades of hiding under wigs and caftans, I'd had enough of living my professional life with the cloak and dagger (the cloak at any rate; I could never quite relinquish my dagger). I would reveal my true physical identity with the publication of *Voracious*. My book publisher loved this idea, of course, because I was seasoning the publication of my book with a spicy revelation. My publisher—for it wasn't just magazines that were feeling the cold, hard economic pinch of the internet—danced a little jig over my news.

Before *Voracious*, you couldn't find a picture of my face. Not on my book jackets. Not in the magazines, not in the newspapers. Not on the web. And, believe me, it was a job of work policing this moratorium on images. Keeping my identity a secret from the restaurant public—whether the people dining at the tables, running the front of the house, or toiling in the kitchen—was imperative to my work as a critic because only if I was just anybody could I be assured of getting just anybody's dining experience. This "anybodyness" is why Gael Greene wore her Bella Abzug hats for so many years, why Sam Sifton shape-shifted in a string of bland button-downs, why Ruth Reichl employed wigs. (Food writers are, by and large, a plain sort; so dowdy, like high school principals.) You can't let people know who you are or you will be treated unlike everyone else, and this is not what you want. I hid from the limelight, and it pained me. Such are the sacrifices of a food critic, at least until she's done with it all and can rip off her wig and tell the blazing world to go fuck itself.

I reworked my career, and as 2008 became 2009, I returned to the slog through hip-deep oatmeal that is freelancing, something I hadn't done since I'd moved to New York two decades earlier. Career-wise, I had been extraordinarily lucky. Hired out of college at the *Boston Phoenix*, I freelanced only a few months before my one-year stint at the short-lived *Gotham Ace*, and during this lean time, I'd had the lofty cushion of my inheritance. In 1990, *Noir* hired me directly from *Ace*; in 1997, I moved seamlessly to *Eat & Drink*, where I started as a featured writer and became a contributing editor after *Ravenous* won the James Beard Award in 2000. Contributing Editor is a largely ceremonial title, but it confers respect and money. I'd had a shockingly easy life for a writer—until 2008, when I got shit-canned.

Now, at the age of forty-six, I had to hustle. I'd always written the odd piece here or there for other publications—you might remember the op-ed in the *Times* on Crisco, American comfort foods, and trans fats in 2006, a prescient piece where I called for a ban that received raging pushback. It's rare I write about healthy food, but I find Crisco and its elastic-waist, artificial culture so repulsive that any excuse to revile it felt like a gift. Middle America and its widening asses and widening car seats and widening highways needs to turn off Paula Deen, step away from the television, and take a long, hard look at its naked, pocky flesh in the mirror. If the denizens of the wide swath of states from Ohio to Nevada were filling their hot-pocket pie-holes with foie gras and burrata, I wouldn't say anything. Those foods may be terrible for your waistline, but they don't cause cancer, and they taste divine. I'll never understand people choosing to eat soulless foods—monsters all, say I, the cannibal.

Freelancing meant that suddenly I had to rely on my wits and my charm to make my money. I had the book coming out, I had consistently kept up my blog, and I had the severance package that, while far from strictly "generous," was something. I was not in critical financial shape, but one does get accustomed to a certain lifestyle, and I'd grown complacent living on a fat paycheck. One enjoys purchasing airline tickets when one wants, one feels validated when one's rituals include hideously expensive face creams, one feels better in Ferragamo pumps, and one likes to avail oneself of all these items while still having the psychological freedom of a tidy nest egg. I had to get hustling.

I thought it would be unappealing; rather, the hustle was energizing. I did some fancy strategizing and managed to monetize my blog—and can we for one moment ponder the violent deformity of that phrase, "monetize my blog"; it's so grotesque that Diane Arbus could photograph it. On the one hand, paid content makes me shudder. On the other, I'd be lying if I didn't admit that duping the slathering hordes into buying things didn't thrill me. To my credit, I never plugged any product I myself didn't like. I mean, every kitchen should have a proper hand blender; Cuisinart makes a fine one. Every kitchen should have a quality eight-inch knife; Wüsthof knives were in my kitchen. Everyone needs a Champagne stopper, a microplane zester, and a laser thermometer—why shouldn't I guide people in their choices? The ethics of bloggers being paid to write about the wonders of a specific Dutch oven is no different from magazines offering glossy four-color consumer porn of items from companies that pay for advertising. Everyone does it. Bloggers just do it for themselves, and that's something I always endorse.

During this time of crafting together my financial crazy quilt, I still dated Gil, the ousted publisher of *Eat & Drink*. Gil was like my stateside Marco, minus Marco's glowering conflict and tortured conscience. Energetic and staunchly nice, Gil was there when I called him, many more times than not, regardless of his marriage status. I like a man who can keep his commitments. Let me rephrase that: I like a man who can keep his commitments to me. Gil and I had come a long way from the days when I taught him the saline pleasures of shad roe, the sweet ecstasy of eel, the sea-swept delectation of abalone, the bitter euphoria of being bound tight to a chair, blindfolded, naked in abnegation, waiting to be hand-fed a delicacy. Gil was fixed as a North Star, and as much as I appreciated the unfettered sensuality of our time together, I believe I appreciated the constancy more.

Thus it was in late June 2009 that Gil, ex-publisher now semi-retired, and I, ex-staffer reborn as freelancer, boarded his sailboat to sail across Gardiners Bay, a lovely half-moon of ocean fitting between the North and the South Forks of Long Island. Gil's family had long owned a house on Shelter Island, and though theirs was a modest in-island cottage, Gil's own home was a sprawling white-wood minimalist villa, all right angles, clean lines, and the thick scent of discretionary income. Gil kept his sailboat, a Hunter 45CC, at the Island Boatyard and Marina; this fiberglass cruiser was the love of his life. Sailing it, Gil radiated a nearly postcoital joy.

A well-appointed boat, Gil's Hunter had a charming galley with a three-burner gas stove and the most adorable oven. I packed the makings for a delightful lunch: a chilled white gazpacho; a savory frittata with rabbit sausage, potatoes, and fresh herbs; a salad of ripe melon, arugula, and mint; and a wonderful *torta ai fichi e limone*, which is a terribly fancy-looking but ridiculously easy pastry that eats like a lemon cake baked inside a jam tart. I brought the gazpacho and the pastry crust, cooking the remainder of the meal in the galley, a most efficient little kitchen—I'm quite sorry to have lost it. I brought a bottle of really nice Prosecco to serve with the meal and a flask of Poli Miele, a lilting grappa liqueur flavored with honey and herbs, to complement dessert.

The weather was guileless as a child's drawing. The sea was calm, and Gil and I ate as the breeze blew and the sails luffed rhythmically. We didn't chat much, intent on enjoying the feel of the boat rocking below us, the sun on our shoulders, and the slow progression of flavors and textures—the fatty cool of the gazpacho, the fragrant weight of the frittata, the fragile crunch of the salad, and the delicate zip of the *torta*. Some meals, simple as they may be, unfurl with the sacred precision of art, and this was one. Nature had conspired to give us a beautiful day, Gil had used his skill to give us a beautiful sail, and I had made a beautiful meal.

Now all I had to do was wait for Gil's anaphylactic shock to kick in before I pushed him overboard and cut out his tongue.

11

Lingua con le Olive

"*A* kiss is the beginning of cannibalism," said Georges Bataille, or maybe he didn't. I haven't read the book this quote is supposed to appear in, *Erotism: Death and Sensuality*, but perhaps I will. I suspect I'd find it interesting, though I don't know that Bataille's book would pass the prison's censors. They'd likely take one look at the title and pull it (while letting far worse tomes slip through the cracks. We're allowed twenty-five books of our own here in prison, and they circulate like rumors. Truth be told, most Bedford Hills inmates have terrible literary taste. They love *Fifty Shades of Grey* and Danielle Steele. *Mein Kampf*, if you can believe it. The complete works of Stephen King. *The Diary of Anne Frank*— she knows about living in close, unsparing quarters with people you don't like; it's an unsurprising favorite. Flannery O'Connor's stories, tellingly, have a following. As do Sylvia Plath's writings, because what con doesn't feel drawn to a melodramatic portrayal of adolescence. If there's a single thread that runs through the fabric of the penitentiary, it's that of arrested development).

Here are a few things I've gleaned from being a penitentiary librarian: prisoners love self-help books. They glom on to religious narratives as drowning rats to the flotsam of a sinking ship. Cons do, in fact, judge a book by its cover; an unsympathetic author's picture is enough to dissuade a convict from reading it. They are credulous with regard to titles. Most find great disappointment in *Of Human Bondage*; a very few will, however, enjoy it.

The incarcerated, by and large, read books that comfort them, which makes them not very different from the world outside. Inmates, like conservatives who strictly watch Fox news or liberals who mainline MSNBC, are vested in their own convictions, by which I mean their opinions, not their sentences—everyone here is innocent, everyone but me. You never see as many innocent people as you do in prison. Everyone here is stuck in the limbo of their own appeal, buffeted in eternal circles with their arms wrapped around sheaves of legal paper. The bubble-wrap of self-delusion swaddles all convicts; they think they're this close to being sprung free. Almost all are wrong. I myself find serenity in accepting my fate. The unapologetically guilty woman sleeps soundly at night.

"Is this fig?" Gil asked, eyeing the slice of *torta limone* on his plate.

"Of course not, darling," I said. "It's quince."

Gil took a bite, smiled with satisfaction, chewed, swallowed, and immediately put another forkful of *torta* to his mouth. Two minutes later, his hands around his throat, his breathing ragged, Gil's face turned red as arterial spray, then the sanguine hue seeped away, and bloomed a mauve, lavender almost. It was interesting to watch Gil's skin grow a sweaty gloss and a pallid hue. It was like a sunset, but with motion. Gil looked at me with pleading eyes. I have mentioned Gil was allergic to figs, or perhaps I have not.

"Epi!" Gill gasped and reached out his hands in the universal gesture of supplication."Epi!" He whispered.

I couldn't let myself get drawn into the spectacle. Gil's EpiPen had hit the water leagues ago. I had things to do.

His body must be found with water in his lungs, assuming that anyone found his body, which in an ideal world would not happen. Hope for the best, prepare for the worst, and make sure there is water in the lungs when a body is fished from the Atlantic. No water in his lungs meant no drowning, and no drowning in a waterlogged corpse meant foul play. I needed Gil to inhale at least one full breath before expiring in order for his death to look like a proper accident, and judging from Gil's ever more livid skin, I had no time to waste.

I sprang at him. My hands hit Gil square in the chest, hard enough to knock him sideways onto the edge of the boat. "Oof," he gurgled. His throat closing, Gil wasn't capable of articulate speech or even inarticulate screams. Gil hit the side of the boat and rested, body splayed diagonally across the gunwale, half on and half out of the boat, his legs stuck at an awkward mannequin angle. He scrabbled at the gunwale to right himself.

Gil was a solidly built man. Though not as tall as I am, Gil was thick and powerful, with big, meaty hands and dense thighs. His surprise, his anaphylactic shock, and his momentary weakness were on my side, but I knew that as Gil's adrenaline kicked in, my advantage would vanish. I grabbed his legs in a fireman's grip and heaved Gil's body up, hefting him above the six-inch railing, and shoving him over the side of the boat. As he fell, one of Gil's hands grabbed the railing. Hanging by one hand, his body trailed toward the water. His legs kicked the water, churning like an aimless egg-beater. His other arm thrashed toward the railing as he reached out his free hand.

I did some quick, brutal math. As the anaphylaxis closed Gil's throat and cut off his air supply, he would pass out and slip into the water. But before that happened, he could pull himself up and over the side of the boat. Neither case was ideal. It simply wouldn't do to let him drop inert into the sea, nor could I risk him getting back into the boat. I wasn't convinced I'd be able to hoist his unconscious body over the side of the boat. I needed him to drop into the drink and take one last, big, conscious breath before he died—Gil's great appeal had always been his cheerful compliance. Whence this new and displeasing recalcitrance, I wondered.

Gil's hand tightened its grip on the gunwale. I spied the winch Gil used to tighten the sails a foot to my right. I grabbed it and started whacking his fingers as hard as I could. One by one, his fingers let go, but not all at once and not fast enough. I could hear his breaths coming ragged and short, desperate painful wheezes. I banged harder at his fingers. They held fast. His body struggled to lift his other arm. It flailed in space, awkwardly reaching for the boat's railing.

Slowly, painfully, Gil was pulling his big, doggy body up the side of the boat. I put my hand in my pocket and pulled out a knife, a cruel, whisper-thin, scimitar-shaped blade made for gutting and boning. Gripping the handle inelegantly in my fist, I jammed the point deep into the first knuckle of Gil's index finger and twisted it, messily severing the finger. A little spray of blood jetted, a tiny scarlet fountain. The joint went flying onto the deck. I'd find it later. Gil's hand released.

Gil slid beneath the water's surface. A sound, high and alarmed, hung in the perfect June air. And then, it quieted. I watched Gil's hands flop like clumsy baby otters. He bobbed up and down, a buoyant jack-in-the-box, a crimson stain wispy as watercolor spreading around him. I grabbed for the boat hook, a telescoping tool that Gil used to snag mooring lines. I extended it to its full length, thinking I could push down on Gil's head, hurrying his drowning, but it didn't reach, even as I leaned dangerously over the side of the boat. I stood upright and assessed the situation. Gil was now safely and proverbially, if metaphorically, dead in the water. I pulled the clever telescoping ladder up from the rear of the boat, leaving him stranded and alone, bobbing in the water, helpless.

I found the fingertip and threw it overboard, sluicing the boat with water as quickly as I could. A few drops of blood shone crimson on the blue indoor-outdoor fabric of the boat's seat cushion. I'd been trying to avoid exactly this. Bloodstain spatter analysis is a killer's worst nightmare.

Let us pause as Gil dies to sing an encomium for the freedom-loving days before Luminol, when homicidal maniacs could kill with bleach-happy impunity. Before the 1980s, when Luminol found its footing in policing, a murderer merely had to clean well to transform a bloody scene of homicide into the very picture of domestic calm. Luminol changed that. Bleach blurs Luminol's traces, and you can never really be certain that you've gotten every splat of blood, and even the miasmic haze of bleach can alert law enforcement to the fact that you've cleaned too aggressively and make them wonder about your motives. A little Lysol, a jug of Clorox, and getting away with murder was easy before the days of DNA and Luminol; these days, even Mr. Clean will bite you in the ass.

I stared at the tell-tale droplets of Gil's bright red blood and reassured myself that the boat wouldn't divulge my secrets—nautical paint is made with copper to help it withstand fading, and copper always reads a false positive under Luminol. Should the authorities find a spot of Gil's blood on his boat's seat cushion, I told myself, homicide wouldn't necessarily be the first thing to leap out at them. It's entirely within the realm of possibilities that an ordinary, everyday accident would cause the dime-sized blot of Gil's blood. Gil fished, he hung sails, he spliced rope—he even carried a little knife on his hip. That splat was entirely plausible. Innocent, even. I couldn't let my morbid flights of fancy run away with me, not at a crucial time like this.

As I watched Gil drown, I stripped to my bathing suit, readying myself for the third stage in this murder. Gil looked at me only once, his eyes pleading and hurt, like a puppy as you drive away from the pound, like the face of a veal calf hung from his hocks, like the face of a nice man you've killed simply because you can. It was only that one look, wounded and dying. And then it was gone. His body was inert, rocking gently as a buoy, but otherwise still, facedown in the great, wide ocean.

I lowered the ladder, popped a life jacket around my chest, and affixed it with a rope to the boat's swimming platform. I threw a second life jacket at Gil and slipped the sheathed gutting knife into a small net bag that I tied to my wrist. I jumped into the water, swam the few yards to Gil, and started wrangling him into the life vest.

This was not as easy as I'd planned. His body didn't want to float on its back, and facedown in the water, his body was hard to dress in the life vest, which I needed him to wear. Prior to the sail, I had schooled myself with YouTube lifesaving videos where lifeguards gracefully slipped a life vest on one unconscious person after another. They'd made it look effortless, like a phalanx of soldiers gracefully sliding slippers on to the feet of insensate Cinderellas. The videos lied. Real life was nothing like YouTube.

Gil's body kept slithering from my grasp, twisting and dropping below the water's surface. He was slippery and his finger was still oozing blood, which was spreading everywhere. I couldn't get the vest to lie flat in the water, and I couldn't slip it around Gil's body without him spinning away like a renegade log. I had nothing to buttress myself against, so I couldn't hoist him up above a vest, and as I was wearing a life vest, I couldn't slip beneath the surface and grab him to hold him still. I tried wedging myself between his body and the boat to get better leverage, but the boat moved, making everything more irritating. It was hard, much harder than I wanted it to be, far harder than either of the other murders. I could have cried.

Gil's body was far more troublesome dead than it had ever been alive. His legs starfished out at every turn. His arms acted like spiteful toddlers, floundering with the purposelessness of feelings. We turned and spun, and we tangled in the rope that tied me to the boat, which, though anchored, floated this way and that. It was very annoying, and just as I was about to give up and carve some indiscriminate pound of flesh from somewhere—anywhere—Gil's body righted itself in the correct faceup position. Holding the body against my hip with the life vest trailing in the water, I swam to the ladder, climbed up two steps, sat down on a rung, and wedged my butt hard on the ladder's step. Crouching over Gil, I slipped the life jacket over one arm and then the other, as if I was dressing a big, sleeping baby. I clipped the fasteners tight around his middle. The body was held tight, secure, buoyant. I was ready to cut out his tongue.

Only then did I realize exactly how poorly I'd planned this murder. The one part of Gil I wanted was his tongue. (I very much wanted his thymus glands, too, but the body tucks those tender little sweetmeats like jewels behind the bony breastplate—and it would not do to crack Gil's barrel chest with him bobbing in the Atlantic.) I wanted his tongue; I had planned to harvest his tongue. I had a charming recipe for *lingua con le olive*, a simple Campania stew of tongue, olives, and ripe, fruity tomatoes, and everything was ready to go, lacking for nothing but the tongue of the dead man in front of me. Yet in all my planning, in all my scheming, in all my research, and in all my dreaming, I had failed to remember that when humans suffer anaphylactic shock, their tongues swell, sometimes three or four times in size. Gil's tongue was so big that I couldn't open his mouth and I couldn't fit my fingers or my knife in it. Indeed, when I pried apart Gil's lavender lips, his giant, bloated

136

tongue lolled like a beached, bleached whale. I hoped that the swelling wouldn't ruin the texture. That would be ironic.

The sun shone down on us like God's own benediction. There was no other boat to be seen. The ocean, tucked as we were near the lip of the Bostwick Bay, lapped with gentle little waves, hardly anything more than meditative in motion. It was a lovely day for a little homicide. I took a deep breath and reconsidered the situation.

If I couldn't take Gil's tongue from above, I'd harvest it from underneath. Sitting on a low rung on the boat ladder, I laid Gil's body across my thighs, lashing him to me and to the ladder for stability. With my left hand, I felt his throat from his Adam's apple to the crease of his jaw, searching for the point where the soft, pliable muscles left off and the hard accordion pleats of the esophagus began. With my right hand, I tipped the knife, aimed at the sweet spot my left hand had found, and from left jawline to right, I sliced through the soft bits where the tongue rooted to the esophagus. The angle wasn't easy. It would have been so much simpler if he were lying on a hard, flat surface. I felt perturbed as I hacked away. This butchering was not my best work; it lacked delicacy. As carefully as I could from that strange angle, I sliced repeatedly through Gil's throat; each time, digging deeper, angling the knife up and back toward the soft palate, watching the blood ebb like warm cherry cobbler into the Atlantic.

I made several passes, working to sever all the connections. The water blossomed with bloody roses that flattened to nebulous clouds. I put the knife between my knees and, with my right hand, I rooted around in the back of Gil's throat, parting the skin, the thin layer of adipose tissue, bright yellow as marigold butter. I kept slicing carefully with the tip of the boning knife until I could feel the tongue wriggle free from its moorings, like a child's milk tooth. When the tongue felt loose and mobile, I put the knife between my knees again and pulled the tongue from its roots through the hole I'd made under Gil's chin. A few tendrils of connective tissue remained, like the stamens of a bloody flower. The knife slipped through them as through tissue paper. How inconsequential they were!

I was surprised at how large the tongue was. I was expecting it to be about four inches long, but it was much longer. Perhaps it was the swelling. Likewise, it weighed much more than the three ounces I'd anticipated. Lying inert in my hand, like a big, pink petal or a giant snail out of its shell, Gil's tongue resembled exactly what it was: a piece of meat. Gil was gone; his tongue remained; and the sun shone not unpleasantly on my shoulder blades. I remember thinking that I needed more sunscreen.

I slipped the tongue into my net bag, sheathed the knife, and tucked it in beside the tongue. Then I removed the life vest from Gil and shoved him off into the Atlantic. He was a good man, Gil.

I have, in my life, been a girl, a daughter, a student, a woman, a writer, a critic, a friend, a mistress, a lover, and a murderer. Now I'm merely a prisoner. This is the alpha and the omega of my identity. Even being a psychopath takes a distant second seat to being a prisoner. I am a prisoner first, foremost, and always. I'm here for life, which is to say I'm here to die, slowly, incrementally, bits of me failing as the New York State Department of Corrections struggles to keep me alive. It's a touch paradoxical, really, the fact that one of my few rights as a prisoner is the right to health care, given that I'm here for life. Unlike you, I will get the best health care that your tax money can provide. For richer, for poorer, in sickness and in health, 'til death do us part: a life sentence is like being married, but without the handholding.

As a nun to her order, I am eternally joined to New York State. The phrase "penitentiary system" comes from the religious term for a place to discipline or punish those guilty of religious offenses. The word naturally shares the Latin root "paenitentia," or repentance. It's a small mercy that some beneficent donor gave the Bedford Hills Correctional Facility a full *Oxford English Dictionary*—it's the OED2, thus outdated, but with "penitentiary" it won't lead me astray. You can't have a correctional facility without the aim to correct, however poorly articulated.

You also can't have a penitentiary system without regret, or so social reformers would have you believe. These modern days, that repentance need not be religious. We inmates are provided with secular methods of confession. It's called "group," and I have joined. I mean, really, why not. It's a weekly break from the tedium of library books, meals, and jogging in circles on the cracked red running track. With their eyes on the prize of a successful appeal, few inmates will directly announce their crimes, but there seem to be four murderers in the group, myself included, though one or two may technically be guilty of manslaughter, or what I like to call "insufficiently ambitious homicide." There are also three women convicted of drug felonies, one arsonist, and one computer hacker—she's the most mysterious, often absent for long stretches in SHU, or solitary.

We sit in a circle. Our therapist, a middle-aged woman named Joyce, has an affinity for shawls and wearing her dyed red hair clipped into odd little animal-ear-sized bunches. Joyce makes something of a fetish of forgiveness. She urges us to forgive us our own trespasses and those who trespassed against us, as if we are tiny, grimy gods. We begin each session by going around in a circle and talking about what "came up" in the past week. Listening, I sometimes wish I had popcorn. These women live rich, complicated lives of betrayal, anguish, and worry. My own life, drab as custard, affords me little entertainment. I must rely on the crises of strangers.

After a brief recitation of the dramas du jour, Joyce picks up her thread of forgiveness and asks us to "talk to" some particular strain—family, friends, loved ones, ourselves, pets. She loves it when we confess some burden of guilt. This is very interesting for me. Group is quite informative, particularly those portions when Joyce asks us to respond to the feelings of others. I remember the day that Luciana, the arsonist, "shared" about her first foster home, a place she lived with three other foster children and a married couple, and how, coming home when truant from school, she discovered that her foster mother was having an affair with the UPS man. It was a funny story—little bed-burner Luciana sneaking in the back door of her foster home, hearing odd squeaking sounds emanating from the pantry, peeking around the corner, only to spy a pile of brown uniform pants puddled on the ground and a big brown ass pumping away at her foster mother bent over the pantry counter.

The group laughed with Luciana as she told the story, her eyes getting bigger in pantomimed recollection, her voice rising with each new discovery—rhythmic squeak-squeak-squeak, syncopated thwap-thwap-thwap, feral ah-ah-ah. Luciana's face animated as the truant twelve-year-old she had left in the dim recesses of her haggard adulthood, she caught us in her story's fist, holding us in the risible grip of pubescent narrative. She talked, we laughed; the foster mother exclaimed, tween Luciana shrieked, the couple turned to face her united *in flagrante delicto*, the UPS man exited the foster mom with a non-erotic "pop!" The foster mother, in one graceful swoop, lowered her dress, scooped her gray unmentionables from the floor, and clocked Luciana a ringing blow across the ear.

The story continued with Luciana being beaten purple, getting sent to another foster home, and then two more after that. But Luciana's story hit its crescendo when, as an eighteen-year-old, she returned to that first foster house, and entered its pantry carrying a pile of kindling, a butane torch, and some accelerant.

She burned that house black, she said. Throughout it all, Luciana didn't stop laughing. Her laugh carried her from uncomfortable fucking discovery to arsonist's flickering blaze, her eyes lit ever brighter the closer she got to striking that match. One by one, we quieted. One by one, we knew what was coming. We saw the train rocketing into the tunnel, and we saw that girl tied to the tracks. One at a time, we grew silent, captivated, and horrified. Luciana kept telling her story, oblivious. She laughed and her eyes snapped, her body tight with recollected ecstasy.

The house was a blazing pile of smoke and shadows, Luciana said. The firefighters wouldn't come in time, she knew, and she laughed. She said she hid in the shrubbery across the street, and she watched. She counted the fleeing figures, silhouetted black against the burning building. Only three people escaped, she said. "Three-hee-hee," Luciana laughed.

Luciana ended her story, her laughter ringing hollow. She rocked back and forth in her plastic chair, wound up by the catharsis of confession. The room was silent, clasped in the chest-clenching grip of awkwardness and horror.

Joyce inhaled deeply. "Thank you for sharing," she said and cast around the group for a reaction. Our eyes met. I saw the desperation in Joyce's eyes. Oh shit, I thought.

"Dorothy, how does Luciana's story make you feel?"

"Feel?" I said. "I guess I would say I feel sorry?"

"Yes?" Joyce looked relieved, bright, a rosy cardinal, with a worm in her beak.

"Yes. Sorry. I feel sorry. I feel bad that Luciana had to..." I searched for words that could fill the expected blank. "Experience that."

Joyce looked so happy and so relieved. Her face twisted with the possibility that she could redeem the horrifying hour with an honorable lesson.

I sighed and said, "I hope Luciana can learn to forgive her foster mother because—" I paused. Joyce nodded, and the group looked at me, expectant. "Because then she can learn to forgive herself."

"Yes!" said Joyce, and turned to Luciana, asking her if she'd heard what I said.

If there's one thing that can help a psychopath learn to become a better, more complete person, it's group therapy. It's like a drug you take with everyone's full, smiling approval.

Just because I'm a psychopath doesn't mean I'm incapable of learning and growing, or whatever.

After I removed the life jacket, I shoved Gil toward the open mouth of the bay, where as the tide goes out, the bay's currents sweep into the Atlantic. I cleaned the boat. I took my bathing suit off and carefully hung it on the ladder. I took a shower and dressed. Then I lifted the anchor and stowed it. Settling myself on the captain's chair behind the steering wheel, my eyes lit on the compass, and I felt the wash of terror run down my spine. A nest of howling fantods uncoiled in my chest, cold as ice water. I'd made a mistake, I realized, a towering, inky black mistake.

My plan had been to motor the boat out and around the Sound, and only then to use the ship's radio to call the authorities when safely away from the site of Gil's demise. The issue was that Gil's Hunter 45CC was, as are all modern sailboats, fully equipped with GPS. A body goes missing, and the Coast Guard will look at the ship's GPS. They'd see how the *Sea Bee Tee* sat still for an hour or more, only then to venture out to sea. They'd see where I was when I called them, how long I'd been there, and how long the ship had stayed anchored at the lip of the Sound. They'd do the intricate nautical algebra in the service of finding Gil, and in doing it, they'd see the boat's movements. There was no way this trip wouldn't look deeply suspicious, primarily because it was.

I had planned to power the boat into the Atlantic before using the ship's radio because if the Coast Guard searched the wide-open sea they'd be unlikely to find Gil's body. Radioing from the bay meant a search in the bay, which could very easily turn up the body. I didn't mind if the body turned up in a few days—the intervening time and the inevitable sea creatures delectating at Gil's tasty throat would easily explain the missing tongue—but it was imperative that the body not turn up too early. If the body surfaced too soon, it would be clear that a knife had been at work, and I couldn't have that. I needed nature to be my cover, and as there were no dachshunds about, I was relying on crabs, fish, and other creatures of the briny deep.

Most of all, the Coast Guard would be able to tell that the *Sea Bee Tee* had gone out into the Atlantic not under sail but under motor. I had no idea how to sail the boat by myself; I couldn't maneuver it out into the open water except by motor. There was no reason for Gil, an expert sailor, to motor into the Atlantic on a breezy summer day; sailing into the open sea was exactly the kind of thing he lived for. The Coast Guard would take one look at the GPS, see by the pattern of blips and blops that the boat was motoring, not sailing, and know that I was lying about something. This single mistake would most certainly bring an investigation, and an investigation would raise the likelihood of my being caught for murder.

My only choice was to drop the anchor again and come up with an excuse for choosing to spend the night in the bay. There was, of course, no reason for Gil and me to do so. We were only about two hours from the marina, a location that made perfect sense for a day sail and absolutely no sense at all for a sleepover. I turned the problem over in my head, but I found no solution other than spending the night on the boat, right where I was. There was nothing I could do that wouldn't read as suspicious to the Coast Guard, so there was nothing to do but stay put and make the call in the morning. And after wrapping the tongue tight in plastic wrap and sticking it in the ship's fridge, that's what I did.

I was, as it turned out, profoundly lucky. I called the Coast Guard early the next morning, having concocted a story of our deciding on a whim to spend the night on the *Sea Bee Tee*, of rising to make coffee, and of finding myself alone on the boat. I sounded appropriately mystified and anxious. The Coast Guard, a lovely pair of men with skin sun-toasted the color of a marshmallow a second before it bursts into flames, arrived quickly, surveyed the scene, called in a search team to look for Gil, and ferried me home from the *Sea Bee Tee*. They let me gather my things before disembarking, which included my faintly blood-sodden bikini and Gil's tongue hidden in ice in my bag, and under their care, I made it back to Shelter Island where a less tan policewoman took my statement before dropping me at the Greenport train station so I could take the LIRR back to Manhattan.

I dropped my bikini in the trash receptacle outside an Au Bon Pain in Penn Station, and I dropped the knife into a trash can on the corner of 7th Avenue and 32nd Street. Arriving home, I was pleased to see that the tongue suffered no damage in its travels.

Tongue, I believe, is an underappreciated bit of flesh. Delicately flavored, intensely tender, incredibly cheap, and absolutely singular, tongue has everything going for it but its discomfiting location. People, fools that they are, seem to have a cognitive block against putting a tongue in their mouths. It makes no sense—a kiss is still a kiss, even after you've dined on tongue. Tongue is an amazing foodstuff: you can roast it, pickle it, sauté it, fry it, or boil it, and it will taste just dandy. The important thing you have to remember as you're cooking tongue is that you have to skin it. I like to scald mine quickly in very, very hot water, then remove the tough outer layer. After that, you can have your way with this fatty, luscious delicacy. It's very difficult, even as an amateur cook, to fuck up tongue.

Gil's tongue was a lovely little morsel, surprisingly delectable for all its swelling. I skinned, sliced, then sautéed it with olive oil and garlic, adding chunks of plump Roma tomatoes, and finishing with green olives. I served it alongside a lovely arugula salad that I dressed simply with olive oil, lemon, and shaved Parmesan. Crostini rubbed with olive oil and layered with anchovy paste, and a cutting, fresh white from Liguria, Bisson Bianco Marea—hard to find, and utterly worth the search—completed the meal. I dined outside on my little terrace, Manhattan like a magical film still, as it can be on a June night, and I thought about all the wonderful times I'd shared with Gil.

He was a lovely man, Gil. So delicate.

About five days later, I received a follow-up call from the Suffolk Police Department. The Coast Guard had found Gil's body. His body, they said, had gotten caught in a current, first swept out to sea, then returned to the coast on South Fork, several miles away from where he had perished. In that time, there had been some damage, they said, but they seemed to have found nothing abnormal. Preliminary findings from the autopsy pointed to a drowning, they said, though they couldn't explain why. They expressed their condolences. I wept, mostly with relief.

In retrospect, as I sit on this orange plastic chair, just another inmate number in this prudently repentant group of my peers, I realize that killing Gil was wrong. Perhaps it's spending time in group, with Joyce and the other inmates, but now I see that I made so many mistakes, beginning with murdering Gil at all. Killing Gil had nothing to do with Gil himself. He was a good man, poor Gil. He was collateral damage. I lashed out at Gil because I felt humiliated when I was laid off by *Eat & Drink*. I couldn't take down *Eat & Drink*, and

I felt pained, impotent, raging with no target. I killed Gil because he was the weakest link. The man ate out of my hand; murdering him was like killing a pet.

I acted like a bully with Gil, but then he always liked it when I took the upper hand. He always enjoyed letting me have my way with his flesh. *La petite mort,* the French call orgasm, so who can say what final pleasures I gifted Gil as he breathed his last at my behest. Dying in that briny ocean, taste of verboten fig eternally on his lips, there are worse ways for Gil to go. You could almost say I did him a favor.

12

Silage

It was the spring of 2011, and I wanted to be in Italy. Marco was being tiresome and monogamous. He and his Borghese *donna* had gone 'round and 'round in infinite elliptical loops that ended with Marco's abjuring my company. We had so much history, Marco and I, sweet years layered like *sfogliatelle*. My time with Marco marked my movement from youth to adulthood, and for this reason alone he was special. I wanted to be in Italy, but to be close enough to Marco to brush hips yet not do it was unendurable. He was, he said, never straying again.

"*Mai. Non voglio attraversare il confine Stigio,*" he said. Never. I will not cross the Stygian boundary.

Marco always had a talent for mistaking the melodramatic for the poetic. It was something I was accustomed to, even if his newly found iron will to adhere to the bonds of his marriage was not.

And yet, if I must be honest, to have Marco go over all monogamous was not entirely unexpected. He ran in seasons, and the time had come for his trudging convention. No doubt, Marco's *donna* had nosed out some particularly juicy bit of inconstancy and had harangued her husband into abstemiousness. Whatever the reason, Marco's current cyclical return to his marriage vows was displeasing and inconvenient to me. I wasn't looking forward to going to Italy and having to seduce a new lover. Nearly fifty, I was beginning to find it laborious—it wasn't the seduction, exactly. I looked good, and I've always been as charming as a hungry cat when I needed to be. It was more that performing the dance had grown tedious. I didn't want to tell someone my history; I didn't want to be bothered to invent a new one. I wanted Marco and all our weight, all our wrinkles, all our textures, all our complexities.

He was having none of me. I wouldn't accept it.

I was therefore forced to do something I had never done before: I pitched a story on a lover. I finagled some contacts at *Gourmand*, I promised them the inside scoop on the hottest "bio" butcher in Rome, and I sold it. I suspected Marco would see me to get a story about his meat empire in a glossy American magazine, and I was not wrong. Was crossing the line between work and my intimate life an untrammeled delight? No. But it was a line that was necessary to get my way with Marco.

As much as my decision to leave restaurant criticism was predicated on my getting fired from *Eat & Drink* and the need to bolster sales of my second book, it was not a decision I regretted. Times had changed in the more than twenty years I'd been writing about food. Everyone in food seemed to know everyone else; it was one long human centipede of fuckwittery, where not only was everyone suddenly a writer or a celebrity, but also chefs and sommeliers and even bloody butchers were stars, crossing oceans and running symposiums, Facebooking and tweeting and Snapchatting about the whole incestuous, writhing mess. It was an ugly, self-cannibalizing machine of gratuitous glad-handing, but who am I to buck convention when convention serves me.

I wasn't happy, not with Marco's moral existential crisis, not with having to create a pretense to see Marco—who was really mine by *droit du seigneur*—not with having to compromise my ethics, and not with having to pretend I was interested in his clever mass disassembling of carcasses. I was not happy at what my life had pushed me to do, but who is.

Yet I had to wear the pretense gladly when in late spring of 2011 I went to Italy to interview Marco, landing first in Lombardia, where he fattened his cattle, moving next to Toscana, where he killed them, and arriving finally in Roma, where he butchered them, a trip ripe with the many smells of livestock. My nose filled with the pointy brown scent of cattle shit and the patient green smell of cattle breath, the acrid vinegar smell of cattle piss and the rich, coppery smell of cattle blood—great shining oceans of cattle blood, draining into sluices arranged in the kill floor. I saw giant pellucid piles of cattle nerves and caul fat, and I watched the peculiar way that the quieted eyes of cows lolled as their throats were professionally sliced. I witnessed the snick of the blade and the mercurial quiver of death running quick through a one-ton animal. I saw hides slick and shiny with gore, and I saw lines of men bent over tables of meat, intent as rabbis over scrolls, taking apart the cows with lawful precision. I saw chickens, too, so many flappy birds, and sheep, bleating like human children, their long-lashed eyes innocent and bright—until they were neither.

I visited Marco's empire and saw it for what it was: a well-planned, carefully orchestrated machine bent on the extermination of animals for our gastronomical pleasure. And I walked through it all, rubber boots pulled over my Wolford stockings, tight smile on my face, feigning interest in order to be closer to Marco, incessantly asking myself one question: Why.

The answer was so that I could kill and eat him.

I don't mean to boast, but I cannot forbear saying this: aside from my two books, *Ravenous* and *Voracious*, killing Marco is my finest achievement. Nearly two years had passed since I had turned Gil into a delicate dish of tongue. I'd gleaned much from that harrowing experience—to research thoroughly, to plan for every eventuality without regard for likelihood, to leave nothing to chance, and, above all, never, ever to go near a boat. Killing Marco took a considerable amount of work, all made more difficult by the fact that I had to plan every step with an awareness of whether it would read as legwork for the *Gourmand* article or whether it would bind me to the crime. Unlike the three previous deaths that were easily ruled accidents, Marco's would look undeniably like a murder—there was nothing accidental about it. It was, as I envisioned it, to be pure, unadulterated, premeditated homicide, so I had to ensure that when the *polizia* came looking for Marco's killer, their eyes would glide off me.

So much depended upon the daft schedule of Trenitalia and the unions so imbued with whimsy and given to strikes. In theory, Trenitalia, the national corporation responsible for rail travel in

Italy, is organized, codified, simple, and comprehensible. In actual lived experience, however, Trenitalia is chaotic, disordered, complex, and arcane. I'm sure there are some who understand the great mysterious force that is Trenitalia; the fascist *conduttori*, for one, and the persons who wrote Trenitalia's adulatory Wikipedia entry, for another. To my thinking, the logic of Trenitalia was the worst kind of Italian disregard for rules. Even the Trenitalia website appears to have been created by workers who have a slender understanding of how humans think. It reads like it was written in Cyborg, fed through Google Translate into Italian, and slapped on to a webpage. More than one time, I've sat in the wrong Trenitalia car, taken the wrong train, or bought an online ticket for a trip other than the one I'd intended to take. And all this even before the trains mysteriously stop running because of a *sciopero bianco*, a work-to-rule strike, otherwise known as an "Italian strike," when workers register protest by doing no more work than is mandated by their employment contracts. A butterfly flaps its wings in Chioggia, and a train running to Siena freezes on its tracks, such is the indescribable strangeness of Trenitalia.

It's a fascist adage: "Say what you like about Mussolini, but at least the trains run on time." This was true neither in Mussolini's day nor today. Trains exist and there are many, which makes Italy already superior to the car-logged, rail-beleaguered United States, but don't set your watch by them. However predictable, Trenitalia's inconstancy is an issue when you're planning a perfectly orchestrated murder from 4,000 miles away. I raise the bureaucratic specter of Trenitalia because much of the success of Marco's murder rested upon it. The remainder hinged on my skill with knives.

I landed in Parma and took a train to meet Marco in Cremona, in Lombardia, Italy's breadbasket, where Italians like to feed their cattle until fat and delectable. Following at Marco's elbow, I visited the farms where his beef cattle, some 800 head of Chianini and Bianca Modenese—a lilting grass-green sea dotted with white, lowing lumps of patient mammal—fed before being dispatched to the slaughterhouse outside of Florence. Rather than raise their cattle from birth, Italian beef farmers mainly fatten the cattle born in other lands, usually Ireland, France, Poland, or Spain, depending on where the beef farm sits on Italy's thigh-high boot. Italy's dearth of large, open plains makes difficult the raising of beef cattle, a suck of land and food even in wide-open spaces. There isn't much grass-fed beef in Italy because there isn't much grass. You want grass-fed meat, you go to the Americas, where there are plains for days; your basic Chianina is going to have grown fat eating corn, some hay, but mostly corn. Organically raised from birth without hormones or antibiotics, Marco's pampered, plump cattle ate a mixture of free-range scrubland, trucked-in dry hay, and organic corn silage. It's very, very difficult to make money as a meat farmer in Italy—in fact, most of the cattle industry lives squarely in the arterial red, hemorrhaging cash and requiring government subsidies. The fact that Marco was able to do it successfully, to do it organically, and to do it so elegantly made him and his business quite the story.

Although I pressed him until the moment I closed the zipper on my suitcase, Marco remained adamantly opposed to seeing me for sex. "*Il mio cuore, anima, vita, cazzo—appartengono alla mia amata moglie,*" he said to me before I left America. His heart, his soul, his life, his cock, they all belonged to his wife, enumerating his parts in escalating importance. Boarding my plane at JFK, I promised myself that if he gave in, gave up, and fell with sweetness into my bed, he would live for me to tell the tale. If he didn't, I would tell a different tale. It was all up to him, you see, whether he lived or died. It was his body, his choice.

Waiting for Marco to unknowingly decide his fate, I learned where cattle were born, how they were fed, how they were moved, and I learned precisely how they were turned from sentient beings into comestible lumps of crimson and white. I learned how big cows were, what went on inside them, and how to calculate their value on the open market. I learned a lot about cattle during my week traveling with Marco, but primarily I learned that a beef farmer's life revolves around two things: food and shit.

A beef cow shits up to fifteen times a day, a total of sixty-five pounds of poop, the weight of the average nine-year-old child. The problem is always, ever, unceasingly, what you're going to do with that mountain of shit, a question that screams for an answer when you're dealing with 52,000 pounds of shit a day, as Marco's operation was—and that's not including the shit hillocks produced by his smaller chicken and lamb operations. From the perspective of the farmer, the meat on our tables comes in the service of finding ways to get rid of the abundance of shit excreted by the animal bound for the slaughterhouse. It's an unappetizing circle of life, but once you see it, you can't look away. An average cow produces 490 pounds of trimmed, edible meat; it also produces about 12 tons of shit, or 24,000 pounds, during its lifespan. Vast truckloads of shit must be moved, somewhere, to get that steak on the plate or that burger on the bun. Think about that the next time you unwrap your BK Double.

As I bided my time with Marco, I learned more than I ever thought I'd care to know about organic meat and the Italian slow food movement, the capitalistic dikes holding fast against the nefarious encroachment of agribusiness into Italy. I learned about dark meat, pH factors, lactic acid, stress, and why you as a meat farmer want your animals to be caressed into annihilation. I learned about kosher slaughter, kosher butchering, and kosher market share. I learned about the regional differences in what makes meat "good" in Italy, and in doing so, I realized exactly how dim and homogenized the American palate is. I learned a lot, and I stored all of it on my computer because, as much as it helped me write an excellent article (titled "Marco Iachino, the Natural King of Chianini," September 2013 Gourmand, nominated for a James Beard Award in magazine profiles), it tied me to Marco as subject of an article, not victim of a homicide.

I also learned many things that would not appear on my computer searches, a distinction I made in case my hard drive were to be scrutinized after Marco's demise. These were things I did not want traced to my home, so I researched them in the last great bastions of public learning, libraries. I learned the precise ritual for kosher killing, memorizing its intricate choreography, its slitting of carotid arteries, jugular veins, vagus nerves, trachea, and esophagus. I mapped out this ballet on a human body, likewise the body's necessary exsanguination, stripping of veins, caul fat, and sinews. I got achingly familiar with human anatomy. A few days with Hollinshead's anatomy textbook, and I knew the inside of the human throat like the back of my hand.

And I memorized all the routes into, out of, and around Florence to Rome; it was dreary, tiresome, and vital information. All the best-laid plans will run to naught if you get caught by train strike, traffic, or accident on a roundabout. One Vespa rider goes splat like the wasp it's named after, and the cold, uncaring universe undoes weeks of meticulous planning. The only thing to do was to learn it, learn it all, the trains, the roads, and the bus schedule; the ins, the outs, the ups, and the downs, because all roads may lead to Rome, but not all roads lead to an airtight alibi.

Prison food is part of the punishment. The food the prison feeds you is almost entirely comprised of meals made from cans, boxes, or mixes, made by people who can't be bothered to care, and served to people who have no choice but to eat it. The meals abide by USDA regulations, which is to say that nutrition waves in its general direction. One thing most people don't fully comprehend is that the USDA, the United States Department of Agriculture, is for all intents and purposes run by big agro. Let me put it another way: the USDA is a giddy dystopian wonderland designed for the pleasure of big agribusiness. There are only a handful of American agribusiness corporations, and they essentially dictate what Americans eat because they essentially control the USDA. For example, the USDA created the nutritional pyramid first and foremost to serve agribusiness's interests—not human physical needs. And thus the meals served to schools and to prisons reflect not what the bodies of growing boys and girls or aging men and women need to thrive and/or survive; rather, these meals, planned and vetted and carefully created by lockstep scads of bureaucratic drones, work to buttress the agribusiness economy—while costing the State (or the corporation running the institution) as little as possible.

Here's another way to look at it: in the 1930s, there were 5,000,000 more American farmers than there are now, not quite a hundred years later, and these millions of farmers grew a wider range of foodstuffs on these predominantly family-owned-and-operated farms. Most important, these farms don't exist today. That cool six-figure loss hides the explosive growth of corporations like Monsanto and DuPont, shrouds the decrease in differing crops that American farmers grow, and obfuscates how what we eat is making us sick because what we're eating is in no small part dictated by the big businesses that grow the raw materials for our meals. We've gained cheap food (and the cheapest food goes to public schools and for-profit prisons), but we've lost everything else.

That said, the food here at Bedford Hills is better than at most prisons. We have a garden, and we're surrounded with all manner of chipper do-gooders, prison education volunteers, religious types, prison reformers and assorted kindhearted saps who want to tell us that they believe in us, they really do. Still, the lionesses' share of Bedford Hills's three meals is white: white bread, white milk, white rice, white potatoes. The meat, such as it is, tends toward the stringy and inedible. It is not, as the common expression goes, "Grade D—Fit for Human Consumption," but that is only because there is no Grade D meat. That's a myth like the organ harvesters that sprung up in chain email in the '90s: a horror that never existed created to take our minds off life's real horrors, like the fact that the pesticides DuPont creates are in essence honeybee genocide. The USDA, for all its questionable wisdom, has eight rather serviceable categories for meat: Prime, Choice, Select, Standard, Commercial, Utility, Cutter, and Canner. Granted, while what we prisoners (and your public-school children) eat derives from the last four grades, there's no Grade D, and the meat on our compartmentalized plate is, all things considered, edible, though not delectable.

That said, only the truly hard-up inmates rely on the three squares that Bedford Hills provides. There is a robust economy in prison comestibles that's like stone soup meets Burning Man meets the night market of Yau Ma Tei. Your can of Goya chickpeas and box of Stove Top stuffing, my tin of chicken breast and can of green beans, someone else's plastic jar of jerk marinade, and between the three of us, we can create something verging on tasty. Some of us, the very lucky ones, have Crock-Pots or rice cookers; we are the one-eyed gourmets in the kingdom of the confined.

To put it very plainly: I'm lucky because I'm rich. Before incarceration, I'd sold my apartment, cashed in my 401k and my life insurance, and liquidated all my assets, so my bank account showed a healthy seven figures. I came into prison with money; I'll die in prison with money. Even after the legal fees were settled, even after I paid out Casimir's kin their wrongful death suit, I was left with lots of money (and the residuals on my published books have exploded; there's nothing like notoriety to sell a book). I'm never going to go short at the commissary; I am well stocked with tinned everything, and my father and my siblings send me lavish care packages of the finest Uncle Ben's and Dinty Moore that their money can buy. In the real world, I'd be comfortable, but in prison terms, I'm unimaginably rich. How much of my personal wealth can Cup O'Noodles consume—not much, even at exorbitant prison commissary prices.

Being a wealthy, smart psychopath with superb cooking skills and the best small appliance that the federal corrections system allows makes me a powerful person. If I were merely rich, I'd be a target. But I'm not, and thus I am left more or less alone, except for when people want to barter, and this is fine with me. I live like an island, apart from, distant from, but also reachable from the mainland. I am Sardinia to their Italy, Corsica to their France, Staten Island to their New Jersey.

In prison terms, I eat well. On my terms, it's wretched. Everything is relative, and, here in prison, nothing is beautiful, except memory.

From Cremona's pastoral feedlots, I followed Marco to Florence, where he had kept an office after his business began to boom, and then to his kill yards in Fucecchio, a drab town about 50 kilometers away from Florence. As Newark is to New York City, Livorno is to Florence, and grotty little Fucecchio, a town with a long history in the smelly trade of leather tanning, sits halfway between the gritty port city of Livorno to the west and the stylish, historical city of Florence to the east. Fucecchio is where loads of lowing cattle, bundles of bleating sheep, and masses of spastic chickens meet their Maker, or, barring that pietistic construction, die in methods that Marco repeatedly assured me were the most humane possible.

Throughout the trip, Marco was the quintessence of politesse. He introduced me constantly as "Dorothea, *la scrittrice per le riviste Americana*," the American magazine writer, and he made very certain never to touch me, never to act as if he knew my flesh and my heart, and never to indicate that I might be the slightest bit attractive. Marco even made sure we had a chaperone! Driving from Cremona to Fucecchio, his majordomo, Silvio Chimichì, rode shotgun; I was stuffed like a child in the back seat. At every lunch and every dinner, Marco surrounded us with others, often in the pretense of helping me on my piece. We dined with agronomists, with bovine specialists, with his regional sales managers, with not one but two Italian food writers, with the regional head of the Italian Slow Food movement. I was fairly certain that if the trip were extended we'd soon be dining not on but with the cattle themselves. Any hot body substituted for a bundling board; Marco inserted people between us like clean sheets. It was never for us to touch, not by accident, not by design, not—if Marco had his way about it—at all.

As Marco had aged, his hair thinned and he had cut it shorter and shorter. Outdoors, he tended toward jaunty hats, brushed-felt fedoras in the cold months and straw Panamas in the warm, which created a weatherproof dome for his yarmulke. Indoors, however, it was usually just Marco and his kippah, Italians being quite punctilious about hatless propriety. It was a marvel, watching him bend over, stand up, practically dance around, his yarmulke fixed and unmoving, but I discovered his secret: double-stick tape. Marco's head was like a starlet's breasts, tethered to the performance of decorum with the help of space-age polymers.

The entirety of the time I spent with Marco, I hung on tenterhooks. Would he lose his resolve, succumb to history's flesh memory, and fuck me like a frenzied bull? Or would he hold fast to his slippery monogamy, carry on the pretense, and keep his hands, his mouth, his cock, and his lust to himself? It was delightful, if excruciating, this constant proximity to Marco. For four days, the span of time I spent with him and his cattle, I shimmered with anticipation. A touch, a word, a brush of the lips, a knock at my hotel room door, some sign that Marco wanted me in his bed, naked and writhing: this was all I needed from him. I got *niente*.

And in a shocking show of exquisite self-control, I did nothing and said nothing in return. I, the provocatrix who had once given him a hand job to completion as he talked breathlessly on the phone to his wife and children, who'd induced him to fuck me while I stood watching an opera at the Arena di Verona, who had perpetrated viciously pleasurable acts upon his body in multiple Michelin-starred restaurants' bathrooms, did nothing. I met Marco's cool, amiable façade, and I raised it to business class. No one watching my behavior would think for a moment that I'd had a history beyond casual emails with the man. It wasn't that I didn't want to; it was that I couldn't run the risk of him getting spooked. If he didn't fuck me, I'd have to kill him; to kill him, I needed him to trust me enough to be alone with me; for trust, I needed to play his game. This torture wasn't without its piercing charms.

Touring his empire, Marco was incandescent with pride, and he was right to feel pleased with his work. The slaughterhouse was a thing of genius, a site that would make Temple Grandin beam. Marco moved only as many cattle as he needed from his feedlots in Cremona to his kill yard in Fucecchio, slaughtering cattle and lambs during the months from October to June, when it was cool enough that flies weren't an issue. *"Le mosche contaminano la carne,"* he said with a knowing glance. The flies contaminate the meat. Whatever that meant.

In the yard, a hundred or so cattle roamed free in two separate pens; one pen farther away from the kill floor allowed for food and water; the other, closer to the kill floor, provided only water. Sheep were held likewise, in smaller pens adjacent to the cattle; Marco told me there were no chickens to be slaughtered that day. Before slaughtering the cattle, Marco explained, he stopped feeding them, lowering the chance that an accidental slitting of intestines could harm the meat; otherwise the cattle were free to wander within their pens. So much work in the service of so many carcasses.

In the pen closer to the slaughterhouse, two distinct groups of men wandered among the cattle with clipboards, one clearly goyim, the other clearly Jewish. The Jewish ones, bearded and behatted, closely inspected a number of cattle, looking in their mouths, up their noses, under their tails, at their feet. When they found cattle that satisfied them, they sprayed a "K" on their hides. The goyim also inspected the cattle; a limping one was led away to a farther pen set apart from the others. "Dog food," Marco said as we watched and his mouth made the downward arc of lost revenue.

Mirroring the two groups of men, the slaughterhouse split into two parts: one held the traditional chase, or chute, leading to the "knock box," a close-fitting metal cradle that held the cow still for traditional slaughter; the other had a chase that led to an open room where three very serious bearded men and a large metal cow holder stood ready to slaughter with the kosher method of shechita. Inside the door to the conventional slaughtering room was a quote from Temple Grandin, "Nature is cruel but we don't have to be"; inside the door of the kosher side was something written in Hebrew. Marco told me it was the prayer that the shochet, the men trained in kosher slaughter, say before they begin their workday.

In the decades since our college time in Siena, Marco had grown not merely to accept his heritage, not merely to embrace it, but to believe in it. "It's a mitzvah," Marco said of his trade, in Italian sprinkled with Hebrew, smiling and gesturing at the three bearded men bent over their shiny line of long rectangular knives, running them repeatedly against their fingernails, like obsessive compulsives. "The shochet pays respect to the animal. He releases its deepest unconscious wish—to be our food, with grace, with respect, with humility." Marco was beatific. "In confronting face to face the animal as we kill it, we assume the moral responsibility for taking the animal's life. It is a holy act of sanctification, not this—what do you call it, genocide of cows. No hamburger should cost less than four euros. I spit on McDonald's." He said the name of the burger empire with a strange English inflection, MACK-dawh-*ahldz*.

On one side of the divide, the traditional kill floor, a cow entered the box, a man pointed a pneumatic stunner at its forehead, the cow dropped, and the cow slid out the side like a piece of toast. Then, insensate, it was unceremoniously hoisted by its hind leg, where its throat was cut, releasing a geyser of blood. On the other side, the kosher side, the cow was given a drink of water and then guided into the big metal cow tipper, which rotated to suspend the cow upside down in its full metal jacket. One technician—not, Marco told me, a shochet—used a rod to hold down the cow's chin, another sprayed water over the cow's exposed throat, and in one perfect, swift slice, the shochet slit the cow's throat. Different, more elegant process; same geyser of blood. The metal jacket turned upright, depositing the dead cow on the floor, where, like its goy-feeding brethren, it was lifted unceremoniously by a hind leg. From 1,200 pounds of living creature to so much comestible meat, leather, pet food, beauty products, fertilizer, wallpaper, tennis racquet strings, biodiesel, fireworks, shampoo, refined sugar, air filters, and fabric softeners. For us it may be ashes to ashes, dust to dust, but for cattle it's so much more kaleidoscopic.

There's no good way to turn animals into meat. Statistically, traditional stunning and shochet killing fail at about the same rate, roughly ten percent of the time. No matter what measures you take, you're killing an animal to harvest its glorious muscles. Death is rarely pretty. Indeed, death's very predilection to go horribly awry gave Marco the genius idea to start the organic conventional side of his business. When his team of expert shochets slipped up, when their knives were nicked, when they cut too close or too shallow, when the trimmers perforated the stomach, when the cow's lungs weren't smooth, whenever something, somehow, somewhere rendered that cow not kosher, Marco had an immediate plan B: feed the goyim. It was brilliant, really. Same cattle, two audiences, and both awash in the clean penny smell of fresh exsanguination.

The processing floor was similarly twinned. On the conventional side, a long line of men in white coats, tall rubber boots, netted heads, and paper arm condoms systematically turned dead cows into slabs of meat and tubs of glistening viscera. On the kosher side, the same thing happened with many, many more steps. The cow was not merely disassembled; it was scrutinized, parts turned inside out, upside down, blown up, and pored over. Any tiny imperfection rendered it unacceptable, and swiftly, like a plague victim, it would be whisked away to the other side of the divide. If acceptable, the cow's carcass was hung on hooks from a conveyor belt, the meat was salted and washed and washed and salted. It was bathed with a languorous precision, like the limbs of a courtesan before an assignation. At the end lay twin refrigerated rooms where rows of dismembered cattle hung, red and fulsome as ripe passionfruit.

I had to commend Marco for the simple, automated vision in recognizing that he would do much more than double his business by expanding it; he would make meat his keening bitch. Marco's empire was death, and in complete, abject, honest regard, he did it ingeniously. So much mechanized precision in the interest of beneficient death made me inexpressibly hot. I wanted Marco. I wanted to fuck him hard on that kill-yard floor. And I couldn't show it. Not a sigh, not a glance, not a whimper, not if I wanted him dead.

Punta di Petto and Tripe

arco didn't soften his hard-line commitment to his marriage, not a bit, not for a moment, not once during our travels. I played along. I flirted outrageously at dinner at Ora d'Aria in Firenze with the third regional sales manager that Marco put before me in that four-day trip. You can't slide tapas-sized plates of three-star Tuscan food before me and not expect me to use my fingers. Really, whose fault was it that my index finger made its way inside that sales manager's mouth, topped as it was with a brown-butter-and-chickpea sauce the exact shade of a maiden's aureole. And what can a woman do with the last morsel of pork belly sauced with a garlic and lavender reduction other than pop it in the mouth of the unmarried man to her left. I was in Italy, after all, and even though Marco was having none of me didn't mean I had to be a nun.

For the record, I didn't have sex with the third regional sales manager. He failed to be intriguing. I kept my relationship with Marco professional. It was all merely part of the game that Marco didn't know he was playing.

The Art Institute of Chicago is home to a lurid painting of a door. Ominously black yet kissed with a candy-pink-flowered wreath, this door looms almost life-sized, eldritch as Victorian hair jewelry, ornate and vaguely threatening, somehow dripping in blood, though none is visible. From its jamb, a hand reaches out; you wouldn't accept it. The work of Ivan Albright, this painting's real name is *That Which I Should Have Done I Did Not Do*. Choices are, after all, the things that haunt us. The moments when we could've turned left but turned right. The times when we could've gone back but forged ahead. The instants when we made decisions that we would live to regret. I don't regret killing Marco. It was, after all, almost his decision.

Had Marco broken with his monogamous pact, had he forsaken his bourgeois conformity to the *donna*, to his faith, to the superego of respectability, had he merely made the easy choice to fall gently into vague dissolution, he'd still be walking and talking, alive to sneak into obscure trattorias to eat prosciutto and finger-fuck my familiar genitalia beneath the table. I'd rub my face into his badger-pelt chest and order another magnum of Champagne. We'd have oysters and anal, not necessarily in that order, and all would be right with the world.

Instead things took another route. Deep in the plum of a Friday night, I opened the back door to Marco's butcher shop in Rome. It was almost too easy, but then I had planned this murder within an inch of its life, and Marco, seduced as he was by the future of seeing his empire spread slick as a centerfold across the pages of *Gourmand*, fell like a complicit lamb into my hands. To cap my visit to Marco's meat empire, Marco suggested meeting at his famed *macelleria* in the Jewish Quarter late on the Friday sabbath because no one would be out; no one would see us; no one could bear witness; and no one could tell his wife that he was meeting a *testarossa* of little good repute. In the religious quiet of the night, tucked as his shop was off the quarter's main drag, we were unlikely to be seen. Particularly if, as we did, we entered separately, and I wore an overcoat and a fedora.

I arrived first, by design. Marco was uncertain of when he would be able to pry himself loose from his familial bosom. We were both aware that our walking in together would raise suspicion, so Marco had given me the keys and the alarm code. From an alley, I approached the rear of the store; next to the gripping maw of the loading platform was a plain metal door, thick and heavy. I unlocked it and disabled the alarm. I skulked quiet through the hallway to the dark-ened front room, the one with the large plate-glass window, which during working hours would have illuminated me like a sweet in a candy case. I looked at the worn wooden floor in the streetlight's

Picasso-blue shadows, the refrigerated cases bare and clean and gleaming in the gloaming, the scales weighing nothing but air. The room held the uncanny silence of a public space empty of people.

Visible to the light foot traffic and the windows of the apartments facing the building, shutters decorously closed as averted eyes, the actual shop was not where my interests lay. I wanted the back rooms. The guts of the butcher shop, deep in the building and sealed tight as a tomb. This is where Marco's team performed the unsavory work of making animal corpses into saleable meat. The abattoir I'd visited earlier that day was merely the overture to the corporeal matinee that played out on these dark stages. I fumbled along the walls and found the light switches, flicking them with a snicker-snack of sound and flooding the room with the hallucinogenic glare of aggressive fluorescent light.

There were essentially two spaces for these theatrics of butchery: one large, clean room ranged with four large tables, each accompanied by a sink and a martial row of knives, sharp as freed felons. Overhead was a complex network of tracks; in a topsy-turvy way, it looked like mass transit, and it sort of was, but rather than trains, sharp metal hooks ran on the tracks, and rather than carrying people to their destinations, they carried dead animals to their tidy dismemberment. To my surprise, there was almost no smell, only the faintest copper taint of blood, just the palest whiff of cleaning supplies. Marco ran a very clean shop.

The other room was a giant refrigerator festooned with a very large number of dead animals, great lumpen halves of steers, split down the center; the discomfiting toddler shapes of lambs and baby goats; piles of chickens in plastic bags. In life, this room would have resonated with barnyard cacophony; in that walk-in still life, with its zinc refrigerator walls and mottled animal bodies, my footsteps fell like cotton balls. A door in the back led to a freezer; my breath puffed in impotent clouds about the corpses.

There's a lot of human labor involved in turning dead animals into palatable slabs of meat. One dead cow can garner more than sixty different cuts of beef in as many as eight grades of quality. This math obscures the work it takes to put that filet on your plate; the back of Marco's butcher shop did not. Technology helps, of course, and the tracks that traversed the ceiling made it easier to swing a cow do-si-do around the room from fridge to table, and the small skill saws ranged like sentinels in the corners no doubt did their parts, but in the end, it's the butcher and his handiwork that makes meals from meat.

I had to say, I was impressed. Of course I'd visited butchers before, but they were never butchers I'd known for decades and seen mature from romantic college boy to industry mogul. Marco's modest shop, the genus for his empire, plied the perfect punctuation to the journey. I had to marvel at the perfection of the narrative loop. This butcher shop wasn't just the humble beginnings of Marco's empire of meat; it was also the big, wet secret he'd kept from me in our youth. I'm no heart-doodling fool. I know full well that being only Marco's mistress—the thrill of the chase, the delinquent deliquesces, the ellipses-studded Morse code of our nearly life-long relationship—had kept us interested in each other. Had either one of us been fully available and thus open and honest, our desire would've died a needful death. You only want what you can't consistently have, at least if you're me. Or Marco, I suspect, at least some of the time.

I heard the rasp of a key turning in a lock, the tapping of expensive shoes on cement flooring, and then Marco was all about me, enveloping my body in his arms and beard and trench coat, like a stingray around a school of fish.

"Mia cara, mia fiamma, la mia stella scarlatto," he murmured into my neck. My darling, my flame, my scarlet star. "I have... *anelare, anelare...* how do you say?"

"Yearned."

"Sì. Yearned. I have yearned for you. *Sono debole. Sono debole. Sono così, così debole."* I am weak, he said, I am so, so weak. He breathed the words into my cleavage, punctuating them with kisses on my breasts.

This was awkward. I had promised myself Marco's freedom if he came to me, bent-kneed and supplicant, primed for fornication. In the days we'd spent together, his conduct was so professional as to be nearly imperious. In truth, he'd been kind of a prick. Marco's reigning supreme in his empire of meat didn't make me an underling, yet his behavior toward me verged on bossy. If this was how he treated women on the regular, he didn't deserve to draw breath, much less be allowed to enter my body. Day after day, as Marco withheld, as he swanned about—as he lorded and puffed his chest and kept referring to me as *"la piccola scrittrice,"* the little writer, as if I didn't have decades of experience, two bestselling books, and fluency in Italian—the more I felt he was sealing his own fate. His death was his doing.

So what was I to make of Marco's erotic penitence, and what should I do with the man, now pooled at my feet, his nose pressed against my pudendum, huffing his deep breaths through the lace of my panties. Did it violate my rules to kill him now? Or had his behavior until now sealed his fate. If Marco had to die because of his choice to kowtow to convention and commitment rather than honor personal history and eros, how should I read his eleventh-hour conversion.

"Let us leave," Marco said into my pudendum. *"Andiamo. Andiamo nel tuo albergo. Non mi interessa. Ti voglio."* His mouth moving compellingly over my vulva, his breath hotter with each *"non mi interessa"*—I don't care. He yearned. I felt it. His yearning was palpable through the silk and the lace, and it shot shivers. My vertebrae trilled like a xylophone, but my hotel was inconveniently located in Toscana.

I grabbed a heft of hair and pulled Marco to standing. I kissed him and pushed him against the wall. I slid his trench coat off his arms, first his left, then his right. I pulled his suit jacket down, pooling it around his wrists. I untied the knot of his tie, and I shucked his shirt like an ear of corn. Marco stood in his pants, his chest bare, his arms bound behind him in a wad of aggressively expensive clothes. The fluorescent light turned him the dainty green of an immature olive.

Marco struggled to free his hands.

"No. Stai ferma," I said. Be still.

I pulled a pair of cuffs from my pocket and, reaching behind him, clipped first one, then the other over his wrists. I pushed him a couple of feet to his left, where a chain hung from the ceiling, part of the track apparatus for sliding carcasses across the ceiling, and I clipped the cuffs on to the chain. I'd brought a double clip from a bondage store in Manhattan with me (I'd picked up the cuffs in Milan, one of the few Italian cities whose commerce is not entirely prudish). I believe I mentioned that I'd planned this murder within a cunt's hair of its life.

Marco moaned, indistinctly. His chest rose and fell, and his skin was taut with want.

I unbuckled Marco's Gucci belt, unzipped his Valentino trousers, pulled his cock free of his Dolce & Gabbana boxers, and I took it into my mouth. I lulled Marco into willing submission, and as I felt his cock quiver with the hardness of near orgasm, and as I tasted the bleach-and-umami flavor of his precum, I reached my right into my purse. Marco spent himself into my mouth, shuddering, groaning; his orgasm echoed in his butcher's room. I caressed his flank with my left hand, waiting for him to go soft in my mouth. Then, I stood and kissed him, looked him in the eye, and I slit his throat with my blade.

I did not hesitate. I did not flinch. I did not press. My knife did not slip; it did not dig; it did not tear. My knife, I had taken care to ensure, was free of nicks, and it was sharp. So sharp it shined, and it sang no pain when I'd tested it, first with the pad of my thumb and then with my fingernails. It was a clean, sharp blade. It made Dorothy Parker's wit look dull.

Precise as a skater, my knife sliced through Marco's throat; a second smile spilled crimson down his chest. Marco's eyes locked with mine, a fast, tense flash—and then they glided off, a dull stare that glanced to nothing. There was no time for terror, no lingering mortality, no slow ebb of life, no time to worry or to watch. Marco was alive, and then he was not. His death was as sudden as a light flicked by a forefinger: here-slash-gone. The fault in that analogy, however fitting, is in the undoing; I could not lift the knife, slice backward through the air, and make him as he was. I should have liked, if only to slice again, to do it again; reverse it and do it again and again. Gone. Here. Gone. Here. Gone. I watched as Marco's blood poured and his pleasure-crying mouth went slack. A great red pool grew on the floor beneath him; I stood to the side and let it flow, then I let it trickle, and finally I let it drip, leaving great scarlet trails down his furry chest, belly, and loins. The air smelled hot and bright with blood.

Was it a shechita slaughter? Obviously not. First and foremost, human meat is most assuredly not kosher. Second, I am not Jewish. Third, I'm not trained as a shochet. And fourth, while it's not technically required that a kosher slaughter needs the knife known as a Hasidische hallaf, it is the industry standard. Not using one in shechita butchery is akin to a pastry chef using a mixer other than a KitchenAid; sure, there's the odd one who prefers a Cuisinart or a Viking, but they're the strange child on the playground. My knife was not a Hasidische hallaf; in all other respects, however, it was fine for the task. It was as close as I, a laywoman, could get. I felt as if I had done what I could to honor Marco in the most appropriate manner that I could approximate. It was his heritage, after all, his faith, his vocation, and the visible parts of his life. How could I have killed him otherwise.

The Butcher of Baghdad, the Butcher of Beirut. The Butcher of Uganda, the Butcher of Congo, the Butcher of Plainfield. Bill the Butcher. We're a culture that uses "butcher" as a disparagement. When you've done a really bad job at something, you've butchered it; no one would go to a surgeon who's a butcher. We bandy about the word "butcher" with regard for the profession, but truths be told, humans would still be screeching apes shitting from trees if it weren't for the transformative power of meat. A long, long time ago, a random Neanderthal found a stick and thumped it hard on the noggin of some dumb animal; then she took a sharp rock and slid it into the animal's hot hide. With these modest actions, human history forever changed. We know that people have been using tools to disassemble animals for at least 2.5 million years. And for the last thousand, we've been using the cleaver.

"Cleave" is an interesting word. A contranym, "cleave" means both to join and to separate; in this regard, it works like "splice," but no one splices another to her breast. We cleave to people, or they cleave to us, yet to cleave a person is self-defense at best and a horror at worst. Knives are flexible things; a chef's blade is among the most versatile tools you have in your kitchen—you can press, slice, chop, mince, cut, and even scoop with it. You'd think nothing of picking up a boning knife to prise out a bit of peach pit lodged in the fruit's tender flesh. Your serrated knife may be made to cut bread, but it works wonders on tomatoes, chocolate, and cake. The cleaver, in contrast, has but one task: it cuts through fat, flesh, tendon, and even bone. It turns a carcass into meat.

It is, therefore, somewhat a pity that this tool—so efficient, so shiny, so sharp—has fallen out of favor. Born more than a million years ago, the cleaver has been replaced by quotidian saws, first hacksaws and then table saws, for the gross work and a series of thin boning knives for the fine. You can still find butchers who rely mainly on cleavers, but most do not. In part, this shift is owing to the fact that more and more packers hot-trim the carcass on the kill floor, not even waiting for the body of the cow, the pig, or the sheep to cool to room temperature before disassembly. ("Hot-trim the carcass" is not yet a euphemism, but what a fine, feral euphemism it would make.) And in part it's owing to more sides of meat being shipped frozen, making it easier for meatpackers or supermarket butchers to use table saws to cut it into saleable pieces. More meat, more mechanization, and the cleaver sits on the side of the block, gathering dust on its shiny, noble blade.

Suspended with his wrists shackled to the wall, Marco beetled forward like a figurehead on a ship. His wrists were bound behind him, by clothes and by cuffs; his knees locked in death. Though at a decided angle, he stood upright. I shook a shoulder to test for stability. Gravity and physics blessed me; the body didn't seem inclined to move. In planning, I had been concerned about turning the carcass upside down and thought it might be more difficult had it fallen to sprawl like a line drawing on the floor. Kosher killing—and standard slaughter, too—places a high value on inverting the body to ensure the blood drains fully. Plus, as I had repeatedly witnessed in the slaughterhouse, it was relatively easy to skin, check the vitals, and porge the carcass as it hung, like fruit turned upside down and inside out. I wanted to engage in as much of the shechita process as I could, if do it more swiftly than is usual.

I located an empty meat hook on a chain in the ceiling trestle and rolled it along the track to where the body was. The butcher room had been designed to minimize the need for carrying large carcasses from the fridge to the individual tables. There were separate tracks for each of the four butcher stations, presumably because the shop delivered to so many of the area restaurants and because of its direct link with the abattoir. Marco never liked physical labor, and his ingenious design mitigated it. The tracks on the ceiling let meat swing from fridge to table, a moribund square dance. But the room's design meant one very large problem for me.

It was Gil all over again. Why is it so difficult to get a man where you want him.

Designed for cattle, lamb, and goat that were impaled and then left to hang, the chains were short. About two feet spanned the space between the hook and the freshly killed body below, no insignificant gap. Presumably the butchers, all big beefy men, could easily jostle and lift the slabs of beef or whole lambs and goats off these hooks, wrestle them to the tables, and be jovial about it. I might be a tall, relatively strong middle-aged woman, but I was no Roman butcher. In life, Marco stood six-foot-two and weighed in the mid-200-pound range. In death, his body looked and felt like a beached walrus, dense and pudgy unto bursting. I couldn't lift it. Even more to the point, the body was slick with blood that I did not want coating me. Red and shining, Marco's body looked like a still from an old movie on the life of Caligula. I gazed at the crimson puddle on the floor. I had a hard time believing that I'd be able to drain any more blood, but I had to try. If there was one thing I'd learned from touring Marco's meat empire and from Andrew's rump roast, it was that exsanguination wasn't merely fun; it was necessary to prime meat.

What to do. What to do. I found a thick rubber apron and put it on, ditto some plastic sleeves that made me look like a dealer in a space-age western saloon. I'd already slipped on rubber gloves, of course, and I'd been careful to not touch anything other than Marco and his handcuffs with my bare hands. My clothes and my chest had been spattered with blood when I slit Marco's throat, but I'd brought a change of outfit and some strong camphor soap. I'd wash later. Looking presentable was a problem I'd prepared for; bridging a two-foot ceiling gap so that I could hang my carcass upside down was not.

Searching through the shop's back rooms, I found two lengths of chain hanging from a wall—likely for this exact sort of emergency. Mine could hardly be the first carcass that failed to fit the pre-strung meat hooks. I hung one end from the hook, looped the other around the cuffs, fit the link into the hook, and carefully lifted the cuffs off the wall. The body swung free, a weighty pendulum, the legs collapsing beneath it.

I slid off the Ferragamo loafers, sliced off the pants, and discarded everything in a heap away from the pool of blood. I took the other chain, wrapping it securely around the ankles in a figure-eight pattern. Then I swung the carcass around, wedged my shoulder under the buttocks, and heaved it up until the ankles met the wrists, slipping the chain over the hook. Now it looked less like a walrus and more like a veal calf, ankles and wrists bound together by the hook; all I had to do was unlatch the handcuffs, and the torso fell free. Inverted, the corpse swung with lugubrious grace. I am nothing if not resourceful.

You'd likely enjoy it if I stopped narrating this chapter at this precise moment. You—comfortable in your chair, snug in your bed, rocking somnolent on the train, curved around your Kindle, or propping your book open in your splayed hands—probably are making a silent wish for me to table the gruesome details. You're tempted to thumb ahead, to skip this section where I detail the skinning, gutting, stripping, and slicing of this corpse that once was my living, breathing, ejaculating lover.

It's for your own good that I tell these bits. It's for your own good that you hear them. You've come too far not to see how the sausage gets made, metaphorically speaking, of course.

The animal has to be checked after it's been shekhted. Add that line to your nursery-rhyme pool. It's no more gory than rock-a-bye baby in the treetop. Separating the gash on the neck just below the perfect beard, I peered into the throat, looking to see if I'd nicked the esophagus or the trachea; both looked white, whole, unscathed as a virgin's hymen. I paused to feel appreciation for my knife skills.

But I'd no time to tarry. Although no one was due into the shop until after sunset on Saturday, my alibi gave me no more than two hours to finish and leave Rome, and I had no way of knowing if Marco's family would raise an alarm at his absence. I didn't even know what excuse he'd given them to pry himself from their Shabbat quiet. I carved a crewneck semicircle across the back just below the neck, added armholes, and slit a placket down the front and another down the back. I also sliced a low waistband. Had I all the time in the world, I'd have cut a cunning little circle around the anus and tied the lower intestine off with a bit of string, but I didn't have that luxury, so I half-assed it, as it were.

With some tugging, the skin slid off like a waistcoat, revealing a lustrous expanse of fascia, craggy fields of butter-yellow fat, and silky sheets of rosy muscle. According to the laws of shechita, I had to check the internal organs. So I cut a lovely arc across the loins, and I slashed down the center of the body. A fine cascade of viscera hit the floor with an echoing splat. You can read the statistic that the human body holds twenty-five feet of intestines, but until you see it in all its red-white-and-blue glory, you can't envision it. Twenty-five feet is a lot of intestines, and I was awash. The pulsating, ferocious smell of innards pressed and throbbed in my throat. I pushed snaking lines of slippery viscera to the side, winding some around the nearby jigsaw. The guts smelled like raw haggis—no, let me rephrase: the air smelled like atavistic lust and honor and jubilance and ecstasy. It was awesome, in the oldest Old Testament sense of the word. It was sublime, in the classic sense of Edmund Burke. It was a sharp, bestial, acrid, and mineral smell, one that wed shit and blood and loins and spit in the most holy of matrimonies. If I'd time, I'd have stripped naked and rolled around in it.

I was supposed to look at the lungs, but tick, tick, tick. Time was wasting, and cracking the ribs was hard work. I let that task go with a brief apology. Likewise, I couldn't really porge the flesh, removing the nerves and arteries. If I'd had oceans of time, I'd have joyfully done what I could to make Marco's flesh clean for consumption from root to tip, but I'd only about an hour to spare. Choices must be made. In life as in writing, you kill your darlings. You kill, anyway, and then you see what you can take with you.

I'd intended to leave with two parts: the brisket (which is closest in kin to human pectoral muscles) and the stomach. I couldn't decide which I wanted to eat more, so I took both, first slicing the pectorals away from the chest wall in smooth, heavy sheets, and next following the intestine trail through the belly to find the stomach. It was swollen as an old boot. I turned the stomach inside out, spilling the contents onto the floor. Chunks of chicken, shards of broccoli, and bits of white somethings, possibly orecchiette. I'd always told Marco to chew his food better. I felt almost nostalgic, seeing how right I'd been.

I brought the brisket and the stomach to one of the stainless steel sinks that lined the wall. I coated the pieces of meat with salt and let them sit. Then I turned to the scarlet slick in the center of the room, dipped my gloved hands in the chilled blood, and I finger-painted. I drew pentagrams and vague goat heads, triangles and anarchist "A"s, something that looked like an infinity symbol topped with an exuberant cross, another figure that was a crescent moon kissed with two intersecting lines, something that resembled a double-bladed axe. I'd raided heavy metal albums and pagan websites for visuals, and I festooned the walls, the floor, even the body with these symbols, drawing them with both my left and right hands, doing what I could to confuse the *polizia*, who as we know, can be deeply stupid.

Before embarking on my art project, I switched on the flash-freezer contraption, a bit dangerous as it was located near the door to the shop and was almost visible from the street.

A half hour later, the room was thoroughly satanized with symbols, including one very large pentagram inside a circle that nearly rimmed the room. I rinsed the brisket and the stomach. Then I dropped first one and then the other into the flash freezer; in time, happy little icy bricks would pop out, already shrink-wrapped in plastic, perfect for any housewife's freezer. It felt tidy to see Marco transformed so neatly into supermarket meat. I washed up in a sink and changed into fresh clothes. When the meat was frozen solid, I plopped these bricks into my purse, along with my washed and sheathed knife, and tucked the apron and sleeves and my discarded clothes into a garbage bag that I later emptied into several trashcans around the city. Then I took a final look at my bloody handiwork, and satisfied that it read as the demented acts of a gang of antichrists, I slipped into the Roman night, leaving the lights on and the door wide open.

Satanists shouldn't seem like a polite, eco-conscious folk.

I didn't use a cleaver, but I also didn't butcher my murder of Marco. You want to know how I got away with it, and I don't blame you. Of course, the *polizia* called me; my voicemail was full of messages from the police before my airplane had even landed in New York, Marco's nicely frozen brisket and stomach tucked deep in my luggage, swaddled in clothing and packed in a pair of boots. I acted appropriately surprised, saddened, appalled, shocked, and outraged as the police informed me of his attack, told me about the murder, revealed the occult component, asked if I'd seen any *uomini misteriosi*.

This, quite frankly, was the moment I'd been waiting for. I didn't have to talk to the police—there's no Italian equivalent to our Miranda rights, but you're not compelled to talk. However, Italian police will presume guilt from silence. It was therefore in my best interest to provide my alibi, and while it wasn't a flawless piece of eternal art, it accomplished its task.

It's classic for a reason: make a drunken spectacle of yourself, and people will remember you. I ordered a split of wine on the train to Orvieto, about a seventy-five-minute train ride from Rome, and I spilled most of the wine (a mass-produced Vernaccia, it tasted like pine needles and banana, an unholy botanic welding) on my suit jacket. I checked into a nice but not excessively luxe hotel heavily scented with wine. After dropping my luggage in my hotel room, I walked unevenly across the piazza, entered a trattoria, and I grew blazingly drunk at a table in the middle of the restaurant, visible to everyone and horrifying to most. To outward appearances, I drank two glasses of Champagne followed by a full bottle of Chianti and most of a glass of Barolo Chinato, all while picking at several plates of listless, pallid food.

While I have excellent alcohol tolerance for a woman, I didn't drink the wine the waiter served me. I'd picked the restaurant for its abundance of potted plants, and I poured more than half of every glass into my dining companion, a robust fern. But I was loud, and I was garrulous, and I wafted vaguely of alcohol, and I did my best to speak with a broad American accent. People will believe what they want to believe, and what Italians want to believe is that Americans are boorish, ill-behaved louts whose perennial sweatpants are the least offensive things about them. I merely gave the crowd what they wanted.

Indeed, I got so faux-inebriated that I slurred and tripped, mumbled hazy indecent proposals to waiters and diners, and finally keeled over, thus requiring a bellhop from my hotel to rescue me, shuffle me up to my room, unlock the door, and push me toward my bed. There was not a person in the restaurant or on the staff who did not remember me. I burned myself into their collective memory.

In my room, I sobered up nearly instantly, changed into nondescript black clothes and a black wig, stepped onto my balcony, shinnied over the side, and dropped the four or so feet to the ground. Then I walked to the train station, boarded a train to Rome, and the rest is Marco's unfortunate demise.

I told the Roman *polizia* of my great shame over my drunken night, apologizing profusely for my inability to hold my liquor, and expressing my deep guilt for upsetting other diners and making the gracious hotel staff work so hard. I then told the police that I had slept in, checked out, and flown home, with no change of plans.

Two or three days later, the police called me to ask me a few follow-up questions. They informed me that my story had checked out. I expressed my sadness over Marco's death. In the years since I'd met him in Siena, I said, he'd grown to be a dear, dear friend. The *polizia* told me they were sorry for my loss.

I'd already defrosted and eaten Marco's stomach and his brisket. The brisket, roasted with prunes and almonds, was divine. The stomach, I'm very sorry to say, was inedible; I had to toss the homage to *lampredotto* I made from Marco after a single bite. It's sad that Marco didn't live to read his profile in *Gourmand*. I feel certain he would have liked it.

14
Steak

"Hiya, Ms. Daniels? This is Detective Kiandra Wasserman calling from the Suffolk County Police Department." From the speaker of my iPhone, Detective Wasserman's voice sounded like she'd just smoked her last cigarette to a nubbin and couldn't wait to light another. "We need to, uh, talk with you about a, erm, Mr. Casimir Bezrukov and hoped maybe you could make it over to Yaphank. Please call us back at your, um, earliest convenience." She left a number and the message ended.

It was early December in 2013, about six weeks since I'd last seen Casimir, first alive and then dead, and I'd left his body in a flamey conflagration. The brisk, crisp potential of October fall had turned to a sullen, pewter-skied winter. In the intervening weeks, I'd not thought of Casimir at all. In his memory's place stood a paper cutout, a generalized form, a slight wisp that could slip into nothingness. I poked the circular arrow on the iPhone and listened to the message again. My right eye twitched.

I opened Safari and searched "Yaphank," an unfortunate name for a town; it sounded like something preteens call masturbation. Yaphank, I discovered, was in Suffolk County. It was not good that a Suffolk County police detective was calling me. If it had been a New York City cop, it would've been fine—my worry would be a missing persons report, a minor thing. That it was Suffolk County, the county that included Fire Island and all its quaint seasonal townships, sniffed of something more ominous. This did not please me. This did not please me at all.

I erased the message and decided that I hadn't heard it. Then I met my friends Ron and Paul at a restaurant I was writing about, Cacciucco, a newly opened Japanese-Italian fusion spot. It was, sorry to say, uneven. It's a food writer's job to keep an open mind to a wide spectrum of foods, but some pose a bigger challenge than others. I'm unconvinced, for example, that miso has a place in risotto; I love uni, but don't need it to garnish my burrata; and I'm not a fan of Madras curry in any food that doesn't derive from Madras. Color me the very arsenic-and-old-lace shade of old-fashioned, but I wasn't feeling it. I had to return, of course, certainly on a better day, a day unscathed by the fried mozzarella tones of Detective Kiandra Wasserman and uncolored by the irony that I was dining with my Fire Island alibi, for Ron and Paul owned the Dunewood house where I recovered my equilibrium after I killed Casimir.

I mentally played back my visit to Fire Island that October, from the time I arrived at Dunewood to the moment I departed four days later. I sifted through the detritus of my Robbins Rest memories, wondered what I could have left behind at that scorched beach house that pointed Detective Wasserman to me. I imagined her sitting at her desk, some sad autopsied deli sandwich splayed open before her, its grinder guts spilling pimento loaf, waxy lipid-yellow cheese, wan shredded lettuce, and squirts of pus-white mayonnaise from a squeeze packet. I could see her, Detective Kiandra Wasserman, with her frosted hair and her pack of Parliaments and her palate dulled by her devotion to nicotine and Olive Garden. I could see her with her can of diet cola and her freezer stacked with lurid boxes of diet frozen entrees, cheating with Marie Callender's chocolate satin pie, still icy at the center because her slippery sweet tooth couldn't wait for a thaw. I could see her, and I didn't like it.

What had led Wasserman and her mom jeans to my doorstep. I'd burned the beach house to the ground, and before I'd left, I'd cleaned my tracks. I'd carried everything with me—my containers of duck confit, my kitchen knife, my jar that had held the wine corks in denatured alcohol. I had cooked the entire meal wearing gloves, except for kneading the dough for the bread (it won't do to compromise some things). The only times I hadn't worn gloves was while eating and making love with Casimir. I had been the very picture of the conscientious modern criminal—if not the consummate houseguest.

I tried to put it out of my mind. I tweeted something about Brussels sprouts resembling alien heads; I updated my blog with a brief rant against flaming drinks; I reviewed my notes for my Cacciucco write-up, tentatively titled "Neither Fish Nor Foul at Williamsburg's Cacciucco." I downloaded the edits for a "trend piece" I'd written on artisanal pop tarts. I couldn't bring myself to look at the edits, however. My editor at DISH was this darling little girl. When DISH hired me, I was turning fifty; my editor was twenty-four. She was born the same year as Photoshop, which tells you something. My editor believes that exclamation points are stylish. She believes that "creatives" is a word. She finds first-person essays about tampons "edgy." The skin on her face gleams, untrammeled as blancmange, which no one makes anymore, which I must admit is one tiny sign of improvement.

America has grown more food obsessed, more slavishly hungry for bits and bobs and scraps and flaps of all things gastronomical, luscious, and savory. And you would think that as we have collectively grown more knowledgeable about food; as our restaurants grow in number, complexity, skill level, and creativity; as we as a nation of eaters refuse to be dull, complacent sheep; you would think that food critics would be lauded, knighted, raised high as voices of all that's true, worthy, and good to eat.

You'd be wrong. As I write this memoir in 2016, we don't get thoughtful food writing, we get Yelp, we get "influencers," we get personal essays that masquerade as recipes. America is more interested in eating and drinking well than it has ever been in its 240-year history, yet never have food critics done so much for so little money and been so soundly ignored by so many. Sure, there are the few reviewers who hold sway—and the *Times* has had altogether too many—but that great engine of democratization, the internet, has steamrolled the playing field. A swamp festers where once stood a mountain range. Everyone who's ever watched *Top Chef* and considered herself adventurous when ordering sweetbreads now thinks she's a food critic. After all, how hard can it be? I mean, it's just, like, *food*, right?

In my twenty-five years as a food writer, I have written two books—both reached the *New York Times* bestseller list—I've been a staff writer at three magazines; and I've written for countless others. But by 2013, I was writing for a website. It doesn't even print anything. There is no *there*, there, at DISH. There is, however, a lot of video because if there's one thing that the people who love food love it's *watching*; the internet has made peeping Toms of us all. It almost goes without saying that, as the first food-specific web glossy, DISH led the pivot-to-video charge.

And, you know, it's fine; it's fine; it's pretty and sleek and fine. The open-air DISH office teems with crema-faced young things who wear T-shirts and slump around in big boots and black leggings and hair the color of Pop Rocks. The money behind the site comes from a twenty-nine-year-old man who invented an app that helps you break up—with a lover, a job, a therapist, a television show, a hairstyle. It doesn't matter from what you want to part, this colorful little phone application helps you do it. It's called, appropriately enough, "BreakApp." Maybe you've used it. I've never needed to. When I feel the need to break up with something, it's simply dead to me.

Times have changed, and, like an octopus, I have tried to match my skin to everything new. I started writing my blog in 2003. I joined Twitter in 2008. I have an Instagram account—for the love of all things sacrosanct and holy, I take pictures of my *food*. I even Snapchat. Any more adaption of youthful technology, and I might as well dye my hair the color of Jordan almonds. I have even appeared more than once as a guest judge on cooking shows. I pretended to laugh when I was supposed to laugh; I developed catchphrases, hurling, "Your taste is disgraced" at competitors. I have absolutely burst with not caring, but I didn't show it.

Despite all my hard work, I must run to stay in place. Every decade, every year, and sometimes every month, I see my money, my life, and my work devalued. Literal devaluation is the most pressing, but figurative isn't much easier. Ordinary people, home in bed with the flu, fall in love with Guy Fieri and his fast food doggerel and, taking a road trip to flavortown, decide that they, too, should be restaurant critics; they start a blog; they stop reading food criticism; and one by one, drip by drip, they have chipped away at everything I've devoted myself to for the last quarter century. And it makes a kind of lunatic sense—if chefs are average, ordinary people who look like Rachael Ray and talk like Emeril Lagasse, then why, too, can't the people who critique them be know-nothing vulgarians. All you need to be a food critic is a mouth and internet access, and almost every asshole has both.

The thing that roasts my black heart crispy is that these Word-Press nudniks don't have the ethics of a high roller who's down on his luck and looking for an angle. They don't care about being incognito; indeed, they don't want to be—they want to be friends with the chef. They want free food; they want to meet the maestro; they want to whip out their iPhones and Instagram their meals *as they're being made*. They want more than to rub elbows; they want to kiss asses. For all the things I've done, for all the questionable acts, for all the adultery, for all the various acts of perversity, for all the callous disregard I've had for men, I have never, ever fucked a chef. Nor would I. Either he would hope for a good review and I'd give it because he deserved it, or he would hope for a good review and I'd give him a bad one because he deserved that. In either case, I'd know that I'd fucked him, and I'd have to live with that knowledge. That's a line I can't cross.

And thus I write for DISH. I have my copy edited by a recent Brown graduate who doesn't know the difference between chiffonade and chinoiserie. She's fine, really, she's fine, but I miss the days when I had an unlimited budget, joyous excursions, and checks as fat and sleek as geese—free-flowing, hot-and-cold running money that I could use to track down the finest offal in Rome, the top tripe in Siena, the best brains in Piedmont. I miss the days when my work appeared in glorious four-color separation, on pages slick as oiled thighs and just as weighty. I miss the days when my work—my words—mattered, and I can't shake the feeling that all the running I do to keep up, all the hobnobbing on the treadmill of the Internet, all the tweeting, blogging, Instagramming, and Tumblring, all the gut-wrenching time I put in to being relevant, isn't just a feeble way to plug a forefinger into the dike, to stall my inevitable slow ebb into obscurity.

I am a whore, but I am a print whore, and I miss cracking spines to see myself splayed open in wet, glossy spreads of luscious, expansive prose. Ask not for whom the bell tolls, it tolls for print media, and for me.

The Kiandra Wasserman situation weighed. I worked, I ate, I drank. I had sex with a charming young man I met in the elevator at the New York Public Library. I told him my name was Patience Fortitude; he believed me. Only intellectuals are more gullible than idiots. He had a fine sheaf of notes on Napoleonic Champagne glasses, and a sweet, thick, upstanding cock. It nearly took my mind off Detective BBQ Corn Nuts. Detective Low-fat Cheese-cake. Detective Spicy Calabrian Wings. Detective Soup in a Bread Bowl.

Four days after Wasserman left her message on my iPhone, my doorbell rang. Only after I opened it and saw the badges flash did I realize that my doorman didn't buzz.

"Hiya, Ms. Daniels," the short woman in front of me said, flashing a badge as she grimaced. It might have been a smile. It looked uncomfortable. She was terrible at putting people at ease. "I'm Detective Kiandra Wasserman, and this is Detective Lou MacDonnell. We're from the, uh, Suffolk Police Department, and we'd like to ask you a few questions. May we come in?" She again made that rictus movement with her mouth.

Wasserman's hair was not frosted as I suspected. It was black shot with gray and ringed her head in snaking dreads that were barely constrained in a bright blue scrunchie. Her body was not round and soft, as I'd expected. Wasserman was small, but fit. This woman had not tasted a blooming onion in decades. Under her navy polyester sports coat, her acrylic-blend sweater, and her brown skin, Wasserman had muscles nearly as hard as her pistol, wherever that was. Her partner, however, was plush as a teddy bear. The hair on his head was thatchy, wiry, a little dandruffy, and thin, giving him the look of an aging chow-chow.

"Sure," I said. I had no choice; clearly, I had no choice. What choice did I have. If I said no, they'd call me in and I'd have to—what's the common parlance—lawyer up. That would be tantamount to an admission of guilt, or so every cop show would have brain-washed me to believe.

Wasserman and MacDonnell entered and followed me down the hall. I waved my hand at the couch.

"Espresso?" I asked. "Water?"

"Water would be great, thanks." Wasserman was clearly the top brass of the pair. I returned to the living room, water glasses in hand, to see them seated in the two guest chairs. This put me on the couch, the apex to their triangle.

"Ms. Daniels," Wasserman said, "we wanted to ask you a few questions about the weekend of October twelfth. Do you mind?"

"No. Of course not." I felt my adrenaline spike. It was interesting.

"Where were you?"

"I was on Fire Island, staying at my friends Ron and Paul's house in Dunewood. Why?"

Wasserman narrowed her eyes at me. "We're investigating a matter involving, um, Mr. Casimir Bezrukov, as I believe I mentioned on the voice mail message. Did you get my message, Ms. Daniels?"

"Yes, I did. I was so nervous that I erased it by mistake. I've never gotten a phone call from the police before."

"Why didn't you call me back?"

Wasserman and her CrossFit thighs. I imagined her skin oiled and salted, apple in her mouth, pirouetting slowly on a spit. "I just got so flustered."

Wasserman looked at MacDonnell and shared a smile. "You don't seem like the kind of woman who gets nervous, if you don't mind me saying so."

"And yet," I said. I was imagining a swift slice through her throat with a nine-inch chef's blade. I paused and summoned the scents of a basket of biscuits steaming floury heat, spread with freshly churned butter. I smiled.

"So. Okay. October thirteenth, you were staying in Robbins Rest—"

"Dunewood."

"Right, Dunewood. What were you doing on Fire Island?"

"I needed to get out of the city. I like the Island in fall. It's so quiet, and the autumn air smells like salt and wood smoke."

"Yeah, yeah. Nothing like the fall. Were you alone?"

"Yes. I wanted some time by myself to write."

"You're a writer."

"Yes." Arranged around me were two heavy quartz ashtrays, a bronze statue, one alabaster lamp, and a pair of hefty silver candlesticks. Any of these objects would make an elegant bludgeon. My right palm itched.

Wasserman looked down at a tiny spiral notebook in her palm. "So. Um, Casimir Bezrukov. Do you know him?"

My thumbs against her throat. Press ten seconds against the carotid artery, and she'd be passed out long enough for me to choke her some undiscovered shade of blue. A minute, and she'd be dead as her partner's intellect. Deader. I'd never eaten a woman's flesh.

"Yes, I do. We, oh, this is a little embarrassing. We met at a hotel bar and, forgive me..."

"We're all adults here," Wasserman said.

"Yes. Well, it's personal." I paused for effect, imagining how a normal woman would act.

"Please go on."

"We—we had sex in his hotel room a week or two before the weekend I was in Fire Island." I paused. "Why do you ask?"

"We're investigating his death. Did you see Mr. Bezrukov while you were on Fire Island?"

"What? Oh, no," I said and tried to look stricken. "How horrible!" I pressed my hands to my face, pushing the heels of my hands at my eye sockets. I took a deep breath. Head in hands, I was playing for time. I hadn't expected I'd need to. I'd prepared myself for this conversation. Since the voice mail message four days before, I knew it was coming. It was fascinating to find myself caught between foreknowledge and a total lack of emotional preparation.

After all, I'd lived much of my life in a curlicue line leading to this point—this conversation, this one, me and the law, and the game of playing innocent. I'd played innocent early and often. My sister's cat that had gone missing. The grades mysteriously changed on my boarding school transcript. The Piemonte *polizia* following Giovanni's impalement. The mysterious circumstances surrounding the kiddie porn found on my competitor's computer. The Coast Guard conversations about the moored meanderings of the *Sea Bee Tee*. Marco. Marco's wife. The *polizia* after Marco's body was found, hung upside down, exsanguinated, guts strewn like Christmas garlands, symbols in his blood painted on the walls. I'd anticipated this conversation in a general kind of way, but the specifics of Wasserman sitting across from me on my own furniture I had failed to predict. How did I act, exactly. What do normal women do when they find out their casual sex *compadre* is dead.

I was accustomed to looking innocent in more than one country, in more than one language, and at more than one stage in my life. But somehow the wealth of my experience, the breadth and the range and the depth of my feigned innocence, seemed to crumble like shortbread under the weighted gaze of Detective Wasserman. Could it be that this steely-flanked, Medusa-haired, Long Island Jewess would best me. Could she, who clearly sustained herself on a diet of horse meat, egg whites, and kale in wet, dehydrated, pureed, and juiced forms, be my nemesis. Had I finally met my match. You'd think I would be thrilled. You'd be wrong.

"How very sad!" I said. "Poor Casimir!!" I didn't want to lay it on too thick. Like swirling ganache on a cupcake, I had to tempt this paleo-CrossFit-fanatic policewoman into swallowing something she'd otherwise feel disinclined to digest. I paused, then asked, "How? How did it happen?"

"He was in a house that burned to the ground." Wasserman turned to her partner. "Lou, grab Ms. Daniels a glass of water, would ya?" MacDonnell lumbered off to the kitchen, and I heard some rustling and the sound of the tap; a large hand thrust a glass of water in front of me. I took it and drank, glad for the silence and the opportunity to hide myself behind the glass, if only for a moment.

"Um, Ms. Daniels." Wasserman looked at me, her eyes falcon bright. "Do you have any idea what Mr. Bezrukov might have been doing on Fire Island?"

"No," I said. "I thought he was in town for business. At least, that's what he told me."

"Yes, well, as far as we can tell, uhn, Mr. Bezrukov didn't know many people in New York. We're unable to locate anyone on Fire Island who might have known Mr. Bezrukov." Wasserman looked at me again and pressed her lips together. "We were hoping that you might have some insight."

"I'm so sorry, but I really don't."

"I see. Well, we thank you," she said. "Do you have any plans to leave the area? Any travel plans?"

I told her I didn't.

"Good." She dropped her card on the table. "We'd take it as a favor if you stayed in town."

"You—you—can't think I had anything to do with it, could you?" I tried to look stricken with innocent fear. I approximated the expression of a deer in headlights.

"No, no, no. Nothing like that. Just if anything crosses your mind, if you remember anything, please give me a call. Lou?"

At the door, she stopped, hand on the knob. "By the way, loved your *Guide to Eating Gloriously*."

"It's me," I said into the intercom. The big red metal door buzzed. I waited in the hallway so narrow that two people couldn't stand side by side and listened to the keening of the elevator. The elevator door shuddered open; I stepped inside and pressed "7." The door shuddered closed. Tick. Tick. Tick. Creak. Creak. Creak. The door shuddered open, and I stepped out of the tiny elevator and into the studio of Emma Absinthe.

Emma was working on a series of paintings of famous women who famously got paid to have sex. "The Whorestep Chronicles," she called them. Aspasia, Nell Gwyn, Madame du Barry, Mata Hari, Cora Pearl, Veronica Franco, Carol Leigh. Women who'd sold access to their bodies and risen to power, fame, or infamy. I was quite fond of the project. So many of these women knew how to carry a knife. Emma was at work painting herself as Calamity Jane; the canvas stood about a foot taller than Emma, and she was nose to about navel with Jane, intent on adding dimension to the fringe that dripped like tallow from the elbow of Jane's buckskin jacket.

"Sorry, Dolls, I have to finish this section." Emma looked and jutted her chin at the bags I carried in my arms. "Is that food?"

"Yes," I said. "Steak."

"Oh, thank the gods. I was hungry. It's like you read my mind. Again." Emma had long ago left her veganism with her gas-mask purse and her anti-capitalist practices.

"Steak. Baby collard greens. Pancetta *stesa*. Eggs for béarnaise. Parsnips, celeriac, and lemon. Castello dei Rampolla Sammarco 1996. Give me forty-five, and dinner is served."

"I love you madly, you beautiful woman!"

I went to the kitchen and began clearing the espresso cups, Champagne flutes, and jam jars out of the sink, tidying the space.

I decanted the wine, and took to roasting the root vegetables with pearl onions, thyme, and lemon, browning the pancetta and sautéing the greens, melting the butter and slowly pouring it while whisking egg yolks, and, finally, searing the steak in duck fat and grilling it bloody. Setting the table and lighting the candles, I called Emma as the steak rested under its tinfoil hat. She sat as I slid a plate before her.

"*Salute,*" I said. Emma raised her glass to meet mine.

Emma scanned her plate. "No carbs! Thanks." She forked a hefty piece of very rare meat into her mouth. "What's up?"

I rolled my eyes. Wasserman the boogie monster floated like Marley's ghost, her snaking dreadlocks glowing spectral in my head, her imagined muscles rippling under her acetate blazer. I could nearly hear the clanking of iron chains.

"Maybe I just want to see you, Emma. Ensure you're eating at least one meal this week that was cooked by a caring hand. Something that didn't come to you care of Seamless or GrubHub or SweetEats, or whatever your dining app of the moment is."

Emma rested her fork on her plate. "Let me tell you about this tedious argument I had with Sebastian Arpante." She sliced off another unseemly chunk of steak and popped it into her mouth. Her table manners were far from Italian.

I looked at her blankly.

She narrowed her eyes at me. "So. Sebastian actually told an *Artforum* writer that I was a 'culturally appropriating virago with the derivative, vampiric talent of Berthe Morisot,' but now that it's printed for all the art world to see, he's whinging and claiming it was off the record—"

I let Emma prattle on about the latest online argument she'd had with some of her many detractors. I poured wine, and poured more, and I listened. Emma held the unique position of being an artist beloved by legions of threadbare art students, pencil-sucking art critics, and collectors padded with wanton wads of cash. As much as she painted for the one-percenters, selling their own hypocrisy back to them at a steep markup, she also painted, sketched, and inked her way into a feminist-anarchist consciousness. She held a vibrant credibility among the art geeks, who are usually the first to denounce any artist who makes six figures a year—and Emma has been making seven consistently for more than a decade. But this very popularity made her a target for the cosseted academic elite, particularly since Emma didn't have an art degree. She'd studied, but not at an art school; she'd gone to college, but she hadn't graduated. She was viciously talented and ridiculously hardworking, and people who truck with elite institutions didn't—couldn't—forgive her reckless attitude toward traditional models of artistic creation.

Emma was often eviscerated, sometimes publicly, usually privately, by people in power. Being a person who didn't forgive slights easily, as well as one who truly never leaves the confines of her own world, Emma has an unfortunate tendency to wrap herself in the drama of her own disparagers. I listened to her unspool, and I poured out the bottle of Sammarco. Then I popped another, and I poured that. We drank it, talking in the shorthand of old friends. An hour or two later, we were curled like commas on her big unmade bed, holding jam jars of crushed ice, raspberries, Limoncello, and Champagne.

"This isn't a social call, Dolls. I can tell from your face." Emma put her jam jar down on the stool that served as her bedside table. "Tell me what's up or I'll be forced to tell you all about my new boy.

He's got a cock that's—and I'm not being metaphoric—exactly like a large Asian eggplant."

"I got a visit from a pair of detectives from the Suffolk Police Department," I said. Emma stiffened, curling reflexively on herself. "This guy, I met him in a hotel bar. We had sex a few weeks ago. Anyway, he died in a house fire, I guess."

"Oh God, Dolls. Are you okay?" Emma sat upright, weaved a bit, unsteady on her elbows.

"That's a good question. I'm not sure." I swallowed a mouthful of the Limoncello concoction. The world moved in an uncomfortable swirl, like a lava lamp. I was drunk.

"Sure, that's a shock. Of course you're going to feel weird and awful. Do you, you know, want a *hug*?"

"Jesus, Emma, no." I stopped. My tongue cleaved to the roof of my mouth. Emma looked at me with big blue eyes. She poked me with her forefinger.

"Go on, Dolls."

"Emma, I can't. It's nothing. He's dead. It's nothing. Really."

I killed him, I wanted to tell her. I stabbed him through the heart with a vintage ice pick. I burned down the house with his body in it. I'm not okay, I wanted to say, because that pony-assed police-woman, Detective Kiandra Wasserman, has found something that pushed her on her trail to get her man, and her man is me.

"Jesus. Dorothy."

"Yeah, I know," I said, and inwardly I screamed, *Emma. I killed him! We were lying around after fucking, and I found my hand wrapped around the hilt of the ice pick; I plunged it into his heart; I didn't even love him.* And this was, you see, the essential difference between Casimir's murder and all the rest: I didn't love him, and I didn't eat him. Casimir wasn't even snack food. He wasn't a bag of airline almonds, a cup of Greek yogurt, a bit of street meat on a stick. He was that treat you chewed and swallowed almost mindlessly, blank to notes of salt or sweet, of silk or coarse, of the caressing cold of ice cream or the blistering spit of pizza. Casimir was a passing thought. There had been Casimirs before; there would be Casimirs after. So why did I kill him.

Perhaps I had merely learned to enjoy the act of killing. The television shows and the movies all say that—you kill a person or two and you get a "taste for it," as if murder were caviar or fugu, sophisticated gastronomical experiences whose enjoyment requires inculcation into a cult. Or as if killing were like potato chips; one leads to another in an endless orgy of mindless indulgence. Before you know it, the whole bag is gone, and you're sitting there with gritty fingers, grease on your lips, and bathed in blood.

In my experience, however, murder is roasting a pig. When you've never roasted a pig, it feels like a very big, very over-whelming undertaking. It seems like something so fraught with difficulties that the sheer number of things that could go horribly awry is intimidating. The pig, from a distance, seems bigger than you. And as much as you'd like to roast that pig, to cook it until its skin is crispy as old parchment, its flesh as succulent as a Vermeer pear, you think the task is beyond you. Yet when you do it, you find out that it's truly not all that hard—if you've roasted a turkey, you can roast a suckling pig—once you do it, you find yourself more than capable. You hardly feel bad for the pig. After all, it's scrumptious.

I never gained a "taste" for murder. I might have gained an appreciation for human flesh, but I've always had a wide-ranging, experimental palate. I might have learned how to kill more efficiently and effectively. I might even have grown a thick layer of protection, not unlike the calluses you'll find on a chef's hand, where I had to butt up against the heated sanctity of human life. None of these experiences is as crass as developing a hankering for murder.

Still, even I had to admit that Casimir was an outlier. His un-fortunate demise did not fit the pattern. So why did I do it.

I remember that moment when, straddling Casimir's long éclair-like body, I had felt an overwhelming weight of banality settle on me like an eiderdown. I felt suffocated, resting there naked in the sex-scented air. There were so many things I could have done. I could have stood up and thrown him out of the house in a crazy operatic act of self-definition, run to the ocean and flung myself into its cold, raging arms, or merely walked to the kitchen and made espresso. I could have done any number of things to tear that banality a new one, but I didn't. Instead I killed him.

Unlike the others—Giovanni, Andrew, Gil, Marco—Casimir was not essential to my identity. With Casimir, I felt pleasure and power, but I didn't feel the sudden solidification of self that I got from the others. These four men I couldn't live without, and now I don't have to. I am all of them; they are some of me. Killing Casimir was rash and useless; his murder was akin to pulling the wings off a butterfly.

And I wanted, I absolutely itched, to tell Emma about this murder. Lying next to Emma in her big rumpled bed, I wanted to disclose the whole of it. I wanted to confess, to tell her about the satisfying heft of the ice pick in my hand, the balletic arc of my arm, the cinematic spurt of blood. I wanted to paint Emma a visceral picture, something so thick and real that she could smell the air redolent with duck fat, pheromones, and arterial spray. I felt my hand cover my mouth, an involuntary act to stanch my story's flow.

It wasn't as if I felt guilt. I felt no guilt for stabbing Casimir, no guilt for gutting Giovanni with a Fiat, no guilt for slitting Marco's throat, no guilt for asphyxiating Gil with a fig, no guilt for suffocating Andrew with carbon monoxide (and no guilt for shoving Liam off the side of the cliff, no guilt for Yves and that remarkably well-timed bee sting, and not even any guilt for letting anaphylactic shock do my dirty work not once but twice).

I searched the parts of my body where guilt was supposed to live and I found nothing, not a whisper, not a peep, not a flicker, not a flutter, not the faintest susurration of anything even remotely like remorse. From what I understood, only a few things compelled people to reveal secrets, and guilt was number one with a bullet. I certainly had no Theodor Reik compulsion to confess, no tics, no blushing, no stammering, no clues. Nothing but the naked and pulsating will to tell.

Emma was talking to me. She was waving her jam jar around in sloppy arcs, making a point, some point I'd missed. She had clearly been talking for a while. "I'm sorry, what?"

"I said you're living a police drama."

"It's a bit derivative. Not my best work," I said.

"Yes," said Emma, "that was the source of my worry—your stunning lack of originality." She looked at me. "Go home, Dolls, you're drunk." And then Emma flopped down on the bed, coiled around a pillow, and fell asleep, snoring gently. I pried the jam jar out of her hand, put it on the table next to her, and wobbled, unsteady, out the door and into the night.

Gamberetto

The morning after my swirling, drunken night with Emma, I woke with a migraine and a burning, restive need to do something—anything—preferably violent. Flashes of the evening popped like firecrackers, while shards of conversation with Wasserman lacerated me. Nauseated, I lay on my bed in the dark, a crimson silk sleep-mask on my eyes, my skin hot and dry, then slick with sweat and pricked with gooseflesh. Every forty-five minutes, I ran to the bathroom and threw up; at first, a lurid, festive mauve; then a clear, acidic stream; then nothing. My stomach heaved, each abdominal convulsion resonated in my head, and the apparitional railroad spike drove deeper into the space behind my left eye. I wanted to pull my brain out through my eye sockets with a buttonhook.

What to do. What to do. The indomitable Detective Wasserman clearly had something on me, but what. I ran through the events of that October weekend over and over, like my memory was a manuscript I could revise. I had taken nothing but remembrances and left nothing but footprints, and those had been scrubbed by the wind and scoured by the house fire's flame. I lay in bed and thought through the Fire Island events step by step, from the moment I asked Casimir to come with me, to my train ride, from food shopping to confit making, from meeting Casimir in the Fire Island twilight to our sharing of flesh, from the moment I stabbed him in the jugular to the time I returned to my Dunewood safe haven. Beginning with invitation and ending with conflagration, I scoured my memory and found it as clean as a proverbial bone.

Maybe there were video cameras at the ferry dock, but that wasn't a problem; I had a legitimate reason for taking the ferry to Dunewood. My friends Ron and Paul truly did own a house, I truly had gotten their permission to visit it, and they truly had given me a key. Maybe Casimir had told someone he was meeting me—but I'd never given him my real cell phone number. I had one phone for business and friends—well, Emma, essentially, but a few other contacts, my family, for example, and publishers. I had a secret other phone for dalliances. When I wanted to quit the man of the moment, I threw away the phone and bought another. It was easy and clean, like flushing a condom. If a relationship lasted longer than the cell phone, I bought a new cell and gave the old man my new number. In this day of taking your phone number with you wherever you went—like a thumbprint, like a food allergy, like a talisman—it was a little odd. Yet no one had felt the need to remark upon it.

I had also been careful with my personal phone. I left it at the house in Dunewood when I met Casimir; I hadn't carried it with me when I scouted houses in Robbins Rest. However, I'd made sure that it sat in my pocket to indicate that I'd been out and about on Fire Island, and far away from Robbins Rest. When I met Casimir, my cell phone had lain quiet and content as a mollusk, in the home of Ron and Paul, wholly unconnected to my whereabouts. It came to this: whatever it was that put Casimir and me together in the bloodhound head of Detective Wasserman, neither my phone number nor my cell phone was it.

Nor, for that matter, was my name. Spending almost two decades as a food critic gave me ample experience in concocting new identities on the fly. My colleagues often bewail the difficulty of remembering their various identities, and it's true that there's little worse than making a reservation at a restaurant, then, faced with the supercilious maître d', finding that the name under which you'd booked the table has, like a terrine from its mold, slipped your mind. This happened to me once, so I devised a system wherein it would never happen to me again. I picked a movie, and I ran through the major characters until I was done. Then I picked another and walked through that cast list. I was Jane Gittes, Evelyn Cross, Nora Cross, Holly Mulwray, and Ida Sessions. I was Filomena Marlowe, Eileen Wade, Mary Augustine, and Jo Ann Eggenweiler. I was Cat

Tramell, Nicole Curran, Beth Garner, Lisa Hoberman, and Roxanne Hardy. Sometimes I'd catch that flickering look of semi-recognition, but only once did a maître d' question me. I remember, I announced myself as Patricia Franchini at an aggressively chic Tribeca restaurant.

"Like the Jean Seberg character in *À bout de souffle?*" asked the host in impeccable French that my mother would have kissed with those Dior lips. The maître d's eyebrows rose toward his improbably high hairline.

"Yes," I said.

"Really."

"Truly." He stared; I returned his gaze, steely. He sighed, swished up a stack of menus, and sat my party at an awful table right by the doors to the kitchen. The food, however, was tremendous, over the top, far better than either of my other visits. Clearly, the host had told the chef or the manager, and someone had puzzled out the ruse. I'd worn a wig and glasses, but it was a very close call. I learned my lesson, and I never again plundered a French film for my fictive selves.

Thus it was that Casimir knew me as Diane Selwyn. He thought I was a casting agent. He thought I lived on the Upper East Side. He thought I was unhappily married to a man named Hank. He thought, in short, that I was someone I was not. He went to his grave certain I was Diane. It was fine. It was fine. It was fine. Diane had plunged an ice pick into his throat, not I.

And that thought brought me up short and cold and sweating in the gloaming of my late-afternoon bedroom. I had only ever been Diane Selwyn to Casimir. When he called out my name in bed—and he had, often, for he was the sort who called your name—he'd lingered on the implosive, hard, interdental "D" and the nasal "aye," drawing a straight line between my fictive name and his impending mortality, before he gasped the final "ann." To Casimir, I was Diane, only Diane, and never Dorothy. So, then, precisely how did Detective Wasserman know me by my real name. How had she connected me to him, when I'd put so much in the way of anyone doing exactly this. Someone, somewhere, or something had slipped, a breeze had blown, a curtain had brushed aside, the scale had fallen, a glove had dropped. The jig was up. I was exposed, and there I was, standing naked before that sculpted, muscular lady cop. I had no idea how my clothes had been torn from my body.

This was so much worse than I had first thought.

Snatches of my conversation with Emma played like a bad movie flashback. I fumbled through my hazy memory as if I were pawing through a jumbled lingerie drawer. I had—I thought—I perhaps remembered—I maybe told her everything. Not *everything* everything, not Marco or Andrew or Gil, or Giovanni everything, but I had, perhaps, told her about Casimir. I recollected parts until a whole assembled before me. Red, raw, and fascinating as venison-heart tartare, my confession sat bloody before me. I felt a murmuration of fear. This was new. Fear clutched my chest with a clawed paw. I don't recall ever feeling fear before this moment. I don't recommend it.

I turned the previous night over in my head. Nothing about my maybe-confession to Emma made sense. Confession is always, to my thinking, like a hot mic, an act of illogic. I knew myself. I was not the kind of person who felt the need to unbosom herself. I kept things high and tight, like the testicles of a young greyhound. I saw myself as an emotional dragon, lizard autonomous, diamond-scaled, fire-bright, and handsomely alone in the world. All I needed was an aerie with a view, the land below me unspooling like an endless banquet. I soared and swept and dropped only to pluck sweetmeats as I hungered. I saw myself above, better than, superior to. I didn't fling off my armor to show the rhythmic beat-beat-beating of my human heart. I had learned better. Years ago, I had learned.

I had said something. I had said nothing. I had said—I'd no idea what I said.

Maybe I hadn't said anything to Emma about Casimir. Maybe I had only wanted to say something. I remembered the straining, leaping longing to tell her, and I remembered going through the story in my head as I lay with her on her big canopied bed. I remembered the jam jars of Prosecco cocktails, and I remembered feeling very drunk. I couldn't, however, remember what specific ideas had crossed the mind's threshold into speech. In my head,

I twisted my conversation with Emma like a Rubik's Cube, trying to line up what I knew I'd said, what I feared I'd said, and what I was fairly certain I hadn't said. I knew I'd said something about Wasserman's visit, and I knew I'd told her about Casimir's death. But the rest of it was a swirling verbal haze, a muddled memory where I couldn't parse what I had said from what I only feared I'd said. What to do. What to do. What to do.

The migraine held me in its gloomy embrace. I rocked in my bed. I willed the railroad spike to remove itself from my head. I counted sheep. I counted breaths. I counted back from 100. I counted on myself. The pain in my head burned lethal umber and gold, shaped like a dagger and sharp as betrayal. I named it Detective Wasserman. I gave it flesh with my worrying, and I flayed it, inch by glorious inch.

Melicertus kerathurus, the Mediterranean or Imperial shrimp, is a different species from its lesser Atlantic cousin. Living in fairly shallow coastal waters, the Mediterranean shrimp lies buried and dormant in the sand during the day; at night, it emerges to feed, swim, and spawn, making it not unlike the festive estival inhabitants of Capri, those bright young beachgoers so driven to taking Molly while frolicking at foam parties. The Atlantic *Litopenaeus setiferus*, on the other hand, lives in deeper waters, and it's active during the day. While all species of shrimp, or prawn—really, the difference is the same as between elevator and lift, boot and trunk, truck and lorry, or apartment and flat, which is to say it depends on whether your English conforms to the Queen's or is American as apple pie— all shrimp are known as "bottom feeders," the truth is somewhat less simple. Shrimp eat plankton, small plants, sea worms, smaller crustaceans, and, yes, decaying matter. Really, they're opportunists. As capitalists, we can hardly blame them.

In point of fact, shrimp are cannibals. This fact doesn't differentiate them much in the aquatic world; about 90% of all aquatic species eat their own. You're harder pressed to find the tenth that doesn't. Octopi won't just cannibalize others; they'll also cannibalize themselves, eating an arm to save the rest of the body, and they'll placidly eat the thousands of baby octopi that hatch every spring. Sand sharks are perhaps the most totemic of all ocean cannibals. Gestating for around a year, a sand shark pup will eat its less developed siblings, and before being born, it'll grow to about a meter in length; the sand shark emerges fully developed and ready to embrace its carnivore nature. They're rather docile, sand sharks. Perhaps they work out their issues before birth.

Like the humans who comprised the Donner party, almost all mammals will eat their own if driven to it, but only about fifteen hundred species naturally gravitate to cannibalism. They belong to three separate subgroups: sexual cannibals, intrauterine, and size-structured, a subset that houses both animals eating smaller or younger members of their own kind and mothers eating their own. Of these groups, we love the sexual cannibals the most—so easy to anthropomorphize. Who hasn't lain in bed next to her lover and wished that, coitus concluded, she could turn her head a balletic one-eighty, unhinge her jaw, and snap off the head of the man lying insensate next to her. Beds, for all their vaunted symbolism of rest and peace, are sites of strife. Show me a human who hasn't silently, stealthily, lain in bed and wished for the sudden horrible death of the person lying next to them, and I'll show you a liar. We can only take so much intimacy before we close our eyes and pray to our gods for a cerebral hemorrhage.

Haters gonna hate, and predators are going to predate. Your purring housecat is but a short genetic leap from lions that will kill and eat the upstart youngsters in their pride. Sea horses make a happy meal out of newly hatched baby sea horses. Tell that to the cute little button-nosed girl with a charming frontal lisp and sea horses painted on her rainboots. Prairie dogs and lemurs are possibly the world's most adorable cannibals. You could just eat them up, they are so cute. Perhaps the larger members of the group feel the same way.

Cannibalism aside, Mediterranean shrimp are not at all the same crustaceans as their pallid Atlantic cousins. They are at once sweeter, more savory, more profound, thicker in terroir. You go to your favorite seaside restaurant in Italy, and you order a plate of *spaghetti con gamberetti, pomodori e basilica,* fragrant with the pointy verdant scent of basil, the piquant acidity of the tomatoes, a pungent strain of garlic, and the sweet thrumming bass-line of shrimp, a sea-swept sweetness that tastes like your mouth at the end of a long August day at the beach. You get the plate, and you find the shrimp intact, from their whiskered heads to their fringy feet. It is a dish of utter beauty.

You delicately pull the fringes of feet off the shrimp, discarding them on the side of the plate. If you're Italian, you do this with your knife and fork; likewise, you remove the outer shell with your silverware, not your hands. (Trust the people who gave us the Medicis to have the world's most exquisite table manners; well-bred Italians wield their knives and forks with intimidating art.) Once you've taken your shrimp from its shell, you cut a bite-sized piece, and you twirl it delicately, tangling it thick and helpless in a net of spaghetti, and then you pop the twisted mass into your mouth. It's a careful operation of sophisticated cutlery, and it is worth it. Next, you swallow your American reservations, lift the shrimp head to your lips, and suck deeply. The decapitated head delivers a shot of pure Mediterranean terroir, a gorgeous briny creaminess held singularly in the shrimp's hepatopancreas, the shrimp version of a lobster's tomalley, and it's this—the shrimp's rich, ruddy digestive organs—that make heads-on Mediterranean shrimp so extraordinary.

I thought of Wasserman, and I wanted to flee to Italy. I wanted to sit myself down in a Ligurian seaside café. Some anonymous restaurant with blue-and-white-checked tablecloths, where I could order a bottle of cold Cinque Terre wine and the most immodest plate of heads-on Mediterranean shrimp, wrap my lips around their bristly, hard heads, and suck until sated. I wanted to stroll in a land where the breeze blew across my face, the sun bore down in a vaguely threatening way, and cobblestones clicked under my heels. I wanted to hear Italian roll like the surf in my ears, and I wanted to smell hand-rolled cigarettes and the stink of men who use a bidet more often than the shower. I wanted to roll myself across coarse Italian hotel sheets and pay too much for espresso because I want to sit at an outside table, and I want to be served. I wanted to be in a place that closed its doors, all but those of its restaurants, between two and four. I wanted to be far, far away from Wasserman's brassy tones and viper mind. I wanted to be free.

I couldn't leave. If I booked a ticket to Italy, I felt certain that Detective Wasserman would know about it. I looked into buying a fake passport—not on my own computer, of course, I'm not an idiot—but while it seemed to be relatively easy to get a fake passport in Hungary, Poland, or Albania, it wasn't at all simple here in the States. I could easily command the money, but then what would I do. I might be a murderer and a psychopath, but, before being imprisoned, I didn't hang out with criminals. This plan, appealing as it was, was out of the question.

I was stuck, confined, caught, if not in perpetuity—not yet—I could nonetheless feel the net pressing, the flesh constricting under its pressure. Invisible lines emanated from Detective Wasserman, unspooling through time to tie me in place, and I was not happy. Wasserman sat in the center, secure in her tensile strength, a jacked and happy spider, and no matter how hard I looked, no matter the angle or the light, I couldn't see the web.

And the web was tightening. Two days after my maybe-confession to Emma, Detective Wasserman called me for a formal visit to the Suffolk Police. I imagined the beige horror that would be a Long Island police station interrogation room. I couldn't bear to think of what that woman had on me, though I'd be lying if I said I wasn't intrigued and even impressed by her tenacity.

"Eat what you love," they say, and I have. But that's facile. It's not merely that I loved Giovanni, Andrew, Gil, and Marco; it's also that I lost them. And it's not merely that I loved and lost them; it's also that I hated them. As much as they were my lovers, they were my enemies, which is more or less all you can hope for from a person with whom you do not share DNA.

Food, if it's at all fleshy, is difficult. Even vegetarians are complicated; after all, the mark of an absence is itself a presence, and vegetarians' sanctimony is a lively chorus of apparitional cows, pigs, sheep, chickens, and fish. Our lives, regardless of our choice to eat meat or not, and regardless of the meat we eat, are so filled with death and killing we might as well plant ourselves atop an abattoir and call it a day; our bodies are charnel houses, memento mori for the countless critters we've eaten, and the American industrial meat complex enables our complicity with its cellophane-wrapped acts of oblivion. Bring us our sirloin, our lamb chops, our veal cutlets, and our chicken breasts snugly swaddled in plastic, thoroughly exsanguinated, wholly dismembered, and completely sanitized for our protection. We won't hear the bleating of the sheep, the lowing of the cows, the hydraulic thwack of the bolt gun. We won't smell the copper rivers of blood sluiced from below kill floors, the acrid tang of the chemical foam that suffocates "free-range" chickens, the florid stench of mountains of fish guts. We eat our meat, and we act as if all animals were always already dead.

I am an unrepentant, unabashed eater of meat. But because I love meat, I'm unwilling to be blind to the acts behind my perfectly cooked steak. Every mouthful is a choice; I like to be an informed consumer. To be otherwise is to be a zombie, mindlessly consuming— good, bad, or egregious. I prefer my meat to come from animals who have been humanely raised and humanely killed, but the truth is that even with my formidable resources, I couldn't subsist solely on humane meats, animals with names, artisanally raised and killed at boutique slaughterhouses. And, really, what was my option. Live on a farm? I get allergic smelling hay. So I lived with the conflict, as humans have done for time immemorial. It doesn't mean that I'm unaware. It doesn't mean I'm going full Michael Pollan, apologizing for my desires, and sequestering my flesh-eating to certain days or times like a hapless, half-assed, rehabilitating alcoholic. It does mean, however, that I'm aware of the choices I'm making. I try to make good choices. I fail. I live to eat another day.

I am what I eat, and so are you. And so was Giovanni, the vegan; Andrew, the gourmet; Gil, the hedonist; and Marco, the nominally kosher. In death, I am closer to them than I ever was in life. I carry them around with me. It's not as if I imagine I can hear them calling, but I do like to converse with their imagined voices. It amuses me to have them agree with me.

The interrogation room at the Suffolk County Police Department was exactly what I'd anticipated: rectangular cement blocks the size and shade of industrial vanilla ice cream, unforgiving overhead fluorescent lights, and a Formica table with two chairs of the sort you'd find in a hospital cafeteria. I was shown in by Detective MacDonnell, aka Lou, the hangdog majordomo to Wasserman's commandant, who waved me toward one of the chairs and left. I waited. I tried to look as if I was trying not to fidget. A person of interest who sits calm and composed, I'd garnered from watching *Snapped*, the show profiling female killers on the Oxygen network, shows signs of guilt. Only the worried fidget; the guilty don't worry; ergo, I was playing at fidgeting.

Ten minutes of waiting and Wasserman swept in like Eisenhower into the Allied command room on D-day, MacDonnell tailing like her seborrheic lapdog. Wasserman bristled with authority and blood thirst. The harsh lights let me get a better look at her, my nemesis. Wasserman was a paleo-CrossFit fanatic for certain—she was short but thick, like one of those tiny draft horses from Norway, all solid curves and no gratuitous elegance. In my heels, I was an easy foot taller than her; Wasserman stood essentially eye-to-nipple with me, but even this math wasn't reassuring. I stood when she came in, mostly for the pleasure of looking down at her hair's twisty brown roots.

"Thank you for coming, uh, Ms. Daniels."

"Of course."

"You remember Detective Lou MacDonnell." Wasserman gestured toward her partner, who looked dazed, blinking slowly like a sloth in a bright light.

"Of course."

"So, Ms. Daniels, we called you in because we still have some questions about your relationship with, erm, Mr. Casimir Bezrukov."

"Certainly. I'm happy to help."

"Super." Wasserman's hard brown eyes had these intense lines around them, like sun spokes. Even in December, her brown skin looked wind-burned, and her eyes looked like she spent a lot of time squinting at the sea. "So, if you would, walk me through your relationship with Mr. Bezrukov."

"Bezrukov," I said.

"Yes, that's right. Casimir Bezrukov."

"No, you're saying BEHZ-roo-kov. It's Bez-ROO-kov."

"Well, how about that, Lou?" Wasserman smiled from the nose down, her eyes glittery and flat. "Walk me through your relationship with Mr. Bez-ROO-kov, if you would, uh, Ms. Daniels."

"Do you mind if I consult my iPhone? I forget what day it is unless I look at my calendar." Wasserman magisterially waved permission at my phone.

I flicked my phone, punched in my code, and loaded my calendar. Naturally, I never use the calendar on my phone, at least not for erotic assignations. I had, however, entered all the dates I had with Casimir, from our fateful first meeting at the bar at the NoMad Hotel on September 23, 2013, to our last night of requited passion in that house on Fire Island on October thirteenth. I wonder how differently Casimir would have lived his life if he'd known he had only three brief weeks left to live it. Probably not much. We all lay claims to John Donne's metaphysical, clock-ticking, carpe-diem action, but it's habit's reassuring arms we seek.

"We met on Sunday, September twenty-third, at the NoMad."

"Do you remember what time?"

"Around nine, I think. I enjoy hotel bars."

"And how long were you at the bar?"

"I was there in total for about two hours; I met Casimir after around forty-five minutes. We left together."

"Did you go home?"

"You know I didn't. I told you at our first meeting that I had sex with Casimir in his hotel room."

"So you did." Wasserman's eyes met mine. I didn't flinch. I wondered if I supposed to flinch. *Snapped* said nothing about flinching. "Did you stay the night?"

"I left shortly after dawn."

"Why?"

"I'm sorry, Detective, but is it really police business to know why I leave my lover's bed when I do?"

"In this case, uh, Ms. Daniels, yes, I'm afraid it is."

"Am I under arrest?"

"No, you're not. You're a person of interest."

I narrowed my eyes at Wasserman, and I took a breath. "I left, Detectives, because it was Monday morning, and I had a story to write. I don't have unlimited free time."

"When did you next see Mr. Bezrukov?" Wasserman placed heavy emphasis on the second syllable.

"Three days later."

"That would be September twenty-sixth."

"Yes. I met him at Eleven Madison Park. We had drinks at the bar, and, if memory serves, we left at about 10:30, when we returned to Casimir's hotel room and had excessively athletic sex. I believe there were ice cubes and candle wax involved. Would you like more details, or can I leave them to your imagination?"

"Did you see him again after that?"

"I did. I saw him on the evenings of September thirtieth, during the day on October second, and again on the evening of October eighth."

"And where did you see Mr. Bezrukov?"

"We met out at various eating and drinking establishments. Then we went to his hotel room, where we had sex. Each time I left in the early morning."

"Was October eighth the last time you saw Mr. Bezrukov?"

"Yes, it was."

"Where were you on the night of Saturday, October thirteenth?"

"At my friends' house in Dunewood, Ron Newson and Paul Landrake. I stayed in and watched Netflix."

"They can corroborate your story?"

"They weren't there, no, but they gave me their house keys."

"So you were alone."

"That's right."

Steely gaze and a crackle of electricity. I was almost beginning to like this little pony.

"Tell me, Ms. Daniels." Wasserman paused and leveled her glittery eyes. "Where do you buy your meat?"

"Ottomanelli's. Why?" Wasserman looked at me and smiled the smile of a hyena sighting a particularly slow-moving wildebeest. My blood coursed icy, falling vertiginous in my gut.

"And you maintain that you did not see Mr. Bezrukov on Fire Island during the weekend of the thirteenth of October."

"I do. I did not." I stammered and took a deep breath. "The last time I saw Casimir was the early morning of October ninth; I left him naked and well fucked." I let the word hang fricative in the air and met Wasserman's hard gaze. "And now, if you don't mind, I'm going to end this meeting, infinitely charming as it has been. If you've anything further to ask me, please call my lawyer."

And as I walked out the door, I tossed a card for Margaret Lately, my attorney, recently engaged, on the table.

16
Soup

argaret Lately, my attorney, looks like Hitchcock's blondes if he'd allowed them to ripen into softness. A luminous woman of a certain age who oozes a sophistication that requires whole teams to manifest, Maggie, as Margaret likes to be called, is an ebullient blonde given to laughing loudly, drinking excitedly, smoking avidly, and talking chummily with just about anyone, but especially with men. She is a broad, and I liked her as my lawyer. If you're going to get a defense attorney—and should you become a "person of interest" I suggest you do—choose one whose company you can tolerate. You spend an inordinate amount of time together.

Tedium is the crux of the judicial process. I have a limited attention span for anxiety; I grow exhausted, and then I become bored, a feeling I envision as Millennial Pink: a faintly labial shade that manages to be both irritating and unobtrusive. I waited weeks after my meeting with Detective Wasserman in Suffolk County before I was arrested; months went by before the trial; more time passed before the sentencing. All told, more than a year elapsed between the day that I killed Casimir and when I went to trial for it. Like a summer vacation, this waiting period seemed to stretch out endless and unimaginable, then it sped up, contracted, and turned small and fleeting. Looking back, I see it was relative freedom bound by inescapable confinement. I wish I'd done more with that time than spend it with Maggie, but few people would be seen with me, and even those who liked me well enough to visit me always seemed to have other plans. Being on trial is remarkably draining, unendurably lonely, and terrifically public. I can't say I cared for it.

I learned a lot about Maggie's sons, whom she loved, and her ex-husband, whom she did not. I learned about her appreciation for Thai food (lemongrass and coconut), and her dislike of Chinese food (too greasy). I learned that some mature women wear only tones of ecru, wheat, ivory, and alabaster because they believe these shades bathe them in "caressing light." And I learned that upon her sixtieth birthday, Maggie had tossed out every garment, every unmentionable, every linen, and every bath towel that didn't fit into this blanched, buffed, and bleached color family. You learn a lot about people when you're trapped in a legal case with them. But spending time with a lawyer is much like spending time with a therapist, which is to say that while your conversations may run to the intimate, when your time is up you never hear from them again. I spent my months immersed in the facsimile of caring for Lately and for the simulacrum of Lately caring for me; I didn't have much else to sustain me.

The truth is I knew I was going to serve time—I held no illusions about carceral justice before my trial, and I have even fewer now. Any fool can do the penitential math; it takes a special fool to believe she won't be found guilty by a jury of her peers, and let's face it: if you live in America, even in New York City, your peers are dim, myopic, vengeful, misogynistic, hungry trolls who want nothing so much as to see the bad witch burn.

Together, Maggie and I went to court; together, she and I ate lunch and often dinner; together, we appeared in the pages of the *Times*, the *New York Post*, the *New York Daily News*, and even *Eater*, *Gourmand*, and *Bon Appétit*. When she was apart from me, Maggie was my avatar on NY1 and the local news affiliates. As we drew close to the trial, Maggie became the closest thing I had to a friend, which was understandable since the last time I'd seen a friend was Emma's ashen face, stricken in blinding lights as a phalanx of cops told me to put my hands in the air or they'd shoot.

How, you may wonder, did this happen. What, you may ask, pushes an otherwise controlled woman to a point where she feels compelled to break into her best friend's loft at three A.M. on a Wednesday night in the middle of January, a meat cleaver in her purse, and no plan beyond the solid certainty that her friend must die. What makes a careful and calculated, if psychopathic, woman give in to the call of hot blood spatter and raw id. To be honest—and, really, when have I been anything but—I'm not sure I know, not even now. I sit on my narrow bunk in Bedford Hills and I think on it more than I like to admit. Emma, I thought, had to die so that I could live. It became almost an algebraic formula in its clarity and self-evidence.

For Dorothy to flourish, Emma must perish: I recall this thought with the lucidity that I remember the severe clear blue sky on September 11th, with the precision that I recall the acrid, oily smell of my mother's tomato plants, with the thoroughness that I retain the heartbeat of Gil's sails luffing in the wind. But even as the memory of this thought—Emma must die—remains crystalline, how I got there is nebulous. It's almost as if one moment I was driving home from the vanilla brick interrogation room at Suffolk County Police, and the next I was standing over Emma's prostrate body, cleaver in hand, wondering where best to strike. Almost—but not quite. I do remember crumbs of my thinking that brought me to doing violence against Emma's sleeping body in the dark—slices, but not the whole loaf. Memory is a tricky mistress.

The week after my trek to the wilds of Long Island was a haze of alcohol and chicken broth, haunted by the pervasive sense that Emma was telling the police everything. The more I thought on it, the more I grew certain that I'd made Emma a drunken confession that night we shared too much Super Tuscan and steak. The more I thought on it, the more certain I was that Emma had felt compelled to do the right thing. The more I thought on it, the more I was convinced that Emma was in cahoots with Wasserman. Emma had betrayed me, I realized. I felt this icy awareness twist steely in my gut.

Emma and Wasserman had so much in common, I thought. Their untrustworthy disavowal of carbohydrates. Their short stature. Their united need to see me in prison. I felt sure that they were conspiring against me. Emma knew me almost as well as I knew myself. Only Emma had known me for decades, had sat privy to infinite secrets, had heard me ring ragged on the men who entered stage left, exited stage right, and were never seen again. Only Emma was as smart, as clever, as perceptive as I, and thus Emma must be the sole reason why Detective Wasserman suspected me.

For more than a week after my visit to the Suffolk County Police Department, I laid up in my apartment, methodically drinking my way through my stash of bourbon and my cellar of wines, compulsively and systematically ordering all of the matzo ball soup that Seamless could deliver to my Upper West Side apartment. My kitchen was awash in remnants of my compulsive soup delivery: little white paper cups, tiny balls of foil, vacant saltine wrappers, and empty wine bottles. The phone rang. I picked it up without looking at the caller.

"Dolls." It was Emma. "What the hell."

"Emma. How are you."

"I've been calling and texting you for the last ten days. What am I supposed to think when you don't answer your phone?"

"Have you. I hadn't noticed."

"Jesus fuck, Dolls," Emma said and then whispered something to someone. I couldn't catch it. I saw her sidling up to Wasserman, their heads together, black and blacker. Emma and Wasserman were twinned together, giggling about me. "Sorry about that," she said. "I'm trying to get the Whorestep Chronicles ready for the gallery."

Sure she was.

"Emma, it's nothing. I'm not feeling well. That flu. You know."

"Really?"

I didn't answer.

"What's going on with that thing?"

"What thing, Emma. You have to be more specific."

"That thing with the detectives."

Was that a click I heard on the phone line? I felt certain I heard a click.

"Oh, that. It's...it's, you know, it's nothing."

"Really?" There it was, that click.

"Yes, really. A mistake. It's all cleared up. It was nothing."

"So. You didn't have to talk to herr-em?" Had Emma elided "her" and "them," had she corrected herself mid-word? Had she made a tactical stumble, given a sign of her collusion?

"Talk to whom, Emma?" Did she say her or him? Did she say them? Maybe both.

"The detectives."

"No. I mean, yes. I did. I went to Suffolk County a few days ago." Why was she asking me questions to which she knew the answers. How much sharper than a serpent's tooth it is to have a faithless friend. She may smile and smile and be a villain. Lie thou there. My right hand twitched. That it should come to this.

"And?" I had to hand it to her. Emma's voice was tense, constricted, as if with actual emotion. I'd no idea she had this level of duplicity in her. (Here in prison, I look back at this moment and wonder whether Emma, too, is a psychopath, whether she, too, inhabits the emotional winter that is an utter lack of conscience—could it be this that brought us together.)

"And what, Emma. It was nothing. A case of mistaken identity. I'm nothing—it's nothing. It's done."

"You sound really strange, Dolls."

"I'm tired. The flu. That's going around." I told her I was going to rest. I told her not to worry about me. And I hung up, certain that my phone was tapped.

My friend's treachery whirred; a hamster wheel that squeaked in the night, it turned obsessively. Emma knows all, I thought. Emma has told all, I thought. The police know everything, I thought. She has betrayed me, I thought. I tried to square everything I knew about Emma—her anarchist roots, her anti-establishment beliefs, her bohemian sensibilities—with the knowledge that she had turned her narrow back on all of it and ratted on me. It felt clear as consommé: I'd horrified Emma with my unremembered confession, and she felt compelled to rat me out. Lying on her bed, I had shown myself to be the naked monster I was, and Emma gave me up, I felt sure of it. She was hardly the first.

Then, creaky and petulant with inertia, the wheels would reverse, and my logic would turn withershins. I'd known Emma for decades. In that time, she'd never been anything but my faithful friend; our bonds were thicker than time, faster than men, more solid than family, and truer than brown bread. Emma was the one person I loved, a thought that felt like a douche of cold water. She was, then, the sole person who could hurt me, and hurt me she did.

And yet, I could think of no other way that Wasserman et al had latched their collective claws into my hide. Only Emma's disclosure of my drunken confession could have kept the rodential Wasserman and her frowzy henchman, Lou, hot on my tail—if, in fact, I had confessed on that night to Emma, and increasingly, I was sure that I had.

Drunk, angry, and aimless, I ponged around my apartment looking for a target. All the furniture seemed to have grown. The sofa loomed belligerent; the bed menaced from the middle of the room. The television glowered black and blank; lamps bowed their heads in judgment; pillows mocked me. I set the nearly empty bottle of Knob Creek down on the counter, and I brewed the company-sized pot of espresso. I sharpened a cleaver. I retrieved my lock picks from the ski boots where I kept them.

Even as I packed my knife and my lock picks in my satchel, I didn't have a plan. I didn't know what I was going to do to Emma. Aphasic with worry, I couldn't form a sentence, much less a scheme. I wanted to frighten her, maybe cut her hair and slash her paintings, make her tell me what I'd told her and what she'd told the cops. I wanted to hear it from her pretty, roseate mouth. I wanted Emma to tell me that she'd betrayed me, and when I had heard her say it, when she told me everything I needed to hear, I wanted to slit her thin white throat. The crimson jeweling would look lovely on Emma's flesh. Aesthetics are important.

I wore a black wig, a slouchy knit hat of indeterminate gender, and a black puffer jacket over jeans. Not recognizing me, the doorman didn't say good night. The winter night was glittery and bright, the streetlamps' lights pointed as shards of glass. Surveillance lurked everywhere in the shiny city, from taxi cameras to traffic videos, from tapes in subway stations to the invisible blips off cell towers. Everywhere you went, someone was watching—the only way to fly beneath the radar was to be dead. I crossed the thirty blocks between my apartment and Emma's, first walking, then in a taxi, and finally riding on a bike stolen from a delivery boy.

The streets were almost empty, oddly silent but for the wind and the sibilant sound of wheels. Light bounced off cold surfaces, pinged off iridescent glass, glowed ghost-like on reflective paint, and stopped dead on matte tarmac. It felt like Manhattan herself, that fine gossamer slut clad in jeweled chokers and black velvet, was pushing me forward, her hand firm on the small of my back. I was waltzing with an invisible partner, nodding in time and smiling. Now that I'd made a decision, everything felt clear as vodka.

I got to Emma's apartment building. An old warehouse, it had a side door that dumped into a very narrow, mostly enclosed alley. I knew that Emma's front door had a jeweler's lock, requiring one of those rolling ball-and-socket types of key. I couldn't pick that lock, but I had a suspicion that the management hadn't gone to the same trouble with the side door, an entryway that the porter used for hauling out trash. I was right; it was a standard Medeco lock. Even better, I didn't see any cameras in the alley. I picked the lock within a couple of minutes, and the door swung open as if it wanted to swallow me whole. I'd have picked it faster if I hadn't spent the last ten days drunk.

Creak-creak-creak went the elevator. The door shuddered open. The door shuddered closed. Creak-creak-creak went the elevator. The door shuddered open. Behind me, the door shuddered closed. I got on my knees and inserted one of my lock picks, feeling around for the tumbler. At no point did it cross my mind to simply knock on the door. At no point did I think I could stop what I was doing and talk to Emma, ask her simply and directly if she had betrayed me. At no point did I stop and wonder at my madness, or kennel the crawling horror-sloth whose incessant growling had edged me into action. I did not think. I only felt, and then the lock whispered its sacred "click."

American girls grow up knowing the intrinsic importance of having female friends; our girlfriends are our bosom buddies, a term that links the girlishly erotic with the emotionally intimate. There is no Emma Woodhouse without Harriet Smith; there is no Beatrice without Hero; there is no Anne Shirley without Diana Barry. *Sex and the City, The Group, Gossip Girl, Sisterhood of the Traveling Pants, Thelma & Louise*—American popular culture is positively lousy with BFFs (not even death can separate that final pair). Men may come and men may go, but in American culture, at least, a girl's bosom buddy will always be another woman.

In America, our girlfriends teach us what love, trust, and desire are; they hold our hands as we navigate the Scylla of sex and the Charybdis of culture. With them we are our truest, most essential selves. We don't have to be pretty, but we heap praise upon one another when we are. We don't have to be nice, and we forgive each other when we aren't. With our friends, our guard tumbles like acrobats, falls like leaves, and swirls in glittery, dusty eddies. That face we keep up in front of everyone else—family, lovers, husbands, or children—we let slide. Our friends see the frailties, the insecurities, the unattractive bits that we have to keep hidden from the rest of the world because—and this is the meat of the matter—it's hard work to be a woman. It's a full-time job. Our female friends, the close ones, are the mini-breaks we take from the totalitarian work it requires to keep up the performance of being female.

And none of this friendship had I known until, inch by creeping, prickly inch, I'd let Emma into my life, or she let me into hers, whichever came first. My girlfriends in high school—the giggling passels of scented fluffs and pastel ruffs with whom I ate junk food and learned how to gloss my lips—were merely people I hated slightly less than everyone else. They were necessary distractions. They were camouflage. Emma was my first—my only—true friend. Anything that was good about me, anything, that is, that wasn't my work, lived in my relationship with Emma. She was the black star to my black hole. She was the reflection I saw in the mirror, for true monsters can't see themselves. Without Emma, I was an empty surface. Brittle and magnetic and lovely, but fragile and horrible, too.

The door swung open. Emma's loft was dark. Pieces of furniture sat in indistinct black clumps. Paintings hung like hovering dark holes. It didn't matter. I knew my way around. I removed my shoes, slipped the cleaver out of my satchel, dropped my jacket to the floor, and tiptoed across the loft into Emma's bedroom. Surrounded by pillows, her back to the door, she slept cat-curled in the center of her big white bed, her eiderdown pulled up and around her body so high that only a semicircle of black hair showed against the sheets. A photograph of Emma amid that luxuriousness would go instantly viral; such was her fame.

She was alone. Good. I hadn't even considered that she might have a lover. I didn't relish collateral damage.

"Emma," I said. "Don't move." I saw a twitch in the sheets. "I want to know what you told Wasserman. Just tell me what you told her."

She was silent. Frozen. Still as custard. Quiet as ice. I couldn't hear her breathe. Good. She should be scared.

"You called her, didn't you. After the night we got drunk. You called her and you told that detective what I'd said. Everything about Fire Island, the dinner, the ice pick. The house fire."

Silence.

"Emma, you little twisted bitch. Don't play games." I stepped forward, pulled the covers down, and swung the cleaver in an arc aimed at her neck.

"I'm not," Emma said, as she flipped on the lights. I saw now the bed, empty but for a mass of pillows in the rough shape of a body, one pillow's pallid guts spilling across a black velvet coverlet wadded where Emma's head should've been. My cleaver quivered in its center.

It was a horrid tableau, and I was horrified. Emma was alive and well, but I was cooked.

A man's voice rang, succinct and rapid-fire with authority. "Hands in the air or we'll shoot!" I heard him as through the rush of waves. I raised my hands high. His voice told me to get down on my knees and to touch the back of my head. Rough hands pushed my face into the soft mattress. I felt one wrist and then the other circled by strong hands and clipped tight into cold cuffs. Hands on my elbows helped lift me to a standing position and spun me around 180 degrees.

I turned to see about five NYPD officers; the one next to me made six. In my ear, this officer recited my Miranda rights. I had the right to remain silent. Anything I said or did could be used against me in a court of law. I had the right to an attorney. I had the right to be firmly guided by my elbow. I had the right to be led through the bedroom door and across my former best friend's studio, now with all the lights blazing. I had the right to walk past Emma, sleep-rumpled in her orchid silk pajamas. I had the right to see her crying. I had the right to wonder what the fuck I'd done to myself.

I turned to the left; I turned to the right; I looked straight ahead. My fingers got inky. I learned how to share a single roll of toilet paper with twenty other women and how to urinate in front of guards, skills that would later come in handy. Even with the bulldog diligence of Maggie Lately, I spent sixty hours in central booking after processing. Time enough to etch the foul stench of decomposing skin, stagnating urine, desiccating feces, and human boredom into my hippocampus. It was also enough time to see the same meal—a lukewarm carton of milk paired with a sandwich of spongy white bread slapped around faintly gray slices of bologna and spread with off-brand mayonnaise—circulate three times.

After Maggie finagled my release, I took a shower as long as the Cenozoic Era. I ate a proper meal at Il Mulino (delicate lobster salad kissed with garlic and lemon; improbably perfect beefsteak tomatoes, coated in eloquent bacon vinaigrette; an immodest, perfectly cooked T-bone steak; and a side of fluffy, pleasantly gelatinous spinach creamed with mascarpone; I ate it all with a lovely bottle of Le Macchiole Scrio, the bad boy of Bolgheri Super Tuscans). And I went home to sleep the heavy, velvet sleep of the guilty and caught. The next day, I presented myself at the Suffolk County Police Station to answer the warrant for my arrest. From one jail cell into another. This one with fewer women and a slightly diminished fecal scent.

Not for nothing, we got soup with our sandwiches in Suffolk County.

17

Duck

*E*arly to bed and early to rise, prison is no place for night owls. I toss in my narrow bed and hallucinate espresso and perfect hazelnut biscotti, I hallucinate luscious scallop cruda and crisp Prosecco, I hallucinate a sloppy Corner Bistro burger and a beer. I hallucinate.

Days at Bedford Hills are as you'd expect: uniform. Each gray morning feels like waking in a nightmare of junior high—the matchy-matchy industrial light and flat gray palette, the burbling sense of fomenting unease, the prismatic instability of pubescent psyches, and the unremitting similarity of one day to another. Visiting hours punctuate our amorphous days, as do jobs, meals, bunk inspections, group therapy, the rare fight and its consequential lockdown. Excitement is movie night, the occasional party, or the infrequent altercation that gets seriously ugly. Blood occasionally gets spilled, none mine.

Bedford Hills, despite its country club name, is a maximum-security penitentiary, and it's awful. No one wants to live by another's schedule, particularly not criminals and especially not writers. We've done everything we could to avoid living by anyone else's rules. But I'm white and educated and these privileges get you as far in this incarcerated world as they do in that free one. I'm lucky, and I know it. I've always been lucky. Yet I still look out windows crosshatched by wire grating. I still wander the exercise yard and curl my fingers around the fence. My fingertips graze freedom. They can almost touch it.

I never will.

Unbeknownst to me, Emma's building had installed a silent alarm, trip-wired to activate if the porter's door opened before anyone keyed in the code. Emma, too, had grown more security conscious. She'd seen an uptick in her hate mail, and she figured it wouldn't hurt to install a silent alarm. As I tickled her lock into springing open, Emma had been sitting on the fire escape, smoking. Her phone signaled an intruder. She called the cops, who, because of the porter's door, were already en route. As for the phantom Emma asleep in her canopied bed, well, it simply happened that her pillows had fallen in the shape of her tiny body—or, perhaps, the pillows were just pillows, and my unconscious created a body out of fabric, filler, and goose down. In any case, Emma was never in any danger, while I was clearly a danger to others, and to myself.

I attacked Emma; I got arrested; and Wasserman pounced. Murder trumps assault, so the trial was moved to Suffolk County, where it began in October 2014, just over a year to the day when Casimir, delicious duck in belly and sharp ice pick in throat, died.

What can I say about the trial that you don't already know. Maggie wore a stunning procession of ecru suits. I wore an expression of "relatability" and an ankle monitor. I did not take the stand because Maggie's team thought it was "not a good idea." Maggie said I'd "damage" my case. She was probably right. I've always been impatient with my inferiors. It's a weakness.

Ultimately, I was charged with a laundry list of offenses: murder in the first degree, assault in the first degree, arson in the first degree, tampering with physical evidence, and two counts of criminal trespass in the first degree. Justice was served hot, fresh, and juicy in the Suffolk County Court in Riverhead, Long Island, where the courtroom seemed built by the same visionary designers responsible for such architectural flights of fancy as the American Airlines Admirals Club lounge at JFK. But what aesthetics can one expect from a committee. No group will ever agree on any design that's truly beautiful; a group will always default to bourgeois blandness.

I sat as the silent star of the theatrical show. My trial was a pageant, a drama, a soap opera. It was *This Is Your Life* played out in grisly photos, cell phone records, guest cameos, and scraps of paper. To be fair, Maggie was gorgeous; she swaggered and swept her hand through the air, seeding it with life; you couldn't take your eyes off her. Spectacled and beaky, the judge looked owlish and conservative, but he had no visible tell. His gaveled hand never tipped, not until sentencing. The D.A. was a man who might have been pretty in his youth; now in his forties, he was faintly porcine, one of those men who moves as if he had fifteen pounds of undigested red meat sitting in his colon. He was adequate, a typical mediocre white male whose career advanced because he was not entirely horrible. Women have to work so much harder than men to appear half as convincing.

Questioning the witnesses early in the trial, Maggie stalked like an ivory-coated cat, but I was looking forward to watching her go head-to-head against Detective Wasserman. I saw the detective almost every day in court. I'd turn my head, and there Wasserman would be, her muscled draft horse's body swathed in yet another polyester-knit pantsuit. I played a solitary game of imagining painful deaths for Wasserman. A creative mind can spot a hundred homicides in a roomful of common office supplies. A ballpoint pen swift and hard to the temple or eye. A superfluity of Scotch Tape around the nose and mouth. A well-strung window shade. The judge's gavel looked heavy enough to serve as a bludgeon. I'd have gamely given it a go.

I waited and waited for the watching Wasserman to appear in her official capacity. I wanted to see Maggie gut her—and I wanted to see what Wasserman had on me. I wanted to hear from Wasserman's own naked mouth that she had colluded with Emma. I wanted to bear witness to my own destruction because how many of us get to see our own undoing. All humans are bad. Most of us merely live our lives with our worst, most unethical acts lying like bodies clad in concrete, undiscovered, quiet, and dark. What is heaven but the hope for righteous acknowledgment, and what is hell but the fear of discovery.

Finally, the D.A. called Wasserman to the stand. Dreadlocks bouncing, she strode through the court in a brawny rush of moss-gray lady-suit, put her hand in the air, and made the solemn pledge.

Sitting in that honey-blond witness box, Wasserman's eyes glinted with profound enjoyment; she relished every second on the stand. She savored each question, and she delighted in each curt, thoroughly professional answer with a nearly libidinal abandon. She and the piggish D.A. performed a practiced dance together, a polished pas-de-discipline capered for my benefit.

I imagined Maggie's slow evisceration of Wasserman. I saw my beige lioness stripping the flesh off the State's evidence, gore staining her maw. I envisioned Maggie the surgeon, Maggie the drone operator, Maggie the butcher.

My imaginary Maggie, it turned out, was more effective than my flesh-and-blood Maggie. Maggie did her best, but Wasserman's wounds magically knit when the D.A. and the detective revealed a singular piece of proof, one incontrovertible testament to my unquestionable presence in that Robbins Rest house on that cold October Sunday, the selfsame night that Casimir met his early end and the house met a well-lit match.

You're wondering what Wasserman had that tied me so inexorably to that place and that night. You're wondering about the thing that cooked my goose, broke my burro's back, sealed my carceral fate. It was a piece of paper. Just one slip. Something that could blow away in a breeze. Something that you or I would toss away without a second thought. Something inconsequential and light, yet weighty enough to lock me away for the rest of my natural life. It was almost nothing, this piece of paper. It was a receipt, if you can believe it.

As the Robbins Rest house burned in a bright and shining conflagration, this bit of paper stayed safe. Unthinking, reflexively, I flung it into a lidded metal wastebasket, and there this bit of paper had lived, protected as if in a vault. The D.A. showed Wasserman and the jury a series of crime-scene photos of the trash can. Outside, inside, wide-angle, and close-up, never has a trash can been so documented. It was like a celebrity on the beach, photographed from every angle.

The trash can was made, appropriately enough, by Simplehuman. Black and sooty, the can's exterior was scorched, and while its bin liner melted around the can's lip, its contents remained remarkably preserved, almost fresh. And there, among the scrapings of the breadboard, the wrappers from the manchego and the Comté, the ends of avocados, fennel, and oranges, lay this pristine piece of paper—a receipt from Ottomanelli's, my butcher of choice, a shop with whom I've had an account for decades, and the place where I had bought the duck breasts to confit. Like a relic of a medieval saint, this slip of paper remained unburned, almost clean, pristine, and undefiled. It defied belief, yet there it lay in the D.A.'s porky hand, carefully bagged in plastic with People's Evidence #547-A2 stamped upon its sleeve.

I thought I'd born witness to some repressed joy in my life, but nothing rivaled Wasserman's when the D.A. trotted out that Ottomanelli's receipt. From her nose down, Wasserman was all cop-like professionalism, thin-lipped and terse. From her nose up, however, she was radiant. Wasserman might've been all clipped No, sir, and Yes, sir, and the redheaded woman at the defense table, sir, but I saw through her detached probity. On the inside, she was singing; though rigid and still, she was practically skipping as she sat in that burnt-umber witness chair. When the D.A. showed the videotape of my answering "Ottomanelli's" to Wasserman's offhand question about where I bought my meat, Wasserman broke. She grinned. She couldn't help it. She could have spontaneously combusted from the effort she required to contain herself.

Maggie gave the swinish D.A. a good fight. I don't blame her for losing. I blame the receipt. I blame the Simplehuman. I blame the tender debris.

Maggie and her team of freshly scrubbed young lawyers worked to undo Wasserman's damage. The Ottomanelli's receipt was bad, but it was circumstantial at best. Little remained to link me to Casimir. His phone logged the number of my disposable cell phone long since disposed of. His calendar lined up with mine as much as I'd said it had—there were no other surprises to put us in the same room at the same time. The room service waiter and the hotel cameras told no tale that I'd not already admitted: Casimir and I had enjoyed an intimate relationship. The waiter and the grainy footage didn't aid my case, but beyond raising the pedestrian hackles of the unenlightened jury of my peers, they did nothing to prove I'd killed him either. The medical examiner proved that Casimir had died before his body had burned, but there was no way to prove murder. His flesh was too crispy to reveal the ice pick's deep pricks.

Even the arson specialists were split—denatured alcohol is a fantastic accelerant; it burns quickly and leaves almost no trace. The investigator hired by Suffolk County argued for arson; the investigator hired by Maggie argued against it; and the one hired by the homeowner's insurance company said the cause was indeterminate. My murder trial was a muddle of evidence, and for a long time, our case looked pretty good. At best, the receipt was secondary evidence for the murder and not enough to convict; at worst, it showed I had trespassed. And, of course, I assaulted Emma. There was no explaining that away.

The smoking gun was Emma, you see—just not in the way I'd expected, for in thinking she had betrayed me, I betrayed myself.

While the hordes of strangers, writers, and murder buffs who crowded the seats of the Suffolk County Courthouse were disappointed that they didn't get to see me take the stand, seeing Emma made up for it. It was, after all, the first time that Emma Absinthe, world-famous artist, had stepped foot outside of her Hell's Kitchen atelier in decades. This in and of itself was news; *Art in America* had never before covered a murder trial.

For the majority of my trial, the courthouse crowd had been comprised of media types and rubbernecking gawkers, but the day that Emma was to appear, the assembly shifted. It grew Goth and glittery, fancy with millinery and festive with tulle. There was an improbable number of waif-like girls, sylphine boys, and humans who refuse easy gender categorization, a group united by their abject worship of Emma, their omnipresent sketchbooks, and their expertly lined eyes. There were adults, too, people who had taken a personal day or had merely called their secretary to cancel the day's appointments. Few art buyers and fewer art sellers ever get to meet Emma. She customarily performed her meet and greets through the remote beauty of Skype. For decades, Emma had grown to be a celebrity while also being a person rarely seen in the flesh. The courthouse almost levitated with the sheer giddiness of her physical presence.

Emma did not disappoint. Called to testify, she swept through the honey-oak doors in a tiny lacy torrent of black taffeta and teetering Louboutin ankle boots. Emma didn't look like a woman who'd not seen the world outside of her own apartment in twenty years. She walked into that party as if she were walking onto a yacht, pale skin glowing almost opalescent under the fluorescent lights, red lipstick an arterial nod. She didn't just take the stand; she owned it. I felt a rush of emotion for my friend. Then I remembered her milk-white face on the night I'd tried to kill her, and my hot feelings slowed to a simmer and cooled. She was not my friend. She was a witness. One pale hand in the air, Emma pledged to tell the truth, the whole truth, and nothing but the truth, so help her God.

Emma has long been an ardent atheist.

The piggish D.A. began by asking Emma about our relationship, how long and in what capacity we had known each other. Maggie poised like a pointer, interjecting objections at almost every turn, calling irrelevant, immaterial, leading, and hearsay. With every point the judge granted, the D.A. narrowed his eyes, as if searching the mist for his lost way home. The courthouse felt like a tennis match, spectators restraining themselves from polite clapping. I could see a trickle of sweat on the D.A.'s jowls. Emma, however, was cool as bisque and twice as satiny.

"Ms. Absinthe," the D.A. said, "can you please tell the court what you heard Ms. Daniels say on the night of January nineteenth?"

"I don't recall," Emma said, her voice steady and clear.

"You don't remember what she said?" The D.A.'s pink tongue flicked wet over his lips. "I will remind you that you're under oath, and ask again. Do you remember what Ms. Daniels said to you just before she struck your bed with a knife?"

"Not exactly, no."

"Let me see if I can refresh your memory. More than one police officer has testified to the effect that Ms. Daniels said—and I'm reading from New York City police officer depositions here—to the effect of 'You told the detective what I said about Fire Island, the ice pick, and the house fire.' Does this quote jog your memory at all, Ms. Absinthe?"

Maggie raised her voice and objected in whisky tones. The judge overruled and directed Emma to answer the question.

The courtroom hushed. Emma looked at her hands and then she looked at me. She had a queer expression, one I hadn't seen in decades, not since we lived together in that Pennistone dorm room and she was just Joanne Correa with the mushroom-brown hair, unfathomable love of cats, and parade of Gunne Sax dresses. Emma lifted her chin and looked into my eyes before she spoke.

"Perhaps. I can't say for certain." Emma looked away from the court, out the window, toward the sky. Everyone's head followed. The D.A. grew flustered and looked at his notes.

"Did you have any previous conversations with detectives, Ms. Absinthe?"

"Only when I called nine-one-one when I was alerted that someone was breaking into my apartment, and, of course, after the arrest."

"Nothing before that emergency phone call?"

"No."

"Do you have any idea to what Ms. Daniels was alluding in referencing, and I'm going to refer to the quote I read you earlier, 'Fire Island, the ice pick, and the house fire'?"

Maggie objected. It was sustained. The question was withdrawn.

"Let me try again, Ms. Absinthe. Did you and the defendant ever discuss the events of the night of October 13, 2013, the night Casimir Bezrukov was murdered?"

"Yes." A thrill ran through the courthouse. A chill passed through my chest.

"You did. Can you please tell the court when?"

"She came over to my apartment some night in late December. She told me that a lover had been found dead. On Fire Island."

"Was that all, Ms. Absinthe?"

"Well, we drank quite a bit." The courtroom laughed. Emma was charming them, or her celebrity was. Either way, I could feel Maggie's delight.

"Did Ms. Daniels tell you anything else about the events of October 13, 2013?"

"Not to my recollection, no."

"You are stating for the court, under oath, that Ms. Daniels told you nothing else about Casimir Bezrukov, neither on that night in late December nor on any other occasion."

"Yes. Dorothy never said anything else."

"Ms. Absinthe, you were assaulted on the night of January 19, 2013. Do you see the person who assaulted you in this room?"

Emma almost rolled her eyes. "Yes, of course, Dorothy Daniels, at the defense table."

The D.A. shuffled papers. "Can you think, Ms. Absinthe, why the defendant might have broken into your apartment and assaulted you?"

Maggie objected—leading the witness. The D.A. retorted, calling for relevance. The judge called them to the bench, where a hushed, impassioned powwow took place. The players broke and returned to their honey-oak tables. The judge overruled and told Emma to answer the question.

"In all honesty, Mr. Lezard, I've no idea."

"None at all, Ms. Absinthe?"

"None at all."

Perhaps Emma had not, after all, gone to Wasserman. Perhaps she had tattled no tale. In fact, it was entirely likely that I had not confessed. I had, perhaps, merely gestured in drunken fuzzy arcs toward the murder, never announcing my guilt. Emma had never betrayed me—unless, of course, she had. Was this Emma a performance Emma, one she was wearing to make herself feel better about my going to jail. Or was this the real Emma, the one who would never forsake a friend. Forgery or authentic, Emma was artful, and I couldn't tell the real from the copy.

And yet, there was no dodging the fact that in my vortex of paranoia, I had attacked Emma. I had picked that first lock, and I had picked the second, and I had uttered a string of incriminating things just before Emma and a phalanx of cops saw me bury my cleaver in her body pillow—points to which Emma and at least three of the police officers would testify. There was no way to side-step these facts, there was no way to wrap them in fondant and pretend they were edible. I had made the trap, stepped in it, and found it clapping closed, steely and cold, around my leg. And it was my attack on Emma, the phrase I blurted before cleaving Emma's pillow, and the receipt that, together, convinced the jury, seven women and five men, that I was guilty as sin.

I'd spent the weeks leading up to the trial out on bail on house arrest. These weeks were dear, sweet, beautiful days. I cherished every single one with a kind of bittersweet, grudging love, feeling each moment melt like chocolate. I couldn't move around much—the terms of my bail included an ankle bracelet and strict travel parameters—but that's what you get when you're a rich, white murder defendant. Still, I could cook, and I could order in from FreshDirect. Sadly, Ottomanelli's cancelled my account, which broke my heart. I could read and sleep in my own bed, and I could pack up the apartment where I'd lived for more than a decade, deciding what would go to charity, what would go to storage, and what I could have with me in prison. I couldn't bring much—a few books, a coverlet, some photos—prison is like death in that whatever you have you can't bring it with you. If I won the trial, I was going to move to Europe; if I lost the trial, I was going to move to prison. I didn't know where I was going, and I didn't know for how long. I knew only that it wouldn't be my choice.

Judges and juries are notoriously brutal on violent female offenders, a category to which I belong without question. Nature abhors a vacuum; jurisprudence hates a violent woman. We can forgive any number of men murdering their wives and girlfriends. But we have a hard time extending the same compassion to women who kill their husbands and boyfriends, even though women have many more reasons to be driven to it. Culture refuses to see violence in women, and the law nurtures a special loathing for violent women. Unfettered violence, anger unleashed, the will to destroy, the need to undo—these acts run counter to everything we like to think we know about the feminine nature. Yet women weren't always the angels in the house, and angels weren't always benevolent beings playing harps on the tops of trees. We like to forget that men imprisoned women in the house and expected gratitude in return.

In the end, the terminally middle-class jury of my supposed peers found me guilty of second-degree murder, first-degree assault, and third-degree arson, along with various minor charges having to do with evidence. I was sentenced to life, plus twenty years; I'll be looking forward to probation about ten years after I'm dead. People have asked and I have yet to answer, but my last meal before going to Bedford Hills was duck. Not duck confit—that dish is tragically ruined. It was a Long Island roast duck, whole, rather naked of frills, but still beautiful and crispy and perfect. It sang of flight and of fall and of lives made of freedom in the water, on land, and in the air. It's likely the last time I'll ever eat duck, and it was good.

Hot Dog

We talk about love like it's an involuntary act. We fall into love, like a hole, a puddle, an elevator shaft. We never step mindfully into love. Love, we seem to think, requires a loss of control; love necessitates that vertiginous giving over to gravity; love wants you to have no choice. Your heart thumps because there's danger and adrenaline in love. You lose yourself in love because you've displaced yourself. But dating sites and yentas, arranged marriages and speed dating, advice columns and blind dates, all argue that love is something we can manage, a losing that we can find. I suppose that if you walk into a minefield, you're more likely to explode; if you walk a country lane in the dark, you're more likely to trip; and if you put yourself in the path of dating, you're more likely to fall in love. I maintain that love can't simultaneously be an accident and a premeditated act, yet we treat it as if it is. It's a necessary fiction, love's oxymoronic nature. Love's a contranym as sharp as "cleave" and twice as dangerous.

I loved a man, once. I didn't merely feel passionately for the man; I loved him. By this I mean that when love is real it's not a noun; it's an action. To love was not something I wanted. My thinking has always been that if love, marriage, and family were intrinsically so meaningful, so exceptional, and so necessary, then we wouldn't need millennia of propaganda selling them to us. As I grew up, I looked at my mother and my father and their plastic fantastic Connecticut world, and I knew my bones were telling me that this—this familiarity, this life, this sham—was not for me. Still, I must admit it: once I loved.

I fell face-first in love. As if I were the kicky, peach-faced lead in a romantic comedy, my love began with a literal tumble. It was a jaunty spring day in 2004. The sun was shining, the squirrels were chattering, the whole of Manhattan seemed to be stretching in a wholesome Disney way. Everyone was summoning excuses to be everywhere but the office. I left mine at *Eat & Drink* to get a cup of espresso, but really, I wanted to be outside, in the winsome air, feeling the leaves unfurl, and smelling the peculiarly fresh, waking city air.

I was stopped by a tourist, map in hands and a confused expression on her broad Teutonic face. "Do you know where is the library?" she asked.

"Yes," I said and walked away, turning the corner onto Madison from 44th Street. I saw a FedEx carrier loaded with a dolly of boxes, and I swerved. Unbalanced and inattentive, I rammed into a man buying a hot dog. What happened next was almost slow motion; it was nearly a ballet. The hot dog flew upward, and as the man reached to get it, my momentum took me forward, spinning me over his leg and toward the hot dog cart. An arm caught me just as my right hand grazed the cart. Hot, slick steel burned my palm. I felt a firm arm around my chest, a firm hand on my shoulder.

I felt myself guided upright, and I felt strong hands steadying me. I looked up and saw blue eyes, thick eyebrows, honey-blond hair. A positively Brobdingnagian head. There was something familiar about these eyes, something reminiscent about his hair. Somewhere, somehow, I remembered those eyebrows, that massive head.

"Dorothy...Daniels?" He asked.

"Hi, yes." I felt oddly flustered. It's rare for me to look up into a man's eyes. These were at least three inches above my own. "I'm Dorothy Daniels." I brushed chunks of green relish off my coat. Napkins were pressed into my hand. I used them to dab at the mustard that was Jackson Pollacked across my bodice.

"Yeah, I know! Dorothy, it's Alex Konings. Remember me?" I looked up from my coat. "From Pennistone?"

I stared blankly.

"I was editor of the paper when you started as an arts writer."

"Alex!" I said. I had no idea who he was. None. I hadn't slept with him, I was certain. Looking at this Alex in his nicely fitting, subtly striped suit, all long legs and slightly receding hairline, I felt I might want to. "Alex, of course! How terribly silly of me."

He laughed. I laughed. We laughed, you know, as people do when confronted by the absurdities of life. Mouths open, sound escaping, we laughed like a man and a woman in a film, the sunshine a warm benediction on our shoulders. What are the chances that you'll turn a corner and run smack into a man you've not seen in twenty years. What are the chances that he'll still be attractive, at least as attractive as you. What are the chances of the kind of cliché whimsy that passes for romance on an aggressively spring-like day in the city of New York.

"What are you doing? Holy cats!" he said and smiled a big, middle-aged grin. He had damn fine teeth, white and hard, glittering like marble. I groped to recall this man, this Alex, this once-editor from many decades ago. I remembered shades of an oddly sincere, quiet fellow. I remembered him hunkering in his editor's lair behind the pane of glass, poring over proofs in the small hours of the morning on Wednesday nights, when we students worked all night to put the Pennistone paper to bed. I remembered being at his apartment for a party once, briefly, and I remembered boxes of macaroni and cheese lined up like squat blue-and-yellow soldiers. I remember riding in his car, squashed into the back seat, some last-minute ride from campus to a show, and I remembered ignoring him as soon as the band started to play. I remember him being remarkably quiet, solicitous, polite.

I remembered a party at a country club, a spring night in Vermont, a night not unlike the one coming to Manhattan in five or six hours. There was a hot tub. I wore a shiny purple Danskin one-piece bathing suit that zipped up the front, and Alex told me I looked like a Bond girl. I let him take my toes in his mouth, the steam rising around us like the small talk, my feet cold in the air, my toes warm in his hot mouth. We talked, or I talked, mildly distracted by the frisson of public toe sucking. It didn't occur to me that Alex was hitting on me. He seemed too innocent, too cherubic, too earnest for carefree fucking. His authenticity didn't match with my gut feeling that all men merely wanted to enjoy me and move on. So I let him suck my toes, and it was splendid, and then I stepped out of the tub and stalked off into that glorious damp night.

"Please, Alex, let me take you to lunch. I made you drop your hot dog. I know a fantastic place around the corner that does amazing Turkish tapas. You'll love it."

If I'd known then what I know now, would I have taken Alex to lunch? Probably. But that day I was suffused with the vivid grass green of possibility, the lush rush of long-gone youth, and the flood of blood to the heart that signaled carnal desire. Here was a man taller than I, big and strong enough to keep me from falling, a man of appetite and well-cut garments and limbs. That day, what I saw was opportunity, and I'd have felt like a fool not to seize it. One thing I've learned since college is that few men will suck your toes. Those who will are men of uncommon bravery, vision, and appetite. You don't let them just wander off to eat street meat.

And that was how it started, innocent as milk. Alex and I shared a long, delicious Turkish lunch. There was smoky eggplant salad, lush and bitter, oily and fresh with lemon juice. There were little bowls of sapid hummus, thick and savory yogurt, chilled spinach sautéed with garlic and lemon. There was a variation of halloumi, a baked cheese made of sheep's and goat's milk, salty and briny and seductively burned. There were thick slices of sausage, burned and crispy on the outside, juicy and feral on the inside. There were mounds of salty, fluffy, oily bread. It was a meal you ate with your fingers, of course. It set the tone for generous reminiscing.

Alex, unlike me, had left the world of writing almost as soon as he had entered it. He'd gotten a job as a stringer at the *Times* after graduation—he had family connections—but he hated it. Hated the hours, hated being called "Tiger," "Sparky," and "Junior" by his chain-smoking editor. Hated not having a byline. Hated cold-calling survivors of minor tragedies for a quotable reaction to something horrific. He hated it all, so he packed it in, took a year at Columbia to fill in the science and math courses he'd missed as an English major at Pennistone, and went to graduate school for engineering. He designed foundations for skyscrapers, he said. He put big holes in the ground, where they lived on in obscurity, quietly supporting the massive structures above them, gathering no glory, garnering no fans. There are few foundation aficionados, but without foundations, those great mounds of glass and steel would tumble like Jenga. He'd married, Alex said, and he divorced. He didn't have children, he said. I was charmed. I didn't want to be, but I was.

And that was the first date. He held one of my hands in both of his as he said goodbye, and he massaged it slowly, casually. He looked me in the eyes as he told me how happy he was to have run into me. And then he kissed me on the cheek, and asked me for my phone number. I gave him the real one, almost without realizing that honesty was the choice I was making.

This first date led to a second date, and a second date brought on a third. We didn't have sex until the fourth or fifth date, Alex and I, and as uncanny as it was to wait, the sex was spectacular. For all his earnestness, Alex was a deep-down dirty pervert, a man who liked to let fucking linger; he spent hours in flamboyant constructions of pleasure. I can't say enough good things about sex with engineers. Sensuality hides in the dark, dim recesses of the mathematical mind.

Before I knew it, I had a boyfriend. I was forty-two, and I had a boyfriend, the first who wasn't merely a convenient cover for federal holidays and family and gatherings, the first about whom I truly cared. Sure, I loved other men, or thought I did—who can say. How do I know if I really loved them, I fucked many—sex is fleeting. I felt certain that at times I loved Marco, and I felt very warmly about Gil. But these were shadow loves, the ambient feelings without the palpating passions. I never lost myself with any man before Alex, and I've never lost myself after. I had never breathed with anticipation like a pet, counting minutes until I'd see him. I had never lain in bed next to a man and wanted to feel absorbed into his body, like a kit into the uterine wall of a rabbit—a gross metaphor, but love is rife with body parts, with wet hearts and thudding rib cages and heaving bosoms and salty loins and velvety genitals. You can't have erotic love without the rank grittiness of dirty bodies, and bodies, like desires, are disgusting. Such was my love for Alex that I liked his morning breath.

Alex thrummed in my bones; he resonated like a sounding charge. He split my heart and made it grow. It was painful. With Alex, I thought I might have a soul; he made me believe that I was a better person than I knew myself to be. And here I must pause—my story is inextricably bound with Alex, yet I want to protect him. My victims rise, herky-jerky, like zombies from the dust as people listen to this, and I don't care; their flesh-and-blood realities are immaterial as shades. I hesitate to admit this, but I don't want Alex to be touched. It's strange to be caught between my will to spill and my desire to protect this man, but here we are, rubbed raw with ambivalence.

The naked, aching truth is that, here in prison's concrete walls, I hold the vestiges of my love for Alex close for comfort. I pull them out like a velvet rabbit and wrap my arms around them. I stroke these remains of love, and I rub their threadbare silkiness between my thumb and my forefinger. I can't tell this story without talking about Alex, yet I don't want to share him. With every iteration of him, he grows thinner, his memory more frayed; his flocking wears down, his form becomes more undefined. Writing about Alex is the opposite of the old wives' tale about mother bears and their babies: my tongue licks him not into shape but out of it. Holding Alex beyond words keeps him safe.

I don't have much in prison, just a very few possessions, and those are always under threat of confiscation or theft. Let me keep Alex. He is mine, even now, even still, even with him gone—alive, as far as I know, but deader to me than those I killed.

Months passed before I realized I was in love, an awareness that required Alex's absence, as so often happens in literature. Alex was out of town, working on a foundation site for a skyscraper in Cincinnati or Cleveland—I always get them confused. I was in New York, living my ordinary life and doing my ordinary things, yet extraordinarily counting days until Alex's return. I remember I was in the Broadway Panhandler shopping for a new mandoline—mine had broken, and I wanted to buy another for shaving fennel; there is no vegetable as flexible, as unsung, and as enlivening as fennel. If a dish is a disco, fennel is the song that a DJ relies upon to make the crowd dance. If you learn nothing else from me, learn to add fennel to legumes when you cook them; it makes lentils sing.

Walking through the store, I saw a pair of egg coddlers, and I thought to myself, Alex loves coddled eggs. I plopped the coddlers into my basket. It was a nothing gesture—the pair of coddlers cost no more than $10—but the moment was an epiphany. In that gesture, I realized that I loved Alex, because in buying those egg coddlers, I was purchasing a bit of domestic intimacy. Of course, I'd purchased gifts for other men before, but I'd always purposefully shopped for them; never before had I spontaneously indulged in the generosity of menial, quotidian pleasure. The gifts I'd bought previously were always for a reason, a part of a larger narrative, and usually something I gave in order to get something back. These gifts were investments at best and emotional blackmail at worst. Alex's pair of egg coddlers—nothing special, just little ceramic cups painted with playful flowers with shiny lids that screwed on—was the first thing I'd ever bought a man for the simple reason that it might make him happy.

With that, I realized I'd fallen in love. Because of egg coddlers. With a man I knew from college and had forgotten. It was wild, and I felt exhilarated. I sensed a stirring in the void where my soul should have been—no great hatching of conscience but a flutter, a breath, a quickening.

Our relationship progressed, a supposedly natural occurrence that I'd read about but never before experienced. Alex and I spent time with each other, and then we saw each other more. We shared weekends, and then we shared holidays. Together, we went on vacation—I brought Alex to Italy, and I spoke Italian for him and we drove the Autostrade. I taught him how to ride the *vaporetto* in Venice, hail taxis in Rome, order raw shellfish in the Maremma, spit wine in Barolo, and buy pizza by the width of your fingers more or less everywhere. His life became my life, and we slept in each other's beds as often as we finished each other's sentences.

With Alex, I shifted to first-person plural pronouns. I became we, and Alex grew closer. He wore me like a second skin, and I was fine with it. I was fine and I was fine and it was beautiful and life was good. For the first and only time in my life, I felt a *there*, there, in my chest, buried beneath my solar plexus. I felt an uncomfortable prickling when I acted in ways that were displeasing to him; a second sense guided my choices, and for the first time ever, I thought about whether what I was doing would make another person happy. I was monogamous. When has that ever happened. Exactly never. Even Emma liked him. She smiled big loopy smiles up at his big Brobdingnagian head because Alex was a smart open book, and even if his big, broad words came easy, they didn't bore you. I read him with my fingers; I read him with my mouth moving in slow, rolling vowels. I read him with delight, and he read me, too.

With Alex, my fortress of solitude grew a Juliet balcony. The balcony became a balustrade, the balustrade a veranda. Before I knew it, the fortress was open, and soft winds blew past gossamer curtains. My heart had become a home, and I did not live there alone.

Have you stayed with me throughout this tale of murder, betrayal, carnage, and meat only to become disillusioned as I tell you of love? I fell in love. I loved. I did not want to. I had not put myself in the path of love; I did not seek gravity. Love found me; gravity took me. Alex was a man so good he was good enough for us both, and I don't like good people. Good is round as a spoon. There's no edge in good. Somehow, though, Alex was interesting. There wasn't a shred of sanctimony in Alex. He was funny, even sarcastic. He could be dark and angry. He was no right little ray of sunshine. His excrement had odor, and I was frequently in a position to smell it. I found I rarely minded. Most of all, Alex was a singular human in his shocking ability to love me without reservation, condition, or mendacity—and not be irksome about it.

Aileen Wournos's last meal prior to execution was a cup of coffee. Before her lethal injection, Karla Faye Tucker ate a peach, a banana, and a small garden salad with ranch dressing—it's almost Spartan. So, too, was Judy Buenoano's final meal: steamed broccoli, asparagus, tomato wedges with lemon, berries, and hot tea. Ruth Snyder, killed in an electric chair in Sing Sing, consumed a meal that is the essence of American Gothic—chicken parmesan with pasta Alfredo, ice cream, two milkshakes, and two six-packs of grape soda. See also: Velma Barfield; her last meal was a Coca-Cola and a bag of Cheez Doodles. It's odd to choose a final meal that you could pick up at a truck stop, but *de gustibus non est disputandum* and all that jazz. Perhaps the most poetic last meal was that of Victor Feguer, a man made interesting only by what he ate. His choice was a single whole olive, and before he was hanged, he placed the olive pit in his suit pocket, wanting to seed the olive, a symbol of peace. Feguer was buried in the suit, pit in pocket, in an unmarked grave. Too bad it was in Iowa, a place inhospitable to olives, a Mediterranean fruit, and too sad that Feguer didn't know that olives must be cured to be edible, rendering their pits infertile.

Divided by what they chose to eat, these people are united by the fact that they committed crimes that caused the State to kill them. What drives killers to kill is a very personal question. We like to think that men kill because they're men—it's as indiscriminate as their wont to procreate. The quarterbacks in the high school of life, men are given a wide berth for murder, as they are for most things. Women, on the other hand, kill for only two reasons, or so the people who study women killers say. We women kill for personal financial gain or to escape an abusive relationship. Of course, this binary stereotype is insulting and inaccurate.

The truth, whether we want to see it or not, is that women will kill for almost any reason. Aileen Wuornos claimed that she killed only men who had raped her; it's more likely that she was a psychotic, angry, and violent human who expressed these qualities through killing. An opportunistic murderer, Karla Faye Tucker killed when a robbery went grisly; her victim, Jerry Dean, was nearly decapitated from the vicious assault by Karla Faye's boyfriend. When Karla took a pickaxe to Dean as he gurgled, drowning in his own blood, it was nearly a mercy—though one woman's mercy is another man's murder. In the nineteenth century, Jane Toppan killed scores of patients while working as a nurse in a Boston hospital; she's not alone: British hospitals have a long, florid history of angels of death. Ditto American nursing homes. Mercy is a wriggling thing. I rarely trust it.

Mothers who kill their children fascinate us—Susan Smith, Andrea Yates, and Diane Downs, child killers all. Fascinating, too, are those women who kill *with* the men they love, women like Karla Homolka, Rosemary West, Charlene Gallego, and Martha Beck, women whose sadism matched or even exceeded that of their husbands and boy-friends, their partners in crime. The couple that preys together stays together, at least until Johnny Law comes knocking and, to save his or her golden hide, one of the previously inseparable two inevitably makes a plea deal and turns State's witness against the other.

Despite their numbers, brutal women catch us by surprise. We expect random acts of violence from men. Men are the people who brought us the golden hits of war, genocide, rape, drones, and foot-ball. We do not expect murder, pain, and sadism from women, but we are co-opted idiots. Our unshakeable belief in women's essential goodness is a wondrous, drooling thing. Despite all evidence to the contrary, we act as starry-eyed as Margaret Keane paintings about the eternal sunshine of the spotless female mind. It's as if none of us ever had mothers who ever acted cruelly, and we all did. Some more than others.

It's not difficult to understand why abusive women kill their husbands or boyfriends (or wives or girlfriends). It's equally easy to understand women who kill for financial gain; money is such a louche, if effective, motivator. The torqued logic behind angels of mercy likewise reads legibly; everyone knows someone with an unhealthy commitment to their work. These are murders that we can imagine with some degree of empathy, if not comfort. The emotional resonance breaks, however, with women who kill their own children or those who kill in tandem with their husbands. We don't get these women, but we are drawn to them. These murder-esses fascinate us most because they take the essential romanticized blocks of human society—family and love—and turn them deadly.

You have to respect an ironic twist on an old favorite. Love makes us do the wacky; it also can make us do the whacking.

Love, as much as any other human passion, made me kill. Love, anger, fear, hunger—take a flashlight to your soul and tell me that these emotions don't burble and stew as one.

Without Alex, I would not be here, neither on the page nor in prison. Without him, I'd not have picked up in 2008 with Andrew where I'd left off in 2000, Giovanni impaled and bleeding like a martyr, the patron saint of vehicular hit-and-runs. Without Alex, I would not have enjoyed Gil's tongue or Marco's brisket. Without Alex and my love for him, this story would not be. It would have ended with the abiding memory of Giovanni's liver, luscious and grainy, salty and fatty, slathered on a piece of garlic-rubbed toast. But Alex came into my life, and he changed everything.

Almost three years passed between Alex losing his hot dog to momentum and gravity, and I losing my heart to Alex. My life was breathtakingly stable in February of 2007. I was writing and reviewing for *Eat & Drink*, where I'd been happily on staff for a decade. I was preparing to write *Voracious*. I was in my mid-forties, child-free by choice, financially independent, creatively fulfilled, in a loving relationship with a man who seemed to accept me entirely as I was. Everything could not have been more perfect—I looked like the late-blooming model of American womanhood. I was living the have-it-all dream I never wanted, and for a while, it wasn't bad. For a while, it was quite pleasant, in fact.

On Sunday, February 18, 2007, Alex asked me to meet him at the corner of Fifth and 33rd at five P.M. A large snowstorm had blown through days before, and Manhattan streets were still piled high with big, dirty mounds of marshmallow snow. I try to avoid Midtown at all costs, unless I have work or an assignation, so this address felt odd. There's nothing there at Fifth and 33rd, nothing but the Empire State Building.

"Dolls!" Alex said as he saw me approach. He had picked up Emma's nickname. "How about this snow?" He laughed. "Come. I want to show you something."

"You want to show me something? Please tell me you're not taking me to the Ripley's museum. I do not need to see a two-headed cow."

"Oh, you are a piece of work. That's closed. It's moving to Times Square. I want to show you something truly spectacular. I want to show you the Empire State Building," Alex said and raised his hand dramatically, like a conductor eliciting a crescendo from an orchestra, or a *Price Is Right* model showing you the splendors of Showcase #1.

"General Motors's John Jakob Raskob wanted a building better than the Chrysler, so he bought the Waldorf-Astoria Hotel, which stood on this spot, and razed it." Alex led me inside the big brass doors into the gilt, marble, and tile interior. "The excavation for the foundation began on the Empire State Building in January 1930. More than three hundred men worked night and day to simultaneously tear down the existing hotel while removing the dirt needed to build the foundation for the Empire State Building."

"Is that so?"

"It is so. The concrete foundation stretches fifty-five feet below street level, the depth needed to hit bedrock solid enough to support the weight of the 365,000 tons of steel, marble, bricks, plaster, and limestone used to make this building. It took two months to finish the foundation, and construction began on April 7, 1930." Alex edged me forward to the kiosk to buy tickets for the observation floor. "Two, please."

"We're going to the top?"

"We are. What else would we do?"

"Good point."

"Although the construction company promised to finish within fourteen months, the teams of 3,000 builders worked around the clock to complete the 102-floor Empire State Building, using state-of-the-art pre-cut girders and steel framework, a mini-train-track system to get building materials to the site, and even individual concessions and restaurants on the various floors so that workers didn't have to descend to get food."

"That's pretty clever."

"It really is. Five men died building the Empire State Building. They fell from girders. When it was structurally completed in April 1931, it stood for forty years as the tallest building in the world." Alex whispered into my ear, as we crowded into the elevator and started our ascent. "A small military airplane flew into the 79th floor in 1945, killing fourteen people. One of the plane's engines shot clear through the floor, out the other side, across the street, and landed on a penthouse roof, setting fire to the penthouse. But the Empire State Building wasn't structurally damaged." We exited the one car and stood in line for the second elevator.

"They don't make buildings like this anymore," I said. I had learned I could play along.

"No, they sure don't." Alex smiled.

"You really love this building."

"I do." He cocked his head like a dog. "Why is that so surprising?"

"I don't know. I don't really think about buildings. They're just... there. I rarely think about their personalities or histories."

"Well, that's how you're a dummy." He gripped my elbow, guiding me out of the elevator and onto the observation deck. The wind cut through my coat and whipped away Alex's voice. "This deck, you likely don't know," he shouted, "was built as a landing place for dirigibles, but the wind is too strong, and then the *Hindenburg* disaster happened, making a dirigible landing dock beside the point. Let's go to the west side."

A blood-scarlet dot, the sun slunk low on the Jersey horizon. Thick swaths of silky rivers and many slabs of satin steel ranged below, making giants of Alex and me. We strode as colossi through the frigid air. Wind knifed through my fur coat and across my face, freezing my tears and sucking my breath. Alex stood behind me, wrapping me in his arms, his cheek heavy on my own, his arms tight around mine. The sunset glittered, turning buildings into chromatic staves, the urban angles glowing in a bonfire of light, ready for the ink-black relief of night. I felt Alex take a deep breath, his chest pressing against my back.

Alex turned me toward him. "Dolls. I love you," he said.

"Yeah, you do."

"Yes. I do. Marry me."

I looked at him, at his big newscaster head, his kind indigo eyes, his menacing eyebrows. I looked at him, and I imagined my life with this man, this Alex. I imagined endless days of waking up next to him, of sleeping beside him, of conversations about whether this tie went with that shirt and how ridiculous he'd find that new molecular gastronomy place. I envisaged days together and nights apart, talking on the phone, and sleeping separately only to come back together. I imagined arguments punctuating our time and earnest conversations where each of us took responsibility for whatever it was the other thought we should.

I saw time passing, us growing old together, Alex's head now more scalp than hair, and my flame mane shot with gray. I saw our hands mottled as corn chips, our skin slack and seamy, Alex's mostly firm flesh gone soft and faintly breast-like. I fast-forwarded to dotage and old-man khakis and old-lady dressing gowns. I imagined staying with this man until one or the other of us died, those decades of dinner parties and vacations, of planning our days and choosing movies, of making beds and folding sweaters, of all those tiny, daily tasks, decisions, and moments that string together to make a life. I imagined, for a moment, that I would share a life—all these days, all those nights, and the long, stunning dots of time that, viewed from a distance, looked solid, impenetrable—with this man.

I imagined being the me who I became when I was with Alex, this kinder, softer, gentler, thousand glimmering shafts of conscience-ridden self. I imagined a life where I would always, ever, be Alex-me because to be the calculating, howling void I was before I met Alex was not an option. I could not be both alone-me and Alex-me; one had to die so that the other could live. I had to make a choice, there as the sky turned plum dusky, and Manhattan grew black and brittle as old glass.

I looked down into the gold-and-red gilt canyons and felt a swoop of vertigo, a sudden, nauseating drop. I saw my former self, the self I'd lived and loved and tended for decades, fall away. My stomach lurched.

"No," I said. "I'm sorry, but I can't."

And I left Alex there on the wind-whipped observation deck of the building that, once the tallest in the world, killed five men in its creation, a skyscraper that will only ever be a building to me.

I never saw Alex again. I'd made my decision, and I saw no need to pretend that it was anything other than the death of our relationship. In the end, it came down to this: Alex made me a better person, but I didn't like her. She bored me. I couldn't imagine forty more years with her. I saw her in my imagination, and I wanted to stab her through the heart with something thrilling and awful. So I killed the relationship instead.

It took me a little more than a year to realize I'd lost something important when I lost Alex. And that was when I decided to look up Andrew. I like being by myself, you see. I just didn't want to be alone. And now I never will be.

Baked Alaska

Joyce, the therapist who leads our group therapy at Bedford Hills, turned to me. "How are you coming with your forgiveness list, Dorothy?" she asked, inquiring after the homework she'd given the group.

"Good," I said, a little surprised to be called upon. "It's coming right along. Yes, making a list, checking it twice." I tried to laugh, thinking that's what normal people do. Sometimes I forget where I am.

"Do you feel like you can tell the group about your list?" Joyce looked at me and nodded, as if nudging my participation with her nose.

"Sure," I said, searching my internal Rolodex for whom I might possibly forgive. "My parents, for one—or two, I suppose. My mother and my father."

"Great!" said Joyce. The group was less enthused. Kaileen-Mae, one of the other murderers, openly smirked. Taryn, the hacker, looked out the window at the sullen sky. The arsonist, Luciana, twirled her hair around her fingers and stared blank-eyed at a spot on the floor. Two Asian inmates, new to the group, signed in secret code to each other, writing messages in their palms. There's nothing like a group of felons for the swift detection of total bullshit. Our ability to sniff out mendacity is as keen as our abilities to lie to ourselves and, more important, to others.

"Actually, Joyce, you know who I forgive? I forgive Emma."

"And who was Emma to you?"

"She was my best friend." Luciana's hands stopped twirling; the convicts ceased their signing. Even Taryn turned her attention from the gunmetal sky. "Yes," I said, "Emma was my best friend. We were friends for years—decades."

Joyce practically bounced with excitement. "And what do you forgive Emma for?"

"I think that she had, um—I thought that she had told secrets to some people. And then I found out she hadn't. Or perhaps she did. I don't know. She might have. Anyway, I forgive her."

Joyce looked at me, her brows knitted together. "I'm sorry, Dorothy. I don't understand."

"I was afraid that Emma had told certain people some information that I'd told her in confidence, and I got angry at her," I said, pausing before I continued. "I thought Emma betrayed me. But perhaps she didn't. So I forgive her."

Joyce's face didn't relax. "I'm terribly sorry. I'm afraid I still don't get it."

"She thought this Emma ratted to the cops," said a tall, Black, middle-aged woman with close-cropped hair. "And she forgives her. Because she found out this bitch Emma didn't say anything."

Joyce shook her head. "No, that's not right."

"Sure it is," said Luciana, the girl who laughed as she burned her foster parents' house to the ground. Our common arson conviction made her feel an affinity I neither shared nor wanted.

"No, no, no, no," said Joyce. "That's not right at all."

"More or less, it is," I said. "I thought Emma had gone to the police. Now, I'm not so sure. Maybe she did and maybe she didn't. I thought she did, and I held it against her. I think I forgive her."

"Good for you," said the Black inmate who had nailed my situation for Joyce.

"Thank you," I replied.

"*ACAB,*" Taryn coughed.

"No," said Joyce, her voice sharp. "This isn't how forgiveness works."

"Sure it is," said Lizzie, another one of murderers, a skinny white woman with tattoos snaking from her chin down her arms. "Some bitch do you wrong, you think about it, you forgive her. That's how you do."

"No," said Laquisha. She'd gotten caught selling drugs to afford medical care for her chronically ill son—we'd often heard about her guilt. "You can't forgive someone for something they didn't do."

"This is my point," said Joyce. "Well said, Laquisha."

"I don't get it," said the tall Black inmate. On the inside, I thanked her.

Joyce's voice rose to that level of patience reserved for the very young, the very sick, and the very thick. "Dorothy's friend Emma didn't do anything, so Dorothy has nothing to forgive her for."

"I don't understand," said tattooed Lizzie.

"Nor, for that matter, do I, and it's my list," I said.

Joyce took a deep breath and looked at the ceiling as if it would give her guidance. "Okay. Dorothy." Joyce's voice was both slow and clipped, equal measures of restraint and exasperation. "If Emma had gone to the police and given them information, then she would've hurt you. You don't know if Emma went to the police, and you aren't sure whether she gave them information. Therefore, she might not have hurt you. You don't need to forgive Emma, Dorothy. You need to forgive yourself."

"Whoa," said Taryn in her thick Brooklyn accent. "That's heavy."

Around the age of nine, I grew obsessed with Baked Alaska. I'd read about the dessert in a novel, and I researched it. It was the early 1970s, well before the internet, so my research took the form of encyclopedias, cookbooks, and microfiche. A tour-de-force of misguided American cuisine, Baked Alaska was exactly the kind of thing to drive my mother around the culinary bend, and I was set on having a Baked Alaska for my tenth birthday cake. A slab of ice cream on a foundation of cake covered in meringue and cooked in an oven, the dish is fussy without being difficult. Anyone with a reliable hand mixer, a timer, and a relatively stable oven can make Baked Alaska—the question is why you would want to.

The answer is being a nine-year-old child. A Baked Alaska is, in many ways, the quintessence of what a child of a certain age would want in a birthday cake. It's hot, it's cold, it's surprising, it's messy, it's unusual, and it's more than a little bit gross. A fluffy concerto of saturated sweetness wrapped in egg whites and delivered on a cake base, a Baked Alaska invites gluttony. You cannot have left-over Baked Alaska. Unlike an ice cream cake, the uneaten portion of a Baked Alaska can't simply be popped into the freezer, because neither the cake base nor the meringue will both freeze and thaw well. And you can't put it in the refrigerator because the ice cream will melt. A Baked Alaska, like cheese fondue, is a dish you must consume in its entirety. Naturally, my sister, then seven, and my little brother, then four and a half, were thrilled.

My mother was not. There is nothing elegant about Baked Alaska. There is nothing chic. If I wanted meringue, she asked, why did I not ask for œufs à la neige, individual lemon soufflés, or a nice raspberry dacquoise? Because, I said, I wanted a Baked Alaska. Simple, American, and what my mind was set upon.

With great reluctance, my mom made it, and out of the oven appeared a swirly mound of caramel-hued egg whites, expansive as a Texan blonde, tempting as fresh-fallen snow. It was perfect. My mom stuck the Baked Alaska with candles, my family sang, I blew the candles out, and I made a wish. I almost quivered with anticipation as my mom set the plate of gooey, melting Baked Alaska in front of me. My research had paid off; my dream had come true, and everything I'd hoped for was on this plate. I delighted in my mother's sweet, sweet capitulation to my childish obsession, all in the service of my special, special birthday.

"You only turn nine once," my father said.

"I'm ten!" I cried.

"Bon appétit!" my mother said, as I lifted a fork, layered with the trifecta of fluffy meringue, yellow sponge cake, and chocolate ice cream, to my mouth. And you know, it was... okay. More an overblown homage to the idea of dessert than an authentic dish, Baked Alaska holds all the charm of a hotel lounge singer—it's obvious, pandering, one-note. Lacking the satiny texture of lemon custard and the gritty crunch of piecrust, the Baked Alaska felt oddly viscous, and lacking the creaminess of frosting, the meringue didn't augment the already superlative combination of cake and ice cream; likewise, the ice cream lacked the bright tartness found in lemon meringue pie. In short, the dessert felt woefully out of balance. Every component in the Baked Alaska acted like a third wheel, a presence without a function. Even I had to admit that Baked Alaska was nothing but a dessert novelty act.

My sister and my brother soon grew bored and wandered away. My mother swallowed a single mouthful and lit a cigarette. My father poured himself a glass of scotch. It was left to me to consume this monster of my own desire. So I sat, and I ate, and I ate, spooning one gelatinous, melting, crumbly spoonful after another into my mouth, hardly tasting, merely swallowing. My mother sat at the opposite end of the table, smoking. I glared and I ate. I ate it all. I even licked the plate.

I glare and I swallow here, at Bedford Hills. Every day, I glare and I swallow. The Baked Alaska was good training.

I got some mail today, a tiny stack of prison-vetted correspondence hand-delivered through a slotted cage. In the slender pile, I found a thin violet envelope addressed in black, spidery handwriting. A letter from Emma. I almost ripped the letter down its spine and tossed it into the garbage, as I've done twenty or thirty times before, tipped off to its sender by Emma's tell-tale palette and her peculiar, spindly hand. But this time, I stopped. I held the cool envelope in my hand. I flipped it over and turned it over again. It was a flimsy thing, nearly weightless, almost inconsequential. I felt its flat weight in my palm. I rubbed my forefinger over the violated wax seal, a burnt blood red, and opened the envelope. Out drifted the scent of Emma's perfume—Nahema, smoky sandalwood and dreamy ylang-ylang. I inhaled and my heart clenched. I could see Emma, small and perfectly dark under a lamp, seated at the Edwardian dining table she used as her desk. I imagined her holding her Rotring Rapidograph in her hand, her pen poised on the lilac paper as she pondered what she would write. I felt her fear (or anxiety or mendacity or ambivalence) shimmer off the page, uncoiling in spirals.

I slid my forefinger between the envelope and the seal and removed the letter's single page and unfolded it. Just four lines written in Emma's thin hand.

"Dolls," it read, "you told me everything. I said nothing, and I never will. Love you to the end, Emma." And there it is, Emma's infinite, unflinching devotion in black and lavender.

I think of agoraphobic Emma, out there in the world, able to walk Manhattan's gray-slick streets. Emma, free to choose an outfit from her expensively monochrome closet, fling open her front door, and wander lustily until she finds a hospitable café. Emma could, if she wanted, reject the café host's offer of a dark table shoved next to the kitchen door, and point her manicured finger to demand the best seat in the house, the one near the window, with a view of the avenue, cars and pedestrians pulsating like blood in the city's veins. Sitting comfily in her restaurant chair, Emma might scan the weighty, cream-colored menu to find the one dish that calls to her. A lobster roll, maybe. Duck cassoulet, perhaps. A sashimi tasting menu. A tomahawk steak—why not. The world is Emma's oyster, and in my imagining, this is literal.

Out in the world, Emma is free to sloppily slurp a tower of shellfish or gnaw a rack of lamb, noisily sucking the delicate meat from each bone; she is free to press her delicate hand to her breast, breathlessly order a bottle of Champagne, and swill it with abandon. Emma has liberties that I must dream about, yet she lives her life bound to her Hell's Kitchen tower, a captive of her free-floating, ambient fears of the wide, wild-open world. Life is bitterly unfair, in short, and Emma's untouched, unfettered freedom is evidence of it.

Shielded by her artist's atelier, famous Emma is seen but not viewed. Secured in penitential Bedford Hills, infamous Dorothy Daniels is watched but not seen. Emma and I are separated by circumstance and choice, yet we're united by experience. As aging Sisters in the Inescapable Order of the Corporeal Skin, we slip into the invisibility of menopause, our womanly faces growing lined, our womanly bodies succumbing to gravity, our flesh slumping, our wombs collapsing, our girlish selves dissolving into bony piles of wrinkles and dust.

The goddess of femininity is cruel to mature women, crushing our brittle bones in her silken, youthful grip. As a girl, when you grow up, you become delectable. As a woman, when you grow old, you turn immaterial—unless you bear children, unless you make art, unless you leave a legacy. As she slouches toward menopause,

Emma has her paintings to stave off irrelevance. My legacy is somewhat more fraught. The choices that we have, the choices that we make—these choices condemn us, constrain us, and create us. This is life at its most essential, a series of decisions that leads to your inexorable end and your desperate, muffled hope that you may be celebrated when it comes. I can live with my choices, as I will live with my legacy.

I write this knowing that I will grow old and die in this prison, and I write this so that no one will forget me. I have carved my place in your memory, cut to the quick of American consciousness. How many women—hungry as we are for immutability—can say the same?

Acknowledgments

One hot night in June 2011, I went to a gay bar in Hell's Kitchen. It's not my neighborhood (and only occasionally my milieu) but my friend Katelan Foisy was reading tarot cards, and I hadn't seen her in four months. I'd been living in Italy. I was heartbroken. I'd fallen in love with a beautiful, cruel, stupid Italian man, as one might do, and I'd fallen in love with Italy, as one will do. Neither, I felt, loved me back.

Wrapped in the prickly Gotham heat, Katelan and I sat outside the bar, and she began turning cards, one after the other, layered like a fresco. Flick-flick-flick went the cards. Katelan paused. "You have two projects inside you right now." Flick-flick, more Rider-Waite tiles in my life's fresco. "Both are good." Flick. Flick. Katelan's eyebrows shot up. She smiled. "And they'd do well. Really well." Flick-flick-flick. A slight scowl, like a tiny cloud, and a toss of Katelan's head. "They'll bring you to dark places." She smiled. "But you'll make money." Flick-flick-flick. "You've got choices," Katelan said as we reached the end of the deck. "It'll take longer than you want it to, but you'll be okay."

Writing this novel was a circuitous, torturous process that spanned more than eight years from conception to publication, first as an Audible Original and now as a print book from Unnamed Press. Writing this novel consumed nights and weekends and holidays and my vacation time. Writing this book was a leap of faith, a jump into the void of my creative unconscious, and a willing suspension of belief that I could do something I'd never done before, that I'd never been trained to do, and that I'd desperately, feverishly, fiercely wanted to do for as long as I'd known that books were a thing that people could make.

As much as I made *A Certain Hunger* (Fiction! It comes from your brain!), I didn't make it alone. I'd like to thank my parents, Frank and Jennifer, who read to me when I was a kid and gave me books that I hated when I was an adolescent; consider this novel payback. I'd like to thank my friend Sergio Esposito, who brought me to Italy in the first place and who served as Italian proofreader because, as it turns out, you cannot trust Google translate. I'd like to thank Margaret Edwards, who has a good story about teaching me in 1980, and I'd like to thank Susan Greenfield, who has a good story about teaching me in 2002.

This novel had several beta readers, and their enthusiasm even when it was in a raw, glistening, and fetal state powered me as I finished writing. You wouldn't be holding this book had I not received love and encouragement from Kat Howard, Lizzy Weinberg, Libby McCurrach, Kim Boekbinder, Tory Jones, and Kathleen Urda, so buy them a drink when you meet them. A cavalcade of glittery adoration to my muse Molly Crabapple, whose memoir kicked my ass and whose work ethic spurred me to finish this bitch.

The road to this book's publication was rocky. The sole reason it's available is the dogged, impassioned dedication of my agent, Jen Udden, who read the raw manuscript over a weekend in 2016 and vowed, "As god is my witness, I will sell *A Certain Hunger*." Roughly 25 rejections later, she did, first to Andrew Eisenman at Audible and then to Olivia Smith at Unnamed Press. I thank Andrew and Olivia for having the outstanding vision and bold taste to take a chance on my gory angel baby of a novel, and I thank Jen for, well, everything.

I cannot forbear acknowledging the following humans: my former therapist, whose first name is the same as my given name; Beyoncé, St. Vincent, and Janelle Monae, whose music has been my constant writing companions; and Elizabeth Gilbert and Brett Easton Ellis, whose works I ate, vomited up, and created something new and splendid and gross. I'd like to thank my hot Swedish husband, who celebrates the magnificent bitch I am. And, finally, I'd like to thank you for reading my book. I'm not great at being sincere, but it means the world to me that you've taken the time to read my words.